MURDER CAN UPSET YOUR MOTHER

A DESIREE SHAPIRO MYSTERY

Selma Eichler

A SIGNET BOOK

SIGNET
Published by New American Library, a division of
Penguin Putnam Inc., 375 Hudson Street,
New York, New York 10014, U.S.A.
Penguin Books Ltd, 27 Wrights Lane,
London W8 5TZ, England
Penguin Books Australia Ltd, Ringwood,
Victoria, Australia
Penguin Books Canada Ltd, 10 Alcorn Avenue,
Toronto, Ontario, Canada M4V 3B2
Penguin Books (N.Z.) Ltd, 182–190 Wairau Road,
Auckland 10, New Zealand

Penguin Books Ltd, Registered Offices:
Harmondsworth, Middlesex, England

First published by Signet, an imprint of New American Library,
a division of Penguin Putnam Inc.

First Printing, March 2001
10 9 8 7 6 5 4 3 2 1

 REGISTERED TRADEMARK—MARCA REGISTRADA

Printed in the United States of America

PUBLISHER'S NOTE
This is a work of fiction. Names, characters, places, and incidents either
are the product of the author's imagination or are used fictitiously,
and any resemblance to actual persons, living or dead, business establish-
ments, events, or locales is entirely coincidental.

For my very dear,
very supportive friend Julian Scott.
You are missed.

ACKNOWLEDGMENTS

A big thanks to—

Major Alan G. Martin of the New York State Police, who, as always, was so generous with his time in acquainting me with police procedures.

Pharmacist Fiana Finkel, whose information on drugs was so vital to constructing the murder.

My fellow mystery writer, artist, and friend Barbara Comfort. What little I know about Connecticut I owe entirely to Barbara.

Dr. Marion Turkish, who never stops helping— and in so many ways.

My editor, Ellen Edwards, whose insights and sound advice contributed to honing this story.

My agent, Stuart Krichevsky, for all his efforts on behalf of the series.

My husband Lloyd for his criticism, his praise, his suggestions, and—most of all—his patience.

Chapter One

Listening to Miriam Weiden's phone message that night, I was totally dumbstruck. Here she was, frantically informing my answering machine that someone was trying to kill her. And it just didn't make any sense. Not from what I knew of the woman.

Of course, I have to admit that I didn't come by most of my knowledge firsthand. In fact, I'd only been in her company once, about three years earlier. The man I was seeing then—although I guess I shouldn't say "was seeing," because I only went out with him a couple of times—had taken me to this formal benefit dinner. He was a high muck-a-muck at one of the television stations, and he went to those things pretty frequently. Me? It was my first—and only—venture into society.

We were seated at the same table—Mrs. Weiden, the muck-a-muck, and I. Initially I had no idea who she was. Her face wasn't the least bit familiar, and it wasn't as if her name were Trump or Tisch or anything. But I learned from some big mouth I met up with in the ladies' room that my tablemate was a rich-as-all-get-out widow. Then later, over the poached salmon *pipérade,* Mrs. Weiden and I chatted for a while. This is when I discovered that she was a true philanthropist—*and* that she refused to take any credit for her generosity. She regarded herself as blessed to have the means to be able to help those less fortunate.

At any rate, after that evening I'd spot a line or two in the New York papers every so often mentioning that she had contributed a humongous amount to some worthy cause or that she'd be chairing an important, star-studded charity event. But most telling of all were the photographs I would occasionally come across. I remember a picture of her reading to the children in a hospital ward. And another showing her carrying hot meals to shut-ins. More recently there was even a shot of her dishing out food at a local soup kitchen.

It's possible you've seen her photo yourself: a very attractive lady somewhere in her forties, with a better-than-average figure, nice, regular features, and dark, shoulder-length hair, the hairline forming a widow's peak. (Some mean-spirited columnist had once written that the hairline had been surgically created. Well, that was Mrs. Weiden's business. And anyway, big deal.) Most likely, though, you'd have had to read the accompanying caption to identify her.

Still, so what if she hadn't achieved genuine celebrity status? Miriam Weiden was certainly the most impressive person I'd ever met. As far as I was concerned, she was maybe one step removed from sainthood. And for someone like that to be a target for *murder*?

I don't suppose that anyone is immune from evil, though. And listening to her desperate cry for help that night, it was apparent that, for whatever reason, somebody wanted Mrs. Weiden dead. And very, very soon that's exactly what she was.

Thanks in part, I'm afraid, to yours truly.

Chapter Two

The thing is, for over a week I had been, as they say in showbiz, "between engagements." So I'd left the office at two-fifteen that Tuesday, after providing a firm reassurance to Jackie, my overbearing, anxiety-afflicted secretary, that I was not in failing health—followed by another reassurance with the same message.

And then I headed straight for Bloomingdale's.

It was what I'd call a successful shopping expedition, too. I wound up with a tobacco-colored silk blouse that didn't go with a thing I own and really couldn't afford. It gave me a lift, though. I mean, it was a lot better than sitting around and dwelling on all the misgivings I was having about ever getting another client as long as I lived. (There's nothing like being secure, is there?) Or, when I managed to move my masochistic little brain off *that* topic, brooding about a recent investigation I'd handled—the most angst-producing case of my career. But those things aside, I honestly feel that once in a while it's good to let yourself know that you *can* be extravagant if you want to be.

I even considered treating myself to a lavish meal at a French restaurant not far from the store. But I chickened out at the last minute and grabbed a croissant sandwich and cheese Danish at an Au Bon Pain.

The first thing I did when I walked into the apartment that evening was just what I always do: check the answering machine. The red light was flickering meaningfully. I pressed Playback.

"It's Harriet. Where *are* you, for heaven's sake?" my friend and across-the-hall neighbor Harriet Gould demanded, her voice a good octave higher than it normally is. "I've been trying to reach you all afternoon. Call me the *second* you come in. It's very imp—"

She sounded so frenetic that I hastily followed instructions. Jabbing the Power button, I terminated her message in mid sentence and picked up the phone.

"Desiree? Oh, I'm *so* glad you're home," she said when she heard my voice. "You have to come over. And I mean *right now*."

"I'm on my way." I scurried over to the Goulds' still in my coat and with a suddenly dry mouth.

Harriet's husband Steve answered the door. He was grinning broadly. And before I knew it, he shoved a glass of champagne in my hand. "Scott got married," he informed me of his twenty-something son. I extended my congratulations and kissed him.

Entering the room, I saw that there were about twenty people milling around, sipping champagne and soft drinks and poised to attack the still cellophane-wrapped deli and pastry platters laid out on a folding table against the wall. The aroma of freshly brewed coffee was a good indication the food would be made available soon. And sure enough, Denise—the woman who "does" for Harriet every other week—emerged from the kitchen at that moment, preparatory, I was certain, to removing the wrappings.

I spotted my friend and next-door neighbor Barbara Gleason then, who waved her greeting as she continued a conversation with a tall man sporting a red handlebar mustache. And hovering conspicuously near the edibles, her eyes positively riveted to Denise, was Mrs. Simmons from down the hall. A couple of other residents of the building were here, too. Plus there were a number of semi-familiar faces. Which means I may—or may not—have met these people before. I took them to be Gould relatives.

Steve was helping me wriggle out of my coat when Harriet rushed over.

"Desiree! Thank goodness you got home in time! Where were you all day? Never mind. Just give me a hug. Did you tell her our news, Steve?"

Her husband nodded. And I gave her the hug she'd ordered. After this she grabbed my arm—which was not yet completely out of my coat sleeve. "Come on," she said, "I want you to meet Hyacinth, my new daughter-in-law."

Hyacinth? Yes, I know; I'm a fine one to talk.

I hurriedly snatched up my champagne glass, which I'd deposited on an end table, as Harriet propelled me over to the corner where Scott and a very expectant (pregnancy-wise, I'm referring to) young woman were standing and talking.

Sprawled alongside the two was the Goulds' retarded Pekinese, Baby, whose many sterling attributes include a chronically weak bladder—which I swear she sometimes employs out of sheer spite. Not being one of Baby's favorite people and reminding myself that I had on a practically new pair of suede pumps, I quickly edged away from her, positioning myself a lot closer to Scott than I normally care to.

"Look, Scott, here's Desiree," Harriet announced brightly.

He barely glanced at me. "Yeah, I can see that." It was the kind of response you could expect from the sullen and spoiled-rotten Gould progeny. The "Congratulations, Scott" I was about to offer never left my throat.

"And this is Hyacinth, Scott's wife," Harriet went on. The girl, at least, stuck out her hand in acknowledgment of my presence, accepting my good wishes with a smile and a polite thank you. She wasn't bad looking, I thought, even in that shiny, too-short navy polyester maternity dress—with a soiled white collar, no less. It wouldn't hurt, though, if somebody could prevail upon her to trim that stringy brown hair and acquaint her with the concept of lipstick. And, of course, once those zits of hers cleared up . . .

"Imagine," Harriet was saying, "these two kids keeping a secret of their marriage for so many months—since May." I'm not certain if the blush originated at the roots of her hair and then spread down to her neck or vice versa, but my friend's complexion was now bright red. "Scott only decided to let the cat out of the bag this afternoon. And about time, too, considering that Steve and I will be grandparents at the end of next month."

I couldn't help it; I did the calculations in my head: May to February. That would make it nine months by the time the baby arrived. Harriet is from the old school. Until you stand in front of the clergyman of your choice and repeat those vows, you just don't conceive. And even if you do—you didn't. If you follow me.

Anyway, Harriet's eyes were imploring me to believe her. And so I joked that at least *somebody* in the Gould family was able to keep a secret. Which seemed to satisfy her. The truth is, I could really sympathize with Harriet's embarrassment. I mean, as modern and independent as I keep telling myself I am, I attended the same school she did. I wondered idly what sort of a bribe it took to get Scott to agree to his mother's creative rechronicling.

"Hyacinth is really a sweet girl, isn't she?" Harriet prattled on when we walked away. "This is the first time we've met her, Steve and I. You know, I've never before put together a party in a few hours like this. I didn't think we could pull it off. Luckily, Denise was available to help out." And steering me in the direction of the food, she promised, "This roast beef is absolutely the best. Just wait till you taste it, Dez."

I discovered that she was right. The corned beef was very good, too. And the potato salad was terrific. Also the pastries. (Look, I barely had a thing to eat at Au Bon Pain. I mean, it wasn't as if it was an actual *meal* or anything.)

*　　*　　*

As soon as I was back in my own apartment I realized that in my rush to return Harriet's call, I'd shut off the answering machine.

I wasn't too concerned, though. If somebody phoned while I was at the Goulds', they'd just have to try again, that's all.

It didn't even occur to me that, earlier, there might have been other messages on the tape besides Harriet's.

And that one of them could be a matter of life and death.

Chapter Three

It wasn't until the following Tuesday that my friend Pat Martucci contacted me at the office.

"Don't you believe in returning calls?" she threw at me. This was not preceded by so much as a hello.

Irritated by her tone, I said coldly, "What calls? Would you mind telling me what you're talking about?"

"I phoned you on Monday. *A week ago* Monday. Or maybe it was Tuesday. . . . Yes, I remember now. It was definitely Tuesday. And I asked you to get back to me."

"I'm sorry, Pat. But Jackie never gave me the message. It must have slipped her mind." Even as I said it, though, I didn't believe it. Jackie is easily the most efficient secretary in New York, and absolutely *nothing* slips her mind.

"Oh, no you don't. You can't put this on Jackie. I left word on your machine at home."

"I don't understand then. I—"

"What did you do? Forget about me?"

"Of course not. I didn't get that call. Honestly. What time did you try me?"

"About five, I guess."

Tuesday. . . . That was the night of Harriet and Steve's party. *Let's see,* I mused, attempting to dope this out. I had come home around seven-thirty and immediately played the tape on my answering machine. After which I'd made a beeline for the Gould apartment. *But wait! First, I'd called Harriet back, turning off the machine before she was even finished carrying on!*

Now, I don't know how your answering machine works, but once I shut off the power on mine—even if it's only for an instant—that's that. What I mean is, when I switch it on again, the unit automatically goes into the "answer" mode and no longer plays back any existing messages. The only way I can retrieve them is by listening to the tape on my tape recorder.

I explained to Pat how I'd "lost" her message, and she responded with a neutral, "Okay," most likely accompanying this with a shrug. Then she quickly got down to business. "The reason I wanted to talk to you was to ask you to a birthday party—Burton's fortieth. It's February ninth—a week from this Sunday—at eight o'clock. You can come with someone if you want to, but it's not necessary; there'll be other singles there, too. And incidentally, you don't have to worry about Bruce's showing up. He's relocated to LA, in case you haven't heard."

Just to bring you up to speed, Burton is Pat's live-in significant other—or whatever they call it these days—and a pretty nice guy. Bruce is Burton's cousin and a former something-or-other of mine and not a pretty nice guy at all (but that's a whole different story). At any rate, knowing Bruce wouldn't be putting in an appearance, I was able to accept the invitation with genuine enthusiasm.

The conversation ended a few minutes later, and I resumed the highly productive activity I'd been engaged in prior to Pat's call: applying a second coat of polish to my nails. I'm embarrassed to admit it, but even at this point it didn't dawn on me that Pat's might not have been the only message I'd missed out on last Tuesday.

It took a full half hour, as I was on my way to the ladies' room, for the light bulb to go on above my head.

*   *   *

Less than five minutes after walking into the apartment, I removed the tape from the answering machine and transferred it to the tape recorder.

Fast-forwarding the earlier messages on the tape, I finally got to Tuesday—and Pat's terse directive to me to contact her. And then I heard this quivering, unfamiliar voice.

"Desiree? I'm not sure you'll remember me, but we met at a charity function two or three years ago—I think it was an AIDS fund-raiser. My name is Miriam Weiden; we sat at the same table. You mentioned you were a private investigator—you even gave me your card. I hung on to it because . . . well . . . because you never can tell. I've had jewelry disappear on me a couple of times—I've always suspected it was this cousin of mine—and I figured that if it should happen again— But that's not important. Anyway, I just tried you at your office, and they said you'd already left."

There was a sharp intake of breath and a short silence here. "I'm calling you for a reason I never would have dreamed of the night of that dinner." Another silence. "Someone is trying to kill me, and I . . . I don't know who else to turn to. The police won't believe I'm in jeopardy. Apparently they don't have what they regard as evidence that the things that happened to me weren't merely accidents. But they weren't. I swear to you that there have been two attempts on my life."

At this juncture Mrs. Weiden was terminated by my extremely intolerant answering machine with its strict sixty-second time limit, and she had to phone again. She resumed her narrative as if there'd been no interruption.

"I desperately need your help, Desiree. I'm terrified there'll be a third try—and that this time she'll succeed. Please, *please* call me. No matter what time you come in." And she left a number.

Somebody wants this wonderful woman dead?

I had to shake myself out of a kind of stupor before dialing.

*　　*　　*

"This is the Weiden residence."

"Mrs. Weiden, please. Mrs. Miriam Weiden."

"Who is this?" the woman inquired gruffly.

"My name is Desiree Shapiro. I'm returning Mrs. Weiden's call."

"When was it that Mrs. Weiden called you?"

"Last Tuesday, but—"

"Don't you read the papers, Ms. Shapiro?" Well, the truth was that I hadn't had the patience to actually *read* the papers lately; *skimmed* was a lot more like it. "Mrs. Weiden passed that same night."

"Passed?" I repeated stupidly.

"Passed. Died." *Well, why didn't she say that in the first place?*

I felt a little sick. "Uh, would you mind telling me who it is I'm speaking to?"

"I'm Erna Harris, Mrs. Weiden's secretary."

"Ms. Harris, could you . . . I mean, I'd like to know the cause of her death."

"The autopsy report hasn't come in yet," she told me dryly. "Were you a friend of Mrs. Weiden's?"

"I only met her once. I'm a private investigator. She phoned to hire me, because she felt that she was in danger."

"She was going to bring in a private detective?" The secretary seemed to be speaking more to herself than to me.

And now, in the background, I heard what sounded like, "Give me the phone." Then the receiver changed hands.

"This is Norma Davis, Miriam's mother. You say my daughter wanted to employ you?"

"Yes. She was afraid that someone was going to"— I scrambled frantically for the most benign way of putting this—"umm, harm her. She left a message on my answering machine last week, but unfortunately, there was this . . . this technical trouble with the machine, and I wasn't able to retrieve it until this evening."

"I see."

"I'm terribly sorry for your loss, Mrs. Davis. I was in your daughter's company briefly a few years ago, and she's—she was—a very special person."

"Yes, she was. Thank you."

I was about to say good-bye when Mrs. Davis added, "I didn't get your name."

"It's Desiree Shapiro."

"I assume there is no longer anything wrong with your answering machine."

"I had it repaired."

"And the problem you did have—is it something that happens often?"

"No. It never happened before." Even this wasn't the truth.

"Good. Then I want you to find my daughter's killer."

"But the police—?"

"The police," the mother scoffed. "They're still waiting for the medical examiner to tell them how she died. Almost immediately, however, one of the detectives was speculating that it might have been a heart attack. Or suicide. *Suicide—Miriam!* And there was nothing wrong with her heart, either. Somebody murdered my daughter, Ms. Shapiro. Probably poisoned her, if you want my opinion. I should have believed her to begin with. Maybe I— At any rate, it's already been a week, and the police don't appear to be getting anywhere at all."

"But once the cause of death is determined—"

Mrs. Davis aborted the protest. "Look, Ms. Shapiro, I'm counting on you to find out who did this. My daughter was a smart woman. A very smart woman. And if Miriam had confidence in you, well, so do I."

Chapter Four

I had a bad case of the *if onlys*.

I went to bed with a couple on the brain, and after I finally managed to fall asleep, I woke up with half a dozen others.

If only I hadn't gone on my little expedition to Bloomingdale's, I'd have been available to receive Miriam Weiden's call.

If only I hadn't been so anxious to get back to Harriet that I shut off the answering machine, I still would have heard Mrs. Weiden's plea for help.

If only Harriet hadn't sounded so agitated.

If only the party for that rotten Scott hadn't taken place *that* evening.

If only . . .

Of course, even if none of these things had happened, there's no guarantee I could have prevented the philanthropist's death. Still, I would have seen to it I met with her that night, so it's very likely the tragedy would have been forestalled. And who knows? There was certainly a chance I could have uncovered the killer before there was another opportunity to strike.

I phoned Jackie at around nine-thirty Wednesday morning to let her know I wouldn't be in.

The response was an "Oh?" that was loaded with implied criticism.

"Look, I have a new client, and I'm investigating the very real possibility that her daughter was murdered. I could be tied up all day."

"A child was murdered?" There was an uncharacteristic catch in Jackie's voice now.

"No, no. She was an adult. Her name was Miriam
Weiden. Ever hear of her?"

"Uh-uh, should I have?"

"It would have been nice," I said softly.

In the taxi headed for the west side and Norma
Davis's Riverside Drive apartment, I mulled over her
decision to put me on the case.

Why would she even consider an investigator who'd
already botched things up once? I mean, even if the
cause *was* a malfunctioning machine, as I'd led her to
believe, the woman had to realize that my delay in
returning Miriam's phone call might very well have
contributed to her demise. So why not go for someone
with a clean slate?

I didn't kid myself. The reason had little, if anything, to do with Miriam's "confidence" in me. It was
simply that Ms. Davis didn't know any other PIs, and
she felt more comfortable dealing with an actual ac-
quaintance of her daughter's than with a total
stranger. (This acquaintanceship, of course, being why
the victim herself had contacted me.)

The fact is, though, it didn't make any difference to
me what had influenced Mrs. Davis. I was still very
grateful to her for the opportunity to look into this
murder that was so relentlessly gnawing away at my
conscience. Presuming, naturally, there'd even *been* a
murder.

Miriam had looked nothing at all like her mother,
a tall, almost gaunt woman in her late sixties or early
seventies, with a wide, flat nose, a sallow complexion,
and coarse gray hair. Her steely gray eyes and gray
tweed suit matched each other and the hair.

It was just going on noon. We were seated in Mrs.
Davis's spacious, high-ceilinged living room—the room's
generous dimensions not untypical of pre–World War II
Manhattan buildings. The furnishings here were com-

fortable, although far from elaborate—an eclectic mix of period and contemporary styles. It was a pleasant setting, I thought. Bright and welcoming. But if whoever decorated the place had had any sort of color scheme in mind, it certainly didn't come off.

Mrs. Davis was occupying a small portion of a kind of puce-colored Chippendale-type sofa, her long legs tucked under her. I had sunk my bottom into the cushy blue club chair opposite her and was now struggling to get my feet to make contact with the floor. (Which, considering that I'm only five two, is all too often the case.)

I noted the wad of tissues clutched in my hostess's right hand, but there was no redness or puffiness around her eyes, no indication she'd been crying. Nevertheless, I instructed myself to tread very carefully.

"You don't look anything like what I expected," she remarked before I could even put my first question to her.

Well, how many times had I heard *that* one? I mean, considering that these days the feminine counterpart to the stoop-shouldered guy in the trench coat seems to be the leggy blonde kickboxer in the tight sweater, I don't suppose I'm what *anyone* expects. Not only don't I meet the height and athletic requirements, but too little of my ample poundage is concentrated in my chest. And then, of course, there's my glorious hennaed hair.

I was about to utter a defensive retort when my new client added, "Your appearance must be a tremendous advantage in your line of work. Nobody would ever know you were a private detective unless you wanted them to."

"That's true," I said, pleased with her take on things. "Uh, would you mind if I asked you some questions now?"

"That's why you're here, isn't it?" she responded tersely.

I nodded, feeling foolish. "Umm, where was your daughter when . . . where did it happen?"

"In her apartment."

"Who was it who found her?"

"Erna—her secretary. At eight-thirty Wednesday morning when she showed up there for work. But Miriam was killed on Tuesday night. And I'm sure it was before ten-thirty, too."

"What makes you say that?"

"Because that's when I telephoned to find out how she was feeling. I got the answering machine."

"Maybe she'd gone out."

Mrs. Davis shook her head decisively. "No. First of all, most likely the doorman would have seen her."

"He *could* have missed her, though."

"I guess so. But what really clinches it for me is that Miriam was extremely edgy those last few days— there had been a second attempt on her life only that Friday. I kept urging her to come and stay with me for a while, but she wouldn't hear of it. At any rate, I'd spoken to her around four that afternoon. I suggested we go out to dinner, figuring it might take her mind off things. I even offered to pick her up at the apartment. But she told me she'd rather stay in." Mrs. Davis's small, sad smile turned me to mush. "I think Miriam had the foolish idea that she'd be safe in her own home."

"Something could have come up at the last minute," I speculated.

"I said that I'd speak to her later, and she knew I was worried about her. She would have phoned if she'd changed her plans. I'm certain of it."

And besides, I reminded myself unhappily, *she was waiting for my call.* "Were you concerned that you couldn't reach her?"

"I wouldn't say I was concerned. I was a little puzzled maybe. But then I figured she might have fallen asleep. As a rule she didn't go to bed that early and she wasn't normally that sound a sleeper, either, but—" The mother gave one of those you-never-can-tell shrugs.

"Mrs. Davis, do you know of anyone at all who might have wanted to harm Mrs. Weiden?"

"No one. Listen, Desiree—Oh, I hope you don't mind my calling you that." (Obviously, however, she had enough confidence in my response not to let it hold her up.) "My Miriam was the most thoughtful, the most generous person in the world." There was a deep sigh. "She was so young, too. Not even forty-eight until next week. It gets you to wondering, doesn't it?"

"Wondering?"

"Why so many of the *good* people are cut down like that—the people who really give of themselves to humanity."

"Yes, you do have to wonder," I murmured, a damn lump beginning to form in my damn throat.

"We thought we'd have a nice, quiet birthday celebration," Mrs. Davis mused. "I made dinner reservations ages ago at Le Bernardin, Miriam's favorite restaurant—you have to call ridiculously far in advance to get a table there. And now she's dead." With this, Mrs. Davis dabbed at her eyes. (I could swear, though, that they weren't the least bit moist.)

"What can you tell me about the previous attacks on your daughter's life?" I inquired—after a decent interval, naturally.

"The first incident took place this past summer. One afternoon Miriam was out on the lake in a rowboat, and the boat started to sink. So she and the person she was with had to jump into the water—I have no idea who this other person was, by the way. Anyhow, my daughter wasn't much of a swimmer, and it was obvious she was in trouble. Well, this companion of hers put an arm around Miriam's neck, and for a second Miriam got the notion she was about to be pushed under. Almost immediately, though, a delivery man came along and saw the two of them struggling in the water, and he swam out to help. And then once Miriam was pulled to safety, she was ashamed it had ever crossed her mind that she'd been in any danger from her friend—or whoever. Especially since the delivery man told them they probably hadn't even needed him, that it looked to him as though Miriam had been in very capable hands."

"You heard about this from your daughter?"

"That's right."

"And you didn't ask who'd been with her?"

"Of course I did. But she refused to answer. She said she couldn't be sure whether the delivery man had interrupted an attempt to drown her or to prevent her from drowning. And she didn't want to do any finger-pointing unless she was certain which it was. How fair would it be, was how she put it, to accuse someone—even if it was only to me—when that someone's only crime might have been in trying to save her life?"

"Any idea why the boat went down like that?"

"It was pretty old, and I presume the wood had begun to rot."

It was also possible, I thought, *that steps had been taken to insure that that boat wouldn't stay afloat.* But I kept the observation to myself. "Where did this take place?"

"At Miriam's summer cottage—at Coral Lake. It's a small town in upstate New York."

I knew *that.* Which is why it was all I could do to suppress a grin. A couple of years ago I'd driven through that beautiful lakeside community, which is known for its stately—and pricey—old homes. And I didn't spot a single residence that could even remotely qualify as a "cottage."

"She was there for ten days at the beginning of August," Mrs. Davis informed me.

"Alone?"

"As far as I know. Deena, my granddaughter—she's Miriam's daughter—was supposed to go with her, but then Deena changed her mind. I'm sure Miriam didn't lack for company, though. I wouldn't be surprised if Erna spent a couple of days with her. No doubt some friends drove up, too—Miriam had a lot of friends. And Deena might even have come up for the weekend with her boyfriend. I never did ask Miriam very much about her vacation. I was in California at my sister's the entire summer, you see. I didn't get back to New York until the third week in September, and by that time we had a few dozen other things to catch up on."

"But Miriam did tell you about the boat."

"Oh, no. Not right away. As a matter of fact, not until the Friday before she died."

"Why then?"

Mrs. Davis moistened her lips. "As I've already mentioned, that's when she had her other so-called accident. She said that it caused her to rethink what had happened that day at the lake."

"The delivery man you spoke of. Any idea who he delivered for?"

"Miriam didn't go into anything like that."

"All right. Let's talk about this second attempt."

"Yes. That morning—Friday—Miriam visited her old alma mater, James K. Polk High School—it's right here on the West Side, only a few blocks from this apartment. At any rate, the school's in the process of being renovated, and Miriam donated fifty thousand dollars toward the renovation. She was there for the ceremonial presentation of the check, which was scheduled for ten a.m. Well, just prior to ten, as she was walking toward the front entrance to the school, a heavy metal ladder came crashing down. It missed her by inches. There were some construction workers nearby, and one of them remembered seeing the ladder a couple of minutes earlier, propped up against the side of the building—right around the corner from that entrance."

"Were the police called in?"

"Oh, yes, they certainly were," Mrs. Davis replied tartly, a disgusted expression on her face. "They went around asking everyone a lot of questions. And then they told Miriam that it was more than likely one of the construction men had started to carry the ladder away and lost his grip on it. Or that someone—maybe even one of the students—had bumped into it. According to the police, it was no big surprise that the party responsible didn't come forward. The bigger surprise, they said, would have been if someone *did* admit to causing what could have been a fatal accident. They promised they'd continue to investigate, though." The disgusted expression was back on her face.

"I take it Miriam didn't see anything. When it happened, I mean."

"She was too shaken to even look around her. Besides, there was an open side door just a couple of feet from where the ladder had apparently been standing, and whoever was to blame could have ducked inside the building within seconds."

"Who knew about Miriam's presenting the check at the school that morning?" I asked.

"She could have mentioned it to any number of people—it had been on her calendar for weeks. Also, there was a little squib about it in the *New York Post* on Thursday, so . . ." Mrs. Davis shrugged.

I took a minute or so to try to digest all I had just learned, after which I said, "Did Miriam tell the police about Coral Lake?"

"She didn't make the connection immediately. Not until later—in the afternoon. Which is when she finally talked to me about it."

"Did she contact the police at that time?"

"At first she decided not to. She didn't have much faith in them, considering how they'd handled things at the school. But on Saturday she had a change of heart, and I went over to the station house with her. We both got the impression that the officers we spoke to didn't put any stock at all in the boating business. Especially after Miriam admitted that she never bothered reporting it to the authorities upstate."

If only she had. I clicked my tongue to commiserate.

"I have to confess something, though." And now two red spots decorated Mrs. Davis's sallow cheeks. "The truth is, I had a problem, too, accepting that Miriam was in danger. Maybe I just couldn't come to grips with the fact that anyone would want to hurt my Miriam.

"Except for that initial reaction, though, she herself hadn't been certain that what took place at the lake was really an attempt on her life—not until last Friday. And even then she wasn't *positive*. At any rate, I got the idea she was looking to convince me that somebody had purposely thrown the ladder at her, and so she dredged up Coral Lake. Besides, she was still distraught—understandably, of course—and I didn't feel she was thinking that clearly at the time. I know she doesn't—she didn't—give that impression, but Miriam was on the high-strung side.

"And Desiree? What the police said about the ladder did make sense to me—initially, that is. Don't you agree that it made sense?"

"Yes, I do." Actually, I didn't know yet whether I did or not. But it hardly mattered. In spite of all that rationalizing, it was apparent the woman was distressed enough at it was. "Tell me, have you mentioned these two incidents to the detectives investigating your daughter's death?"

"Naturally. And they did say they'd talk to the officers who were on the scene at the school. A lot of good that'll do, I'm sure. From our conversation at the precinct, I could see that those policemen had already pretty much concluded that the ladder came down by accident."

Norma Davis bit into her lower lip. "They were wrong, of course. But instead of putting some stock in the word of my own flesh and blood, I chose to believe them." Then in a voice barely above a whisper: "I'll never forgive myself for that."

And she dabbed at dry eyes again.

Chapter Five

My stomach was protesting its deprivation at top volume. I was hoping the taxi driver couldn't hear it, but unless he was stone deaf, this was wishful thinking.

I checked my watch. After two. Well, I suppose I couldn't blame it for bellyaching. (And yes, the pun *was* intended. Forgive me.)

Fortunately, I wasn't that far from Little Angie's. At least, that's how I chose to look at it. But really. Traveling across town and then heading over fifty blocks south isn't that big a deal when New York's thinnest, crispiest pizza is calling your name.

I took a seat at the counter. A wise move, considering that there are no tables at Little Angie's. And after deciding that three slices topped with pepperoni, onion, and mushrooms should do me just fine, I shamelessly ordered a fourth ten minutes later. Listen, I was going through too much angst these days to deny myself a few extra nibbles of sustenance.

I finished eating, took one last swallow of Coke, and then dug into the suitcase-size accessory I call a handbag and into which I cram everything it's even slightly conceivable I might have use for some day. I wound up dumping half the contents of the bag on the counter—luckily, the place wasn't that crowded at this hour—before I was able to lay hands on what I was searching for: the slip of paper on which I'd jotted down a couple of telephone numbers supplied by Mrs. Davis.

Little Angie's doesn't have a pay phone—there's barely room for Little Angie—so I had to hunt one up on the street. I could hardly believe my good fortune when, on only my third try, I located a telephone with the receiver and all its other essential parts intact.

Erna Harris, the dead woman's secretary, picked up at once.

"I definitely can't meet with you today," she informed me, the firmness in her voice precluding any attempt at persuasion. "I was just on my way to Mrs. Weiden's. I have so much to do at the apartment that I intend staying until nine or ten tonight." It was almost as if she could see my lips begin to part, because she immediately warned, "And don't even suggest it."

"I wouldn't dream of it," I lied. "You'll no doubt be worn out by then. Perhaps you could give me a few minutes tomorrow."

"Look, I have weeks of work ahead of me if I'm going to get everything in order, and—"

"I have some work to do myself," I responded curtly. "I'm busy investigating the possible murder of your former employer. Or doesn't that interest you?"

Erna reluctantly reconsidered, agreeing to see me at Mrs. Weiden's apartment at ten the next morning.

I had another quarter in the pocket of my trench coat. I used it to dial Miriam's daughter Deena.

There was no answer—not even by a machine.

Well, it wasn't yet four o'clock. Nevertheless—and Jackie's strict work ethic notwithstanding (besides, she'd never know)—I decided to call it a day.

"White," the voice on the other end of the line proclaimed without preamble.

I had been sipping that indisputably horrendous brew referred to as coffee at my place when the phone rang. And while I'd been deep in thought on the Weiden investigation, I had no difficulty at all in identifying the significance of the word. "You're sure?"

"Definitely." But then just to be on the safe side: "Ninety-nine point nine percent sure, anyhow. I figure you only get married once—or *I* will, at any rate—so why not go all out?"

"Does this mean you've also decided on a big wedding?" I asked my niece Ellen, who had recently (and finally) gotten engaged to her longtime boyfriend.

"You bet."

"What does Mike say?" Mike being the longtime boyfriend.

There was a moment of hesitation. "Well, I haven't talked to him about it yet. I figured I'd wait a few days."

"Good idea," I concurred, grinning. I had no doubt— and I have a feeling even Ellen suspected—that as the week wore on she would go back and forth at least half a dozen times between her latest preference and a small, immediate-family-only ceremony at which she'd be attired in an understated little off-white number.

"Umm, you'll be wearing a gown, too, I hope," she put to me.

"I'll wear whatever you'd like me to wear," I answered, still ecstatic about Ellen's having chosen me as her matron of honor.

"Chartreuse would be nice."

"Chartreuse?"

"What's wrong with chartreuse? It'd be great with your coloring."

"Oh, Ellen, I . . . I—"

"Just kidding," my niece clarified, giggling as only she can giggle. "Only—you know?—it's not really a bad idea. Try to picture how it would look with your red hair."

I wasn't certain whether she was continuing to give me the business or not. But I wasn't taking any chances. I got off the phone before this latest notion had time to take up permanent residence in her head.

And then I made another attempt to reach Miriam's daughter.

Still no answer.

So I poured myself a second cup of coffee. Which was a lot more palatable than the first—thanks to the heaping dish of Häagen-Dazs macadamia brittle that accompanied it.

It was just after nine o'clock when the phone rang again.

"Missus Shapiro?"

"Yes?"

The voice was halting, the information delivered with a heavy accent, most likely Eastern European. "My name Hilda Popov. I . . . I vork for Missus Veiden. Two years now I come to clean five times during veek. Yesterday I hear Harris voman telling to somebody on telephone dat you are inves— Vot is dat vord?" She gave up before I could help out. "Harris voman vas telling to person dat you look into death of Missus Veiden. Dat you tink she vas maybe . . . *murdered.*"

"That's right." My adrenaline had already begun to kick in here—it doesn't require much of an incentive—and I waited expectantly.

"Pipples dey . . . dey tink because I don't spik so good English, I don't understand nothing, neither. But I understand plenty."

"I'm sure you do," I said, pleased with myself for that instant having translated *pipples* to *people.*

"Vot I vant tell you is you should maybe spik to Missus Hartley, who used to be friend to Missus Veiden, but no more. Dey have terrible fight. Dis summer, it vas."

"About what?"

"I don't know. Maybe you ask her—Missus Hartley. You vant telephone number?"

"Yes. *Please.*"

"Umm, one more ting. You von't tell nobody I call you?"

"Ms. Harris doesn't know about your getting in touch with me?"

"No, I find number in book of Missus Veiden."

"Don't worry, I won't tell a soul. You have my word."

Apparently satisfied with this, Hilda relinquished Mrs. Hartley's phone number.

"I really appreciate your contacting me, Ms. Popov," I said. "I'd also like to ask *you* a few questions about Mrs. Weiden, though. Can we set up an appointment to meet?"

I could have taken a nap during the pause that followed. Finally, Hilda Popov mumbled, "No appointment. I . . . I vorking at Missus Veiden's apartment dis veek. Until all hours I stay. You try me next veek or veek later. Maybe can see you den."

The prospect did not seem to excite her.

Chapter Six

The door to Miriam Weiden's Park Avenue duplex was opened by a tiny, birdlike woman with a thin face, penetrating brown eyes, and a small nose that had a slight hook at the end of it. *Almost like a beak,* I thought uncharitably. Her short, blunt-cut brown hair was lightly streaked with gray and topped off by straight bangs that completely covered her eyebrows. She was dressed in baggy chinos and a blue-and-green flannel shirt that was at least two sizes too large for her, which she wore out, over the pants. She was of indeterminate age. (But if you forced me into making a guess, I'd put Erna Harris at close to fifty—on one side or the other.)

"Excuse the work clothes," Erna said. "I'll be spending most of the day packing stuff in cartons." And then hanging my coat in the foyer closet, she groused, "The way things are going, it doesn't look as though I'll ever be through here." This last, I was certain, was to let me know—in the event yesterday's conversation had left any doubt—how intrusive my visit was.

I followed the bird lady down an almost endless center hall with marble flooring and walls crammed with paintings of every conceivable style. I could hear the hum of the vacuum cleaner behind one of the closed doors. *Most likely Hilda Popov,* I informed myself.

We entered an enormous kitchen at the rear of the apartment. The instant I saw that room, I wanted to cry. And not only for the space it afforded, either. All around me were the sort of state-of-the-art industrial appliances that—with my love of cooking—have been pushing their way into my daydreams for years. There was a large platter filled with pastries in the center of the long wooden table there—which, to my astonishment, was set for two.

Erna motioned me to a chair. "We'll talk over coffee," she announced. I had no problem with the authoritative tone, since the dictate suited me just fine.

Crossing over to the counter, she poured two mugfuls of the steamy aromatic liquid from a large urn and brought them to the table. Then she sat down herself and waved her hand. "There's cream, milk, sugar, artificial sweetener—whatever you want. So help yourself." And grudgingly: "Try the prune Danish. It's excellent."

I was soon able to confirm the excellence of the prune Danish. And minutes later I could attest to the merits of the cheese Danish as well. The coffee, too, was outstanding, a delightful change from the stuff you-know-who prepares.

The conversation—which was paced to accommodate countless sips and chews and swallows—was fairly general at first, gradually segueing into more specific areas. I began by telling Erna how I'd met her employer at that benefit dinner and how I had been so impressed with the woman that I'd been checking the papers for news of her ever since. Erna then commented that Miriam had affected a great many lives with her generosity.

"You have no idea how sorry I am about what happened to her," I murmured. "I suppose you know about my answering machine's malfunctioning?"

"Norma—Mrs. Davis—told me. But look, if you *had* spent that evening with Miriam, then someone would have just gotten to her the next day. Or the day after that. *If* it turns out that she was a homicide victim at all."

Well, it was nice—and certainly unexpected—of her

to take me off the hook, even if I wasn't willing to do the same for myself. "I understand from Mrs. Davis it was you who discovered the body."

"That's right. I let myself in that morning, as I usually do. I figured I'd find Miriam in the study, but she wasn't there. I could hear the TV blaring upstairs, though, so I went up. I found her in the den, sprawled out on the sofa." The secretary looked at me intently. "At first I thought she was asleep, that she had dropped off watching television. But as soon as I tried waking her . . . well, I knew. Not that she was dead, but that something was terribly wrong."

"Did you touch her?"

"Just her shoulder. After saying 'Miriam, Miriam' a dozen times, I shook it a little. There was no response."

"And then?" I prompted.

"I called 9-1-1." Erna reached for a pastry. "You know the rest."

"How was Mrs. Weiden dressed that morning?"

"In street clothes. Same slacks and shirt she had on the day before."

"Was there anything unusual about the room itself?" I put to her.

"No," Erna responded tersely.

"How about food or drink? Any indication she might have had a drink or a snack of some kind?"

"None."

"When did you last see Miriam alive, Ms. Harris?"

"At just after five on Tuesday afternoon—when I left for home."

"Did she complain at all about feeling physically ill when you were with her?"

"No." Giving the woman the benefit of the doubt, I opted to regard this economy of speech as to the point, rather than just plain rude.

"Tell me, was she expecting any company later?" I anticipated the answer.

"She was not."

"The doorman who was on duty Tuesday evening—what are his hours?"

"Jimmy's on from three to eleven, and then Dave takes over from eleven to seven a.m."

Then it would be Jimmy I wanted to talk to. Because if I believed Mrs. Davis—and I didn't see any reason not to—Miriam was either dead or in deep trouble by ten-thirty that night.

"Mrs. Davis is certain her daughter was murdered," I said at this juncture. "Am I wrong in feeling that you don't agree?"

"Look, Ms. Shapiro—"

"Call me Desiree."

"All right. And you may as well call me Erna," she invited with an obvious lack of enthusiasm. Apparently in a more expansive mode now, she continued. "At any rate, what I want to make clear is that Miriam was . . . well, I can't even imagine anyone having a motive for killing her. Everyone adored her."

Not everyone, I countered silently, Hilda Popov's little nugget in mind. "There was no one who might have had it in for her? No one at all?"

"Absolutely not!" the secretary came close to shouting. "It must have been a heart attack—something like that. Those things have been known to come on very suddenly, in case you haven't heard."

"I've heard," I responded a shade testily. "But you are aware, aren't you, of the two previous attempts on Mrs. Weiden's life?"

"*Supposed* attempts on her life. Miriam was a nervous person, and when that ladder came so close to falling on top of her, it really shook her. I think her imagination just ran away with her—I mean with regard to what happened at both the school *and* the lake. She never really believed anyone had intended to drown her at Coral Lake—not until the ladder thing. She wouldn't have waited until that last weekend to tell me about it if she had."

"Do you have any idea who might have been in that boat with her?"

"Miriam refused to say."

I really hadn't expected anything else, so I shouldn't have been disappointed. But I was. "Did you spend any time at the lake with her during those ten days?"

"Yes, but let me set you straight. I don't even swim as well as Miriam did, and you must already know she wasn't any Esther Williams. Which is why, if you wanted to get me in a rowboat, you'd have to lift me in bodily—*after* hitting me on the head and rendering me unconscious."

"That wasn't the reason I asked. I—"

"Anyway," Erna broke in, dismissing the protest, "I went up with her on Friday to help her get settled, and then I drove back to the city with the chauffeur and housekeeper on Sunday night."

I was surprised the chauffeur and housekeeper hadn't remained with Mrs. Weiden, and I said so.

"Miriam gave them the week off. She made arrangements with a couple from New Cedars—that's the town right next to Coral Lake—to fill in for them. The wife came in every day and prepared the meals and did the cleaning, and the husband drove Miriam around."

"Would you happen to know the couple's name?"

"Yes, Reilly. But he died in September, and I understand Mrs. Reilly moved out to Arizona someplace to be near her son."

Figures. "Did Miriam talk to you about having company during her vacation?"

Erna frowned in concentration for a moment. "I remember her telling me that Willie Johns stayed with her for a couple of days—that's *Wilhelmina* Johns. And Carrie and Bill Oxner stopped in one afternoon. They have a summer home in that area, too, about forty miles from Coral Lake. I don't recall her mentioning anyone else."

"What about her daughter?"

"Miriam never said anything about Deena's being there."

"You'll get in touch with me if something occurs to you later on?"

"Sure." The offhand tone of voice, however, did not inspire confidence.

"Let me ask you something else. Who benefits financially from Miriam's death—any idea?"

The answer was slow to come—and reluctant. "Deena gets the bulk of the estate." Immediately Erna added hurriedly, "But she doesn't inherit everything. A nice chunk of the money goes to Miriam's favorite charities. And she told me she'd taken good care of her mother, too. Plus, there were a couple of smaller bequests as well."

"To—?"

"Her housekeeper Margaret and Frank, Margaret's husband, who was Miriam's chauffeur and general factotum. Frank fixed everything from the electricity to the plumbing around here. Those two were indispensable to Miriam—they'd been with her about twenty-five years."

"Are either of them in now?"

"No," Erna said. "I didn't see any reason for them to come to work for the next few days."

"They don't live here?"

"Miriam liked her privacy. They have an apartment on East Ninety-seventh Street."

"Then Mrs. Weiden lived alone?"

"For the past nine months, ever since her daughter moved out. Like practically every other eighteen-year-old girl in this world, Deena decided she wanted her own place."

"To get back to the will. You mentioned *smaller* bequests—what does that mean?"

"I can only guess; Miriam never got specific. But I would think, say, twenty or thirty thousand. But maybe it's less." Erna shrugged. "Or it could be more."

"And you? Did Miriam talk about leaving you anything?"

The secretary's face instantly turned crimson. "Yes, she did."

"And did she give you any indication of the amount?"

"No."

"You know, Erna, I really don't have a clue as to how much Mrs. Weiden was worth. And I'm not being nosy," I assured her. "I'd just like to get some perspective on what's involved here. I mean are we talking about ten million dollars? Twenty?"

Erna snorted at this. "Listen, I don't know exactly, but I *can* tell you it was a hell of a lot more than ten or twenty million."

I wasn't even curious about how *much* more. I mean, from where I sit, when you're talking that kind of money, what difference does another twenty or thirty million make? "I have just one more question for you," I said then.

That "one" was a lie, and evidently Erna didn't place any stock in it, because she pushed her chair away from the table. "I'm having another cup of coffee." At the counter, she turned around. "Can I get you some?" she inquired perfunctorily.

"No, thanks." Actually, I would have loved another cup, but I was offended by what I considered the grudging nature of the offer. (My sensitivity can kick in at the most inconvenient times.) Still, I was considerate enough to hold off until the woman had taken a few swallows before I asked, "Incidentally, what was the source of Mrs. Weiden's money?"

"Her first husband made a fortune in steel."

"Her *first* husband?"

"Malcolm Conyers. He was killed in a skiing accident a couple of years after they were married. That was before I came to work here."

"And her second husband? Was he also wealthy?"

"I guess you could say he was fairly comfortable. No more than that, though. He was a clothing manufacturer."

"Did you know him?"

"Yes." And almost defensively: "He was a very fine person, too."

"How did he die?"

Erna looked down at the table and brushed the crumbs on her place mat into a neat little pile. After this she straightened out the place mat itself. Following which she had another sip of coffee. At last she met my gaze. "Five years ago he committed suicide. Hung himself."

"Oh, God," I mumbled. "Why? Does anyone know?"

"His business was failing, and he was a very proud man. And besides that, he had lost his only brother a few months earlier. They were extremely close, and Dan missed him a great deal." Erna turned away from me then and, with her forefinger, surreptitiously wiped a tear from the corner of her eye.

This was even more of a shock than her providing the Danish had been. "Did Dan leave a note?" I asked gently.

"Yes. It said, 'Life is too painful.' That was all."

"Mrs. Weiden must have been devastated."

"She was."

And now Erna made a show of looking at her watch.

"Just one more question," I said one more time.

"I *do* have work to do," she responded irritably.

"Yes, I realize that. This will only take a couple of minutes, though. Okay?" I put on the kind of pathetic expression that's practically a guaranteed resistance melter.

Erna rolled her eyes and drummed her fingers on the table. But at least she was still sitting there. "All right. One more question—and that's it. And make it snappy, will you?"

I plunged ahead. "Mrs. Weiden was a very attractive woman. There must have been other men in her life since the death of her second husband—uh, I'm assuming she didn't marry a third time."

"She didn't. And she hadn't had any serious involvements since Dan died, either."

"Had she been seeing anyone lately?" I persisted, my thinking being that the victim might have been in a relationship that was more intense than her secretary suspected.

"Nobody at all."

Erna was, I could see, about to rise when I threw in the zinger—the thing I always have to work up to (and which, by the way, never seems to get any easier). "Umm, just for my records, would you mind telling me where you were a week ago Tuesday evening?"

"Would I *mind*? Damn right, I'd mind. What reason would *I* have for murdering Miriam? Have you asked yourself *that*? And if you think it had anything to do with the money she was leaving me, why would I suddenly decide to cash in *now*? Ask yourself that, too. Listen, I've been working for Miriam Weiden for nineteen years, and she's had me in her will for a good part of that time. What's more, I was well aware of it." She laughed without any mirth. "You know what the funny part of this is, though? It's very likely that *nobody* killed her, that she died of natural causes."

"You could be right, Erna. My problem, though, is that I have to assume Mrs. Weiden *was* the victim of a homicide." I went on quickly before the woman—who you could tell was poised to speak—had the chance to interrupt. "It's already been nine days since her death, and it could be weeks longer before the autopsy report comes in. If I were to wait until then to start my investigation—presupposing, of course, there's anything to investigate—the trail would be even colder than it is today."

For a minute or so Erna sat there without responding. Then she gave in. "Okay, Desiree, I'll put you out of your misery. Mostly, though, because you're beginning to look like a sick basset hound." (A very unkind observation, I thought.) "I was home all night that Tuesday. Alone. And to save you the trouble, on the morning of the ladder incident I was also alone. Right here in my office. And no, there weren't any phone calls or visitors either time. At any rate, not that I remember." And with these last words she—literally—sprang to her feet.

Erna made no bones about being anxious to usher me to the door. But she gave me the telephone numbers I requested before handing me my bag.

"Here," she said with a straight face. "I wouldn't want to keep you."

It had been a disappointing morning, I assessed in the elevator. Not only had I learned very little, but I'd seen practically nothing of the apartment. And how often did I get to visit a place like this, anyway?

Dummy! You should have at least asked to use the powder room!

Chapter Seven

It was a few minutes past noon when I arrived at the law offices of Gilbert and Sullivan. (That's right, Gilbert and Sullivan. Would I lie to you?) I rent space there, and thanks to my agreement with those two very nice gentlemen Elliot Gilbert and Pat Sullivan, I am also able to avail myself of the services of a secretary of Jackie's caliber. Just then, however, I had to seriously wonder what kind of a blessing this was.

I had no sooner gotten my left foot over the threshold—with the right one still on the other side of it—when Jackie looked up and glared. "You said you'd be in by eleven-thirty," she reminded me, utilizing her most put-upon tone. "So that's what I told everyone who's been trying to reach you, and they've all called back already, too. Here." She thrust a few pink message slips in my general direction, then very deliberately turned back to her computer.

On the way to my cubbyhole I checked the messages. There were two from my friend Pat, two from Ellen, and two—and *this* was a real surprise—from Deena Weiden. Deena had left the number of a friend's place. I could contact her there after three, the slip read.

I elected to return Pat's call first, our little misunderstanding regarding telecommunications still fresh in my mind.

*   *   *

Her reason for phoning, Pat said, was because she didn't remember if she'd mentioned that I was not to bring a gift to the party.

"Why not?" I had intended to start shopping for Burton's present next week—although what I was going to buy, I had no idea. I suppose I was hoping that once I hit the stores, I'd experience some kind of epiphany.

"Burton really doesn't need a thing. Honestly," she informed me.

"That doesn't matter. I want to get him something, well, just because it's his birthday and I want to."

"Look, if you absolutely insist, I'm sure that the gift he'd appreciate most would be a donation to his favorite charity."

"What charity is that?"

There was what is known as a pregnant pause. "Umm, you might think it's a little way out . . ."

"That's all right, if it's what Burton would like."

"It's . . . uh . . . Save the Cardinals."

I was taken aback. "You mean like in the football team?"

Pat laughed. "The Cardinals are a baseball team, you idiot. And no, I don't mean *those* Cardinals. I mean the birds."

"I didn't realize they were an endangered species."

"They may not be, for all I know. Somehow Burton got involved in this thing through a friend at work and— Anyway, don't ask."

"Okay, where do I send the check?"

"You don't mind?"

"Of course not. Hey, it's his birthday—and his charity." But I was scratching my glorious hennaed head as I said it.

The call to Ellen revealed the not unanticipated news that she had pretty much reversed her latest decision concerning the size of her forthcoming wedding.

"What got me to reconsider," she told me, "is that I was in Saks this morning looking at bridal gowns, and I came across this beautiful cream-color dress. It's silk *peau de soie,* and it has a scoop neck and long sleeves, and right below the waist there are these tiny seed pearls, and—"

I didn't let her finish. "It sounds lovely. But what does it have to do with the size of the wedding?"

"Well, as you know, we were planning to pull out all the stops, have a really lavish affair."

As of yesterday, anyway, I countered. But not out loud.

"For something like that, though," Ellen declared, "the bride should wear white."

"And where is this written?"

"I just think it's more appropriate." I could picture her thrusting her chin out now. I swear, sometimes that girl can be so obstinate. (And she didn't inherit that from me, either. I mean, she and I don't even share the same gene pool, Ellen actually being related by blood to my husband Ed, may he rest in peace.) At any rate, after a moment's hesitation she provided herself—as she usually did—with a loophole. "Of course, I'm not completely set on that dress, and if I find something in white that I like better, then we might still end up having a big 'do.'" She was giggling at her choice of this last word when, apparently, inspiration struck. "Hey, wait a second. I have an idea! Considering the way Mike and I have been vacillating on the kind of wedding we want?"

Mike vacillating, my eye. It was another of my silent comebacks.

"Suppose we just let my dress determine the sort of reception we have. White dress, large gala. Off-white or cream or ecru? Something smaller, more intimate. That makes a lot of sense, doesn't it?"

"Sounds good to me." But once again I was scratching my glorious hennaed head.

The instant the conversation with Ellen was over I switched my focus to the murder that might not even have *been* a murder.

First I got in touch with Miriam's visitors to Coral Lake.

Willie Johns agreed to see me at noon on Friday—and without any verbal arm-twisting, either. And while Carrie Oxner appeared to be somewhat puzzled at being contacted by a private investigator, she nevertheless assured me that she and Bill would be happy to talk to me about their friend Miriam. Could I come by at nine that evening? I certainly could, I said.

I was beginning to feel I was on a roll—until I dialed the Browns, the couple who'd been Miriam's housekeeper and chauffeur. No answer. And when I followed through on Hilda Popov's contribution to the investigation, I struck out again.

"This is the Hartley residence," a very proper baritone voice announced.

I asked to speak to Mrs. Hartley.

"Mrs. Hartley is vacationing in the Dominican Republic until Sunday. Would you care to leave a message?"

"No, thank you. I'll try her then."

"May I tell Mrs. Hartley who telephoned?"

"Uh, well, she doesn't actually know me."

"You don't care to leave your name?" He made it sound like an accusation.

I relented. "All right. You can tell her Mrs. Shapiro called."

"Would you mind spelling that?"

Spelling *Shapiro*? Oh, what the hell. "S-h-a-p-. . ."

Now, while you may have heard some nasty rumor about my taking taxis just to go around the block, believe me, this is a big exaggeration. (Well, maybe not *that* big.) But okay, I admit that walking is not one of my favorite pastimes. Sometimes, though, it does become a necessity—especially on a beautiful day like this one. The thing is, I could hardly window shop along Third Avenue by cab, could I? So at half-past one, right after stopping off for a quick sandwich, I went for a little stroll.

I was really proud of myself for resisting a pair of

gorgeous silver-and-onyx earrings in the window of a tiny boutique near Thirty-seventh Street. In fact, I didn't even go into the store to price them. (Earrings being one of the most major of my many major weaknesses, I figured that the greater the distance between *them* and me, the smaller the likelihood of any bonding taking place.) It wasn't more than two minutes later, however, that I was admiring a leopard-print scarf in another shop window. It was on sale at fifty percent off, too. I mean, they were practically making a gift of that scarf, for heaven's sake. Still, I am pleased to report that I moved on. And without dragging my feet all that much, either.

As soon as I returned to the office I made a second unsuccessful stab at getting ahold of the Browns. Following which I turned on the computer and began transcribing my notes.

At three-fifteen I broke away to phone Deena Weiden.

The man who picked up said that Deena should be in any second. "Can I have her call you?" he offered.

I told him it would probably be better if I tried her again.

And then it was back to my notes.

It was close to a half hour before I temporarily abandoned Mrs. Davis and her description of the ladder "accident" in favor—hopefully—of a minute or two with her granddaughter.

This time I was able to reach the girl.

"Grandmom told me that you're investigating my mother's death and that you wanted to speak to me." The voice was soft and pleasant.

"I'd really appreciate it if we could get together." Deena didn't immediately respond, so I added an inducement. "I'll keep it brief—I promise."

"It's not possible to do this on the phone?"

"I think it would be preferable to talk in person."

Her disappointment was evident. "Well . . . okay. I won't be able to see you tonight, though. And I have a couple of errands to run tomorrow morning, and after that I've got classes until five in the afternoon— I go to NYU. But I suppose I could make it around six, if that's good with you."

"It's fine."

She gave me the address of her Greenwich Village apartment, verifying, just prior to hanging up, that my visit would be a short one.

I was at my bathroom mirror, applying fresh makeup preparatory to my appointment with the Oxners, when I began to reflect on this morning's meeting with Erna Harris.

Why had she insisted that Miriam was so universally loved? Surely if the cleaning woman knew about the argument—or whatever it was—between Miriam and this Mrs. Hartley, then Erna was aware of it, too.

I figured that most likely she was protecting the victim's reputation. And directly on the heels of this, I had to wonder—feeling guilty about its even crossing my mind—if there were others, too, who might have harbored some animosity toward Miriam. And while I found this difficult to accept in view of my regard for the woman, I was forced to acknowledge that it was a possibility, anyway.

At what cost, though, I asked myself now, was Erna willing to shield her employer? Would she actually take a chance on Miriam's killer going free? But of course Erna—according to Erna, at any rate—didn't believe the deceased had been murdered at all. So she'd have no problem with stuffing a harmless feud or two in the closet.

I'd been engaging in these speculations while wielding those indispensable little tools that, when properly employed, do such sensational things for your eyes. But right after the mascara wand landed in the middle of my eyebrow, I decided it might be a good time to go to the phone and give the Browns one last try for the day. I counted eight rings before I put down the receiver.

Well, I mused as I attempted to sop up that giant glob of mascara—and wound up smudging my forehead almost to the hairline—at least Miriam had supplied a clue to her killer. In the message she'd left me that fateful Tuesday she had said she was terrified there'd be a third attempt on her life, "and that this time she'll succeed."

Knowing that the person Miriam suspected was a woman should certainly make my job easier, shouldn't it?

The face in the mirror smiled sardonically at me. *Sure. You can eliminate almost half the population in America,* that smile said. *So all you have to be concerned about is the other half.*

Chapter Eight

Entering the Oxner town house, I found myself in a small, octagonal-shaped foyer that was completely mirrored—up to and including the ceiling. The cheerful little maid who had answered the bell led the way to the study, which was right off the foyer. "Please make yourself comfortable. I'll tell Mr. and Mrs. Oxner you're here," she said.

For a few moments I paused just inside the doorway, admiring the unusually large and handsome room. Rich, dark wood paneling covered the lower portion of the walls, and above this was green felt—an ideal background for the striking collection of pastel watercolors here. A massive mahogany desk stood at one end of the room, and a floor-to-ceiling bookcase dominated the opposite end. All the upholstered furniture—and there were two seating groups—was in the same nubby beige fabric, with batik throw pillows in different prints of green and beige and cream decorating both sofas. Beige tieback draperies under a matching valance provided the window treatment, while on the floor was beige velvet carpeting bordered in the green of the wall covering.

Now, all of this is probably more than you wanted to know about the Oxners' study. But I can't help it. I swear I must have been an interior designer in my past life. If not, though, it wouldn't be a bad profession for my next one.

I crossed the room for an up-close view of the paintings and was soon joined by Carrie Oxner, who solemnly shook my hand, then invited me to sit down.

I settled into the chair she indicated. And after offering me something to drink—which I politely declined—Carrie took the chair across from me. Between us was a huge glass cocktail table that held four stone figurines of varying sizes. No doubt priceless pre-Columbian artifacts, I postulated. (It's funny. In another, less impressive home, I might very well have viewed these sculptures as merely interesting conversation pieces or even—if the Philistine in me surfaced, which it does on occasion—as sort of quirky-looking souvenirs.)

Anyway, I quickly reminded myself why I was there. And I was just debating whether to delay my questions until Carrie's husband came in, when he appeared.

The Oxners were a study in contrasts—physically, anyway. Carrie was blond and fair, a slim, small-boned woman who had to be still in her thirties. Dressed in a purple silk pantsuit that was almost formfitting—but not quite—she managed to let the world in on what a terrific figure she had without blatantly advertising the fact. If you know what I mean. Bill Oxner, who was *the* most successful real estate mogul in New York—according to Erna Harris, at any rate—was a bear of a man, easily two or three inches over six feet tall, and more than a little overweight. He had a florid complexion and about a dozen long dark hairs that were carefully arranged on an otherwise bald pate. I estimated him to be past sixty.

"Can we get you some refreshments?" he inquired, standing alongside his wife's chair. "A glass of wine? Some coffee?"

A frowning Carrie preempted me. "I already asked Ms. Shapiro that, Bill," she said, without looking up. "She doesn't care for anything."

"Sorry, love, I should have known you would." He smiled indulgently at the top of her head before moving over to the sofa, which was at right angles to the chairs. Then he sat down heavily and casually draped his arms across the back cushions. An instant later he turned to me. "How can we help you, Ms. Shapiro?"

"It's Desiree," I corrected. "I understand you and Mrs. Oxner were friends of Miriam Weiden's."

"That's right."

"Miriam and I served on quite a few of the same charity committees," Carrie embellished, "and we became very fond of each other. We—Bill and I—would often see her socially."

"Do you have any idea who might have wanted to harm her?"

"Why?" Carrie said sharply. "Has there been . . . was there some kind of foul play?" And before I could get in a word she switched her focus to Bill, glaring at him. "I *told* you it was strange that a private investigator would want to talk to us about Miriam. But *you* said it must be something about the insurance." And to me: "My brother sold Miriam a life insurance policy a few years back. Although why you'd contact us about *that* . . ." Her voice trailing off, she favored her husband with another glare.

"Mrs. Weiden's mother hired me to look into her death," I explained, now that I had the chance. "It's possible she may have been a homicide victim."

"Oh, my God." It came out in a whisper.

"It's only a possibility, Carr," Bill murmured soothingly.

"The police still aren't sure how she died," I informed them. "We have to wait for the medical examiner's report."

Carrie locked her eyes with mine. "But what do you *think*?"

"It's really too soon to say."

"But what do you *think*?" Her voice had grown shrill.

Well, couldn't let myself be pinned down like this. While I certainly had some very strong suspicions, that's actually all they were: suspicions. "I honestly haven't formed an opinion at this point."

I was about to repeat my still-unanswered question

when Bill Oxner spared me the trouble. "We haven't told you what you want to know yet, have we, Desiree? The truth is, I'm not aware of a soul who wasn't crazy about Miriam. Isn't that a fact, love?"

"Yes, it is. Miriam made a difference to so many people: the sick, the elderly, the indigent. . . . And I'm not only talking about the money she donated, either. She worked tirelessly to make this city a better place—visiting hospitals, taking food to the needy . . . I can't even *imagine* anyone wanting to end the life of a person like that."

"It *is* hard to believe," I agreed. "Uh, maybe you can help me with something else. I understand you visited Mrs. Weiden at her vacation home last August."

Bill was the one to respond. "Yes. We have a summer house not far from Coral Lake. Miriam invited us to lunch the Tuesday after she got up there. Right, Carr?"

"Right. Except it was Wednesday. You played golf with Richie Ivers on Tuesday, remember?"

"She's a hundred percent correct, as usual," the husband confirmed, beaming.

"What do you know about a boating incident that took place that week?"

A puzzled expression appeared almost simultaneously on both faces. "What kind of an incident?" Bill asked.

"Mrs. Weiden was out on the lake in a rowboat, and it capsized."

There was a brief silence before Carrie ventured fearfully, "It . . . it was an accident, though, wasn't it?"

"I'm afraid I can't say. That's all the information I have."

"What day was this?"

I hunched my shoulders. "I have no idea."

"Well, it was probably after Wednesday," she concluded, "or I'm sure Miriam would have spoken to us about it when we were there."

"Very likely. Umm, let me ask you something else," I put to Carrie. "Are you acquainted with a Mrs. Hartley?"

"Of course. Ernestine and Miriam were quite close."

"I was under the impression they might have had an argument of some kind."

"If they did, it's news to me."

I couldn't postpone it any longer. So inhaling deeply and then stiffening my spine, I forged ahead. "I hope you realize that there are certain things I have to check out . . . uh . . . for my records," I began. "It in no way means that you're suspects in Mrs. Weiden's death—either of you. What I—"

"It's okay, Red," Bill cut in, grinning good-naturedly. "Don't sweat it. You want to know where Carrie and I were the night Miriam died. Right?"

I breathed a sigh of relief. "Right."

"My wife had better handle that one. She's the one with the memory."

Carrie obliged. "That was a week ago Tuesday. We had an early dinner with friends, and then the four of us went to the opera—*Don Giovanni*. And afterward we all stopped off for coffee."

"See? What did I tell you?" a doting Bill demanded.

"We were out with Brett and Chuck Korman," Carrie went on. "Why don't I give you their phone number? They live here, in Manhattan." She rattled off the seven digits, which I hastily jotted down.

"Well," I said then, gathering up my shoulder bag and attaché case, "I've taken enough of your time." But even after I thanked the Oxners warmly, I was not yet prepared to leave. Recalling my oversight at the Weiden apartment, I asked to use the powder room. (I mean, occasionally I do learn from my mistakes.)

As it turned out, though, I wasn't able to give myself a mini tour of the house, since the powder room was directly across from the study. But it *was* a lovely room—from the moiré wallpaper with its delicate white ferns printed on a chocolate background to the white-chocolate-and-gold marble floor. Plus, there were thick white towels, a fluffy white throw rug, and white marble fixtures with gold fittings—including a sink counter that offered up all sorts of luxury toiletries. (I wish I knew the name of that hand soap—I'd love to get it. And, really, how expensive can a bar of soap be?)

I was standing at the curb, attempting to hail a cab, when I concluded that visiting the rich and richer can really be a downer. I mean, even from the very little I'd seen of the Oxner town house (Carrie mentioned that there were twelve rooms), the place had to be one step away from a palace.

And while I don't consider myself any more envious than the next person—after all, hadn't I dealt with those fabulous Weiden kitchen appliances without the aid of a single Prozac?—just then I was definitely covetous of the way Carrie and Bill Oxner lived. I don't know, maybe it was a cumulative thing.

All I can tell you is that after spending an hour or so here, I couldn't wait to go home and kick the furniture.

Chapter Nine

Unfortunately I had to hold off on the furniture abuse. Right now my priority was Jimmy the doorman. And he would be through with work at eleven p.m.

I glanced at my watch. It was after ten, and the Weiden apartment was eight blocks away. I warned myself that if I wanted to have enough time to question him, I'd better not walk there. (As if I'd actually had any serious intention of putting that kind of stress on my lower extremities to start with.)

I caught a cab immediately. And in practically no time I was standing in the vestibule of Miriam Weiden's building, talking to Jimmy. A short, powerfully built man of about fifty, with a swarthy complexion and dark, curly hair, the aforementioned Jimmy seemed to have more teeth than I had ever glimpsed in a single mouth before.

The instant I told him who I was, he asked if the autopsy report had come in.

I was surprised. While I've always marveled at the way information spreads from apartment to apartment in multiple-dwelling residences, for some dumb reason I hadn't expected luxurious accommodations like these to be equipped with a grapevine, too. "Not yet," I answered.

"They think Mrs. Weiden was murdered, though, don't they? The cops, I mean."

"They think it's a *possibility,* that's all. But I'm trying to gather all the information I can to get a jump on things—just in case."

"I'll tell you one thing. Nobody got up to her place that night during *my* shift." Jimmy clucked his tongue a couple of times. "Damn shame about Mrs. Weiden. She was a beautiful lady. And I'm not talkin' only on the outside. She was beautiful on the inside, too, where it counts. Damn shame," he repeated. "But anyways, you said you had a few questions."

Okay. So "a few" wasn't exactly accurate. But would it have been better to cause the man anxiety? I began with: "I know it was more than a week ago, but I'm hoping you can still remember something about that night."

Jimmy held open the door for an elderly gentleman who was about to exit with three toy poodles. Then after flashing his mouthful of teeth at the little group, he turned back to me. "Try me," he invited amicably.

"Do you recall seeing Mrs. Weiden on Tuesday?"

"I recall. Only I didn't see her."

"And you say no one visited the apartment?"

He looked me full in the face. "The cops asked me that same thing. And I tole them what I just tole you: not while *I* was on duty. A course," he added, "the secretary was up there that day. Like usual. I seen her when she left—around five, that was."

"You're certain there wasn't anyone else?"

"Look, I'm paid to make sure nobody who don't have any business gettin' in here *does* get in. And I take my job serious."

"It's evident that you're very conscientious," I responded truthfully. "You *are* only human, though. Isn't it possible someone might have slipped by you?"

Holding the door open again now, Jimmy exchanged smiles and good evenings with a young couple on their way into the building before uttering his denial. "Nope. You know what my wife tells me, Miz Shapiro? She says I even got eyes in the back of my head. Believe me, nobody sneaks past me."

But somebody had to, I insisted mutely. I mean, it was essential that I proceed on the assumption that Miriam Weiden had been murdered. And actually, in spite of all my hedging, I suppose that in my heart or gut or wherever, I was virtually certain, right from the beginning, that this was true. Also, in the absence of any visible telltale signs, I considered it probable that she'd been poisoned. Unless, of course, we were dealing with a truly creative killer who'd conjured up a more esoteric means of doing away with her. Like, let's see, scaring her to death, for instance. (I'd read this in a mystery story once.) And come to think of it, there was a homicide that I myself had investigated where . . . But never mind that now. I was still willing to go out on a limb for poison.

At this moment I had another idea—one that stopped me cold. What if Miriam had been given a *slow-acting* poison? It could have been days before the stuff did the job.

I mentally lectured myself. *For heaven's sake, don't start complicating things. In the interests of expediency, for now, at any rate, just go on the premise that the woman had ingested your normal, everyday kind of death potion sometime between five and ten-thirty that Tuesday evening.*

"My shift ends in a coupla minutes," Jimmy was saying, putting an end to my theorizing.

I tried to be pragmatic. Okay, so I hadn't learned how Miriam Weiden's killer might have gained access to her that evening. But what did it matter, really—except to satisfy my own obsession regarding loose ends? It was painfully obvious that someone *had* managed to evade Jimmy's watchful eyes—all of them.

Just then I realized there was an alternative. One that did not make me happy. The perpetrator could be somebody who *belonged* in this apartment house, somebody who lived or worked here. Considering all the suspects I would be faced with, it's no wonder my head started to pound.

Now, I've heard people claim that it's better to be lucky than smart. And while I, personally, had never given the subject much thought, it's a sentiment I was about to share.

After generously compensating Jimmy for his time, I was maybe two seconds away from heading home when a thin, bald little man strode into the vestibule, a big stogie clenched between his teeth. As he left the building and went down the walkway, I became aware that Jimmy was observing him intently through the glass doors. So I observed, too. As soon as he reached the sidewalk, the man stopped to light his cigar, tossing the match carelessly over his shoulder.

Jimmy muttered something under his breath.

I glanced at him curiously. "What's wrong?"

"Nothin', really."

"You're upset."

"Nah. It's only that these people never pay no attention to what they do with their matches. Only last week somebody threw a match into one of those pots out in front." I peered at the two giant stone flowerpots at the end of the walkway, one on either side of it. The containers were about three feet high and square, and each held a large, identical plant—or maybe it was a small tree, for all I know.

"Was there a problem?" I asked.

"Some other joker musta ditched his newspaper in the pot before that, and the paper caught fire."

The instant he said the words, I could tell that something had occurred to Jimmy, because suddenly his expression changed completely. It was, in fact, almost identical now to the look on the face of my beloved and long-departed German shepherd Brewmeister that time I caught him chomping on my favorite sweater.

A little *ping* sounded in my head. "Who put out the fire?"

"I did. Listen, Miz Shapiro, I know what you're thinkin', but it didn't take more'n a minute," Jimmy maintained, a part of him still in denial. "And anyways, I had one eye on this entrance the whole time."

Naturally, I recognized—even if the doorman refused to—that this was virtually impossible. But I clamped down on my tongue. And for a brief while, neither of us spoke. Then shifting uneasily from one foot to the other, Jimmy put in, "Besides, I'm not even sure that was on Tuesday night. Honest."

But his cheeks—which had turned as red as those flames must have been—were calling him a liar.

Chapter Ten

So I had my answer.

I mean, one look at Jimmy and you *knew* the fire had broken out the night Miriam died. What's more, as close as Jimmy could recall, it had happened around nine o'clock. He'd just never connected the two incidents. Very likely because he hadn't wanted to.

Of course, it was hardly serendipitous that the murderer should attempt to gain entry to the place at the precise moment the newspaper burst into flames. No, that little flare-up in the flowerpot was obviously the perp's own handiwork. After putting the match to the paper, she'd concealed herself (by crouching behind the second stone pot maybe?). And then when our friend Jimmy rushed out to extinguish the blaze— voilà!—it was the perfect opportunity to dash by him undetected.

As to how she'd also managed to leave unnoticed, it's been my experience that doormen rarely pay that much attention to those exiting the premises. And if you really want to tip the scales in your favor, try to attach yourself to a group that's on the way out.

Well, naturally, I was relieved to establish a viable scenario as to how the perpetrator was able to gain access to Miriam's apartment. The only trouble was, it didn't do diddly to help me identify her. Still, at least I wouldn't have to resort to interrogating everyone in the building. Not yet, anyway.

* * *

As soon as I was settled in my cubbyhole the next morning I phoned Brett Korman to verify Carrie Oxner's alibi, although the truth is, it was next to impossible for me to imagine that woman murdering anyone. But then how often had I come up with this same kind of assessment—and gone on to prove myself wrong?

Mrs. Korman confirmed that the two couples had been together that Tuesday evening. "My husband and I met the Oxners for dinner at five-thirty, and we were with them until almost one," she told me.

I was inordinately pleased that my judgment had been confirmed. I would not even let myself think those two totally unnecessary words: "for once."

A couple of minutes later I called Norma Davis.

"Do you have any news?" she put to me immediately.

"I wish I did. I've been questioning people, but you realize that without the autopsy findings it's sort of like groping around in the dark."

"Of course. I don't even know why I said that. Have you been to see my granddaughter yet? I asked her to get in touch with you."

"We have an appointment for tonight."

"A wonderful girl—Deena," Mrs. Davis murmured, a rush of warmth in her voice. "She's the love of my life. But I'm sure you phoned for a reason?" Her inflection turned it into a question.

"Uh, listen, Mrs. Davis, do you think I could talk to Miriam's attorney, the one handling her estate?"

"Certainly. Let me give you his number—his name is Ward Reeves."

I suggested that it might be a good idea if she spoke with Reeves first to request that he cooperate with me.

"I'll call him as soon as we hang up."

I decided to wait until later in the day before attempting to contact the lawyer, in the event Mrs. Davis had a problem reaching him. For now I would try the Browns—again. I gritted my teeth as I dialed. I was still gritting them when I put down the receiver—after listening to that telephone ring. And ring. And ring.

Moments later Pat Sullivan (of Gilbert and Sullivan) stopped by to say hello. Pat spends so much of his day in court that I rarely see him except in passing. But today he sat down in my office, and we chatted for quite a while. When he left I had just enough time to repair my lipstick, comb my hair, and leave for my meeting with Wilhelmina—aka Willie—Johns.

Ms. Johns's apartment wasn't nearly as impressive as the Oxners'. (And thank God, too! I can't stand a malcontent—particularly when it's me.) But don't get the wrong impression; the place was still nothing to sneeze at. I will, however, spare you the detailed description.

The lady herself could have been anywhere from sixty-five on up, a handsome, substantially built woman with salt-and-pepper hair—about half salt, half pepper—and bright blue eyes. The moment I looked at her I decided that Willie Johns had a sort of *presence*. This impression was furthered as soon as she spoke in that resounding voice of hers, which, I would soon learn, quite frequently communicated in commands.

We were holding our conversation in a small study, sitting across from one another in matching maroon leather club chairs separated by a low table.

Once we'd both gotten comfortable Willie said, "You'll stay and lunch with me."

"Oh, that's very nice of you, but—"

She waved off the objection. "It's cream of potato soup and shrimp salad sandwiches."

"Sounds great, but—"

"Coffee or tea?"

Well . . . it wouldn't be nice to hurt her feelings. "Uh, coffee, please."

"I want to be sure we get all this nasty stuff about Miriam out of the way first, though. We should be through in an hour, shouldn't we?"

"Oh, I would certainly think so," I answered, in

total agreement with the scheduling. I mean, I hate to eat at the same time that I'm concentrating on work. I take my enjoyment of food too seriously to give it such short shrift.

Walking over to the desk now, Willie picked up the phone and pressed a button. "My guest and I will be having our lunch at one. And, Gertrude? Coffee, please, for both of us."

I noted at this moment that there were already two place setting on the little table under the window. And for some reason I found myself smiling.

Willie returned to her seat, and before I had an opportunity to speak, she did. "I understand Miriam's mother has you investigating the possibility Miriam might have been murdered." I guess it was evident that this took me by surprise, although it really shouldn't have. "Carrie Oxner gave me the report," Willie offered by way of explanation. She leaned toward me. "What makes her mother suspect something like that?"

"It's because Miriam herself suspected that someone wanted to kill her—she'd already met with two very questionable 'accidents.' And now, of course, she's dead."

"*Two* accidents?" Willie responded sharply. "Carrie only mentioned *one*—some boating business. But that was months ago. Did something happen more recently?"

I realized then that this woman hadn't given me the chance to ask a single question yet. Nevertheless, I related the incident with the ladder—but as succinctly as I could.

"Did Miriam have any idea who was doing those things to her?" Willie demanded the moment I was through.

"Not that I'm aware of," I lied.

"And you believe these previous *accidents*—or whatever they were—are related to her death?"

"That's what I'm trying to find out."

"When do you anticipate that the police will have the autopsy results?"

"I don't know. Soon, I hope." I was becoming more and more frustrated at this point. After all, wasn't *I* supposed to be interrogating *her*? "Listen, I—"

It was a futile attempt. "So tell me, Ms.—" Willie broke off. "By the way, is it Ms. Shapiro or Mrs.?"

"It's Mrs.—I'm a widow. But I hope you'll call me Desiree."

"I'll do that. And you call me Willie, hear? I'm a single lady myself, Desiree. Only met one man in my life that I considered worth giving up my independence for. The trouble was, he was already taken. But that's a long story. How many years were you married?"

"Five." And before she could utter even one more syllable, I slipped in, "What day did you visit Mrs. Weiden at Coral Lake?"

"I drove up on Monday—she had only arrived that weekend—and I left the next afternoon. Miriam tried to persuade me to stay another couple of days, but Wednesday was my nephew's birthday. And, no, nothing untoward occurred while I was there. I doubt she'd even been out on the lake yet."

I was all set to bring up something else, but I wasn't speedy enough to preempt Willie. "Carrie said I should be prepared for you to ask where I was the night of Miriam's death. But I'll save you the trouble."

I swear, this Carrie was a human tape recorder. At any rate, you know how unlikely I considered it that Carrie Oxner could be a murderer? Well, I had even more difficulty casting Willie Johns in the role. Still, I couldn't totally disregard the possibility. "I'd appreciate it."

"No problem, kid." And with this, Willie jumped up and strode to the door. Flinging it open, she bellowed into the hall at earsplitting volume, "Gertrude!"

Minutes later a middle-aged woman in a black cotton shirtwaist hurried into the room.

"This is Gertrude, my housekeeper," Willie apprised me, taking a seat again. "Gertrude, do you recall where I was a week ago this past Tuesday?"

The housekeeper, who had positioned herself along-side Willie's chair, nodded. "Of course."

"Tell Mrs. Shapiro, please."

Gertrude obliged. "Ms. Johns was at home—in bed with the flu."

"I'd been to a big charity dinner on Sunday," Willie elaborated. "It was catered by one of the top firms in New York, too. Me? I wouldn't have those people do my Pomeranian Sadie's birthday party. But at any rate, one of the waiters there was coughing and sneezing all night long. And apparently, whatever he had, I got." Shaking her head in disgust, she looked up at the housekeeper. "I was a mess, wasn't I, Gertrude?"

"You certainly were." And to me: "Ms. Johns couldn't go out of the house for a week."

"Did you see her at all on Tuesday evening?"

"Naturally I did. I took her some tea and toast around seven. She barely managed a few sips of the tea. And at nine I brought her her medication and tried again to get her to put something in her stomach. But she still wasn't up to it."

"And was this your last visit to Ms. Johns's room that night?"

"No. I poked my head in later, too—at ten o'clock. She was sound asleep, so I tiptoed in very softly and shut off the TV. But I woke her, anyway."

"How can you be so sure of the times?" I inquired skeptically.

"Seven's when Ms. Johns usually has her dinner if she's at home, so that's when I brought her her tray. And I remember thinking before I went up at nine o'clock that it had been two hours since I'd last checked on her and that maybe by then I could coax her into having a few nibbles of toast."

"And when you went into her room for the third time?"

"*NYPD Blue,*" Gertrude informed me with a smug little smile. "The opening credits were just going on when I switched off the television set."

"Satisfied now that I'm not your killer, Desiree?" Willie challenged.

"I never thought you were, honestly. But I had to establish that. It's what Mrs. Davis—Miriam's mother—hired me for."

"It's okay, kid. You gotta do what you gotta do." Then she glanced up at Gertrude. "Thanks a lot," she told the woman. "You can go now."

The instant the housekeeper had closed the door behind her, Willie was ready for more. "All right," she put to me, "what else do you want to know?"

"Can you think of anyone who might have wanted to harm Mrs. Weiden?"

"It's a funny thing. If you had asked me that question a couple of months back, I'd have told you absolutely not. In those days I regarded Miriam as practically a national treasure. Recently, though, I've had reason to reevaluate this impression. Damn good reason."

It was a totally unexpected and unsettling response. "What made you change your mind?"

"Hold your horses. I'm about to enlighten you. One afternoon we were having a committee meeting at Miriam's, and I got there rather early. So this Mr. Brown—he was Miriam's butler or some such—showed me into the kitchen, where Miriam was seeing to the last-minute preparations for our luncheon. Well, a little while later I had to use the powder room, and on the way back, instead of returning to the kitchen, I wound up taking a wrong turn—I have *the* most pathetic sense of direction. At any rate, I found myself right near what must have been the office of Miriam's secretary. And apparently Miriam had stopped in there to talk to the woman for a moment. I heard Miriam say—and these may not be the exact words, but they're pretty goddamn close—'Did you alert the media to my visiting the hospitals tomorrow?' I didn't catch the secretary's answer, but then Miriam said—and none too sweetly, either—'How many times do I have to remind you to stay on top of these things? If

I left it to you, there wouldn't have been anything in the papers about my paying for that little cancer girl's surgery, either.' "

Willie's expression did an admirable job of communicating her feelings, and she gave me a moment to absorb her disgust before continuing. "Let me tell you, kid, my mouth dropped open so far my bridge almost fell out. Actually, though, I was a little skeptical of all that goody-goodiness when I first met Miriam. She was a tad too self-effacing for my tastes, if you understand what I mean. I *thought* all that humility of hers might just be a clever little shtick. But then right away I accused myself of being a cantankerous old bitch, and I shoved my suspicions aside. I should've trusted my instincts in the first place. Anyone who's lived as long as I have—assuming they've got so much as a thimbleful of sense—develops a feel for those things. You'll know what I'm talking about when you get to be my age." She looked at me appraisingly. "Although you're no sweet bird of youth yourself. How old *are* you anyway, Desiree?"

Now, my mother used to contend that any woman who reveals her age once she's past twenty-five is just plain crazy. And my mother did not give birth to a dingbat daughter. "What if I said I don't have any idea?"

"What kind of an answer is that?" Willie shot back irritably.

"You see, I always lie about my age, and I never pay attention to what I say. By now, I don't even *remember* the truth anymore."

"Touché," Willie responded, laughing heartily. "I'm a nosy old thing if there ever was one, aren't I? Here's something that may make you glad I don't mind my own business, though: I heard a rumor not too long ago that Miriam was seeing a married man."

I was about to follow up on this little bombshell when Willie cut me off at the pass. "And don't bother throwing a bunch of questions at me, kid, because that's all I know."

"Thanks for the lead. Thanks very much."

"It's okay. And listen, you might want to talk to Ernestine Hartley. She and Miriam used to be like *that*"—to illustrate, Willie crossed her third and index fingers—"and then they had some kind of falling out. At any rate, there's no saying *what* that one could tell you. And whatever it is, she'd probably be only too happy to do it, too."

When I returned to the office I spent a few minutes mulling over the day's visit. Willie Johns was something else, all right. *Kid* notwithstanding, I really liked the woman. And not only because she'd fed me that delicious lunch—honestly. Or offered this new slant on Miriam's character. In fact, considering my admiration for the victim, I have to admit that I was reluctant to accept Willie's information as being totally credible. After all, it was possible—wasn't it?—that Willie had misunderstood what Miriam said that afternoon. And as for that married-man rumor, it was just that: a rumor.

But what was the matter with me, for God's sake? I had been given a couple of potentially fruitful avenues to explore. Still, when I thought about meeting with Ernestine Hartley, who, according to Willie, probably could—and very likely would—fill in some blanks for me, it was with more than a little anxiety.

At any rate, it was now close to three o'clock. And that morning I'd disposed of the very few matters requiring my immediate attention, so I had to concede that this would be a good time to transcribe a few additional pages of notes.

Before getting started, though, I figured I should really try the Browns again. So I did. With the expected results. Which was maybe just as well, being that there's a fair chance I would have passed out cold if I'd met with any success.

After this I got out my checkbook. Before I forgot, I'd better make out that donation to Save the

Cardinals. (Although save them from what, I had no idea.)

These things attended to, I glanced down at my nails, noting that the polish had begun to peel. There was no getting away from it; they were a disgrace. Of course, since I was wearing a colorless enamel, someone would have to be sitting on my lap to make that same assessment. But this was not the point. I mean, regardless, a person has to take some pride in her appearance, doesn't she? I nodded in agreement with myself as I rummaged around in the drawer for the polish remover.

As you've no doubt gathered, I wasn't what you could consider fired up with ambition that afternoon. Once I'd applied a third coat of nail gloss, however—and, in the process, exhausted every semi-legitimate excuse I could think of for procrastinating any longer—I began to reach for my note folder. But with my arm in mid air, I glanced at my watch. It was four-ten. Better put in that call to Miriam's attorney.

Ward Reeves's greeting when he got on the phone was "I've been waiting to hear from you, Ms. Shapiro. Just what is it you'd like to know about Miriam Weiden's will?" He wasn't exactly unpleasant; *brusque* would be a better word. At any rate, his manner had the effect of making me speak at a greatly accelerated speed.

"I understand that we're talking about the distribution of a considerable sum of money here," I said, the words spilling out in double time.

"A *very* considerable sum," Reeves remarked dryly. He didn't elaborate, and I didn't ask him to. His response provided all the information I really needed.

"Can you tell me who Mrs. Weiden's beneficiaries are?"

"Hold on a moment." I heard the rustle of papers, and then he was back on the line. "Mrs. Weiden's daughter Deena inherits the bulk of the estate. There are also bequests to Frank and Margaret Brown, Mrs. Weiden's housekeeper and chauffeur, and to—"

"How much will the Browns be getting?"

"Twenty-five thousand dollars each," Reeves answered. "Miriam's secretary—Erna Harris—receives seventy-five thousand. In addition, money has been designated for various charities. Would you like me to be more specific there?"

"No, that's fine."

"Mrs. Weiden's will also grants her mother one hundred thousand dollars a year for life, with the proviso that on Mrs. Davis's death the balance of the funds set aside for this purpose be divided among those charities she—Miriam—supported." And now the lawyer said abruptly, "Is there anything more I can help you with?"

"No one else is mentioned in the will?"

"No one."

"I guess that about does it, then." I thanked him for his time.

"My pleasure. Don't hesitate to call if I can be of further assistance."

But I *know* he had his fingers crossed when he said it.

Well, nothing I'd just heard had left me any wiser.

As I'd previously been informed, Deena was the victim's principal heir. And no doubt the girl had been aware that she would be coming into a fortune on her mother's death. This didn't mean Deena had had a hand in speeding up her inheritance, though. Conversely, it didn't mean that hand of hers was clean, either.

And there was certainly a very nice stipend for my client. But I really couldn't buy her killing her daughter and then hiring me to find the killer.

As for the other, lesser beneficiaries, I wondered if the amounts stipulated in the will (or the amounts they were expecting, at any rate) were sufficient to induce them to commit murder. I decided they could be. But as Erna had pointed out, why now? By the same token, though, why not now?

All of which left me precisely where I was before I telephoned Reeves.

Chapter Eleven

My rotten luck! Deena Weiden's Greenwich Village apartment was a fourth floor walkup!

Dedicated professional that I am, however, I opted to risk a coronary to question the girl.

Heading for the stairwell, I thought it advisable to remind myself that I'd been through this kind of thing before and managed to survive. After all, I was still here, wasn't I? So clinging to that thought, I began my climb. Naturally, this took some time, due to the fact that I had to pause for four or five rest stops—two of them seated and each of them somewhat longer than its predecessor. But I finally did make it to Deena's floor—although I had to practically *crawl* up that last flight.

Deena Weiden was aware I was in the building, since I'd rung the downstairs buzzer, so the door to 4A was already partially open. A pretty girl in a short navy skirt and pale blue sweater was standing just inside the apartment, her hand on the knob. She was of medium height, with a curvy figure and dark shoulder-length hair, her attractive features set into a perfectly-shaped oval face. She was at least part African-American.

I was puffing like crazy. Believe me, Sir Edmund Hillary couldn't have been more pooped after ascending Mt. Everest. "I'm here to see Deena Weiden," I managed to get out.

The girl smiled. "You're seeing her."

"Oh," I said, nonplussed. (No matter what the situation, you can always depend on me to come up with the appropriate response.) But overcoming my surprise a moment later, I extended my hand. "I'm Desiree Shapiro. I suppose you've already gathered that, though." I tittered.

Deena gave the outstretched hand a brief obligatory shake, then opened the door wider and stepped aside. "Come in. You sound a little out of breath. I'm sorry, I should have warned you about the stairs."

"No big deal." But I didn't even wait to be invited to sit before I sat, collapsing on the sofa.

"Can I get you anything?" she offered, hovering over me. Judging from her expression, she might have been viewing someone in intensive care.

"No thanks. And don't look so concerned. It's only that I don't normally get much exercise. In fact, I make sure of it," I joked.

Deena ignored the attempt at humor. "Are you positive you wouldn't like something? Some coffee, maybe?"

"On second thought, I *would* like a cup of coffee, if it's not too much trouble."

"Uh, it's instant. I hope that's okay."

"Absolutely."

A few minutes later she was speaking to me from the kitchen, which, this being a very small room, was no more than a couple of yards from the sofa. "Grandmom is certain my mother was murdered."

"Yes, I know. That's why she hired me."

"So you agree with her."

"It's really too soon to say. Right now I'm just looking into the *possibility*."

She poked her head into the living room. "You're aware that my mother was an extremely charitable person?"

"Yes, I am."

"I just can't think of a reason anyone would have for killing her—she did so much for so many people. Of course, this one detective who came to see me thinks that maybe she committed suicide, which is equally ridic—"

The shrill whistle of the tea kettle aborted the sentence, and withdrawing her head, Deena called out, "How do you take your coffee?"

"Milk and sugar, please."

"How many?"

"How many?" I repeated, exhaustion no doubt having retarded my thought processes.

"Teaspoons," she said patiently. "Of sugar."

"One's fine, thanks," I answered, remembering at last to shrug out of my coat.

Deena was soon back to hand me a bright green mug. Then she fetched a stack table from a corner of the room and placed it in front of me. I had a couple of sips of coffee—and came close to gagging. *How much sugar had she put in this thing, anyway?* The girl was certainly generous, I'd say that for her. I set the mug on the stack table.

"If you're curious about why I have so little furniture, it's because I haven't been living on my own very long," Deena explained, joining me on the sofa. "There's just this"—she patted a sofa cushion—"which was a must since it's also my bed, plus I have a small kitchen table and two chairs."

"Well, it's a start," I told her encouragingly.

"I finally got around to ordering some other stuff about a month ago, mostly to keep the family quiet. My mother and grandmom and Erna—who's my mother's secretary and also my *second* mother—were always after me to furnish the place. So now that I've done my part, what happens?" she demanded with a wry little grin. "The stores are taking forever to deliver."

This brought to mind how I had once waited seven months for a taupe-and-blue rug—only to have it come in in green and beige. "Oh, I know all about that," I sympathized.

"That kind of thing doesn't bother me, though; I'm not really into material possessions. Whenever they send the other pieces, they send them. What's the matter?" She was looking at the mug on the table now. "Is anything wrong with the coffee?"

"Oh, no, it's delicious. I'm just waiting for it to cool off a bit." (I am really *such* a talented actress. I mean, becoming a member of my high school drama club had definitely paid off. Although most likely it only served to polish my innate gift for lying.)

"Anyway," Deena continued, her voice dropping to a more confidential level, "I'm not in the apartment very much. I stay at my boyfriend's a lot."

"No wonder I had a problem reaching you. It was his number you left for me yesterday?"

"That's right. I did have an answering machine at one point, but then it broke, and I still haven't gone out to buy a new one. I'm a terrible procrastinator," she informed me unnecessarily.

"I gather your grandmother doesn't know you aren't here most of the time."

"Oh, no!" Her eyes opened wide. "I call her every day so she won't keep trying me and get suspicious. I guess I shouldn't have said anything to you. You're not going to tell her, are you?"

"Of course not."

"It would probably break grandmom's heart."

"Don't worry, it'll stay between the two of us," I promised.

And now I finally got down to it—to the reason I'd come. "I realize this will be difficult for you, Deena, but I'd appreciate it if you could answer a few questions for me—just for my records."

"Fire away," the girl responded nonchalantly.

"Uh, I understand that your mother left you a great deal of money."

"Yes."

"How long have you known about being her heir?" She shrugged. "Forever, probably."

"You and your mother were close?"

"*Pretty* close. Until the last year or so. She didn't approve of my going steady or of the fact that my boyfriend is a carpenter instead of a Harvard man or the son of some big shot. And she denied it, of course, but she wasn't crazy about Todd's being black, either. Silly when you think about it, right? Plus, she did everything but take to her bed when I told her I wanted to move out of the house."

"So your relationship had become strained?"

"I wouldn't say that. Not really. She got over those things." Deena smiled mischievously. "More or less."

"How was she with your boyfriend?"

"You mean how did she treat him?"

I nodded.

"Fine. My mother was always cordial to people." Now, you can't always depend on my antennae, but they seemed to pick up a trace of irony in the tone.

"And your boyfriend? How did he feel about your mother?"

"Well, knowing *her* feelings, he was a little uncomfortable when they were together. But not so uncomfortable that he'd kill her, if that's what you're getting at."

"I'm not, believe me. Until the medical examiner's findings come in, we have no evidence there was even a murder."

It was at this moment that we heard a key in the lock. "Todd," Deena informed me. I turned to face the door just as a tall, twenty-something man entered the apartment.

He approached the sofa and bussed Deena's cheek. "You're early," she apprised him matter-of-factly.

"Uh-huh," was all he said.

Deena quickly took care of the introductions. "Desiree, this is my boyfriend Todd. Todd, Desiree Shapiro."

I half rose from the sofa and held out my hand. Todd shook it awkwardly, confining his gaze to a spot somewhere over my left shoulder. There was something kind of endearing about his obvious shyness. "We talked on the phone, I think," I told him.

I noted the merest trace of a Caribbean accent when he responded. "Yes, I remember that." And he smiled. It was an attractive smile. But then this was an attractive man. I took inventory: muscular build; close-cropped black hair; skin the dark, rich shade of Häagen-Dazs Belgian chocolate (you can tell where my head is); and—what was most striking—warm brown eyes fringed with the kind of lashes for which I'd have gladly forfeited a year's supply of Egyptian henna. Besides, I admit to having a "thing" for men in neatly pressed chinos and crisp white shirts. Yes, I could see where Deena might brush aside Miriam Weiden's wishes—and probably half a dozen Harvard men—in favor of this Todd.

"Would you like Todd to wait in the kitchen?" the girl was asking. "He wasn't supposed to be here until a half hour from now."

"I don't mind sitting in the other room while you and Deena talk," Todd assured me, staring down at his brown suede moccasins as he was addressing me.

"That isn't necessary. Please stay."

Nodding, he plopped down on the floor—the only alternative seating in the room.

"I was about to ask Deena if you two were at Coral Lake this past summer," I said.

Deena answered the unasked question. "Yes, in August. The weekend before my mother came home."

"Did you go boating at all while you were up there?"

She shook her head. I thought I saw Todd glance at her quickly and then look away. But maybe I was mistaken.

"And you, Todd?"

"He couldn't," Deena interjected quickly. "Neither of us could. My mother told us the boat had sprung a leak that week."

"Did you know that she almost drowned?"

"No, she never said a word about that. What happened?"

I can't say I was convinced by the denial. Nevertheless, I recited what little I knew of the incident.

"My mother believed this person deliberately tried to push her under?"

"She couldn't tell. But she did have her suspicions."

"And you think *I* might have been that person? Or Todd?" She was glaring at me.

"No, I don't. Please understand. If it turns out your mother's death *was* a homicide, it's possible that what happened at the lake was also an attempt on her life. I wouldn't be doing my job if I didn't find out everything I could about that."

"I suppose that's true," Deena conceded reluctantly.

I gave us both a short breather before my next question—another biggie.

"Umm," I began (and it was an extended *umm,* too, since I wasn't very happy to be asking about this, either), "I imagine you've heard that a heavy metal ladder came close to falling on top of your mother the Friday before she died."

"Yes, I did hear about it."

"Again, I'm not saying this wasn't accidental, but would you mind telling me where you were that morning?"

"At Todd's place. I don't have any classes before twelve on Fridays."

Now, while Miriam had been suspicious of a "she," it was certainly possible that this "she"—whoever it might be—had recruited some help. I was poised to check into Todd's whereabouts that day as well when he volunteered, "I was home all morning, so I can vouch for Deena."

For all that's worth, I thought.

Anyway, one more to go. I sat up a little straighter to make clear to myself that I had a backbone. "And the Tuesday night your mother died?" I said to Deena. "Do you recall where you were that evening between, let's say, eight o'clock and ten-thirty?"

"I was at Todd's—sleeping; I was totally wiped out.

I'd had a test that morning, and I was up most of the night before studying for it."

"She wasn't able to concentrate during the day on Monday," Todd put in, "because of the kids upstairs."

"Monday was a holiday—Martin Luther King Day—" Deena explained, "and they were off from school. I'd never have believed two little boys could make such a racket. I kept waiting for the ceiling to come crashing down." She smiled impishly. "God! How I wanted to crack their adorable little heads together."

"You were also at the apartment from eight to ten-thirty?" I asked Todd.

"No, I got home around five. Deenie woke up when I came in, and we had something to eat. She almost fell asleep at the table, though, and right after dinner she went back to bed. I didn't want to disturb her by putting on the TV or anything, so I took off for the movies. That was at a little after six."

"What time did you return?"

"About ten. I ran into a friend coming out of the theater, and we stopped off for coffee."

This, I decided, had to be the most honest guy on the planet—or the dumbest. *Unless* he was actually the most cunning. I mean, could be he was attempting to establish his truthfulness. But at any rate, for whatever reason, Todd had blown the chance to alibi his girlfriend. (Not that I'd have put much stock in a verification like that anyway.)

Deena shot him a disgusted look before making her case. "Listen, Desiree, I had no reason to kill my mother. Money is no big deal to me—or to Todd; the two of us have very simple needs. Besides, I'm extremely grateful to my mother. Who knows what my life would have been like if she hadn't adopted me."

Ahh. So the girl had been adopted.

"Don't you mean if she and Mr. Weiden hadn't adopted you?" I asked, trying to get a fix on the nature of the relationships here.

"Daddy didn't have anything to do with the adoption. He and my mother weren't married then. She didn't even meet him until about six months after she got back."

"Got back from where?"

"From Switzerland. You see, right after I was born, my parents—my natural parents, that is—were killed in this horrendous automobile accident just outside Bern. I was in the car, too, but I didn't get so much as a scratch, which, according to my mother, was mind-boggling—a miracle. Anyway, my mother happened to be spending her vacation in Switzerland at the time—an old college friend of hers had married a Swiss man—and she read about the crash in the newspaper. She said that she'd always wanted a baby and that as soon as she saw my picture in the paper she fell in love with me. I really don't know all the details, but my mother's friend's husband had a brother—are you following this—?" she asked, grinning, "and this brother, who was a very high-powered lawyer, arranged for the adoption. My mother stayed over there for months until everything was worked out."

"And when did she marry Dan Weiden?"

"When I was almost two. He—" She smiled forlornly. "He was a wonderful father."

Making it down those stairs was a lot easier than the climb up had been. But don't get the idea it was any picnic. I mean, I proceeded at a rate not even a snail could take pride in. The one plus, though: I had plenty of time to think.

Aside from my initial discovery of Deena's race and the fact of the adoption, what surprised me most about tonight's meeting was the girl's almost complete lack of emotion when discussing her dead mother. This mother whom, Willie's (unproven) accusations notwithstanding, I still regarded as a singularly admirable human being—and whom Deena herself credited with securing her future. The young heiress's dispassion was all the more evident, too, when you compared it to the sadness she had displayed when speaking of her father.

The thing was, though, hadn't Miriam's longtime loyal secretary reacted pretty much the same way? Hell, even my client appeared to be mourning her daughter with dry tears.

What was with these people, anyhow?

Chapter Twelve

Ellen called at a little past noon on Saturday morning, about two minutes after I'd stuck my head in the oven.

No, life hadn't become unbearable. It's just that I'd been meaning to clean that damn stove for more than a week now, and over the past couple of days things had reached the critical stage. Whenever I went to heat up a pot of anything, I had to avert my eyes—or risk acknowledging that I must have the greasiest, grungiest burners in the entire building. So, really, it was time.

Anyhow, I was so intent on my labors that it took a few rings before I could even be sure I'd heard the phone.

Extricating myself from the depths of the oven and gagging from the fumes of the spray cleaner, I picked up the receiver. Ellen's response to my strangled "hello" was a tentative "Gee, did I wake you, Aunt Dez?"

"You did not," I snapped, offended that my niece could suspect me of still sleeping at this hour. (Not that I haven't been known to do this, you understand. It was just that I was feeling particularly bitchy at that moment. I mean, only scrubbing the toilet ranks ahead of oven scouring as my number one most-hated household chore.)

"Oh, good," my niece responded, either oblivious to or ignoring the waspish tone. "Uh, I have a favor to ask. I'm at the store right now"—Ellen is a buyer at Macy's—"and I've been thinking. Could you possibly meet me in the bridal shop at Saks on my lunch hour? I'd really like your opinion of that dress I told you about. I have an appointment there at one-fifteen."

Well, as much as I hated to turn her down, I didn't see how I could make it. Start with my arms being covered with black gunk from the point where my rubber gloves ended to right above the elbows. Add to this that I was sweaty and tired. And cap it off with my desperation to get this lousy job over with.

"I'll see you then," I told her.

After all, Ellen is one of the people I love best in the world. To say nothing of the fact that it would have been very unmatronly of honor of me to refuse her.

Never before have I accomplished so much so fast. In less than an hour I was clean (well, mostly, although a little of that black gunk refused to separate from my right forearm), dressed, and fully made up. And while I did a pretty slapdash job of things—I didn't even take the time to change my pantyhose after I noticed the run—I have to admit that there have been more than a few instances when I've looked worse.

I was in Saks's bridal shop at precisely one-fifteen. Ellen was already there, waiting anxiously for me. I accompanied her to the fitting room, and only moments later the gown in contention joined us via a very pleasant saleswoman.

Now, I should tell you something about Ellen. She is really an unusually attractive girl (and I don't care if it's not politically correct, she'll always be a girl to me). In fact, everyone thinks she looks exactly like the late Audrey Hepburn. Well, maybe not *exactly*. And, okay, maybe not *everyone*. But I have heard I-don't-know-how-many people make that observation.

At any rate, while the dress itself was lovely, it just wasn't that flattering to Ellen's reed-thin figure. The truth is, it just kind of hung on her. And this, in spite of the saleswoman's almost heroic efforts to gather in the fabric to show how becoming the lines would be once the skirt was tapered. But what really put the kibosh on the gown for me was how the low scoop neckline accentuated Ellen's . . . well . . . bony chest.

Apparently, however, my niece didn't see what I was seeing. To my amazement, she seemed positively enthralled with the image in the mirror.

As soon as we were alone in the fitting room, she grabbed the back of the dress herself and twirled this way and that, admiring her reflection from every angle. She was actually beaming when she turned to me. "Isn't it elegant?" she said, her tone close to reverent.

I was reserved in my response. "I suppose it is."

I doubt if she even heard me. Facing the mirror again, she murmured, "Once it's altered, it should be just perfect. I love the way the little seed pearls come to a vee in back, too, don't you?"

"That's a very nice touch."

"And I just *adore* the neckline. I'd kind of been thinking of something with a higher neck, but I really like the way this looks, don't you?"

Well, if I continued to bite my tongue like this, it would probably start to bleed. Besides, Ellen wanted me here for my opinion, didn't she? Still, I had a flashback to when she was in high school and that rotten kid Barry from two houses down the block told her the boy she liked had a thing for this busty little blonde. And he made it clear, too, that a major magnet for this devotion was the blonde's substantial upper protuberances.

I was about to be Barry.

"It's a pretty neckline, Ellen, but, umm, it really doesn't do that much for you."

"What do you mean, 'doesn't do that much'?"

"It's just that . . . uh . . . that kind of neckline is more suitable for someone who's . . . who's . . . What I'm saying is, a turtleneck or even a boat neck is so much more attractive on someone slender."

"You don't mean slender; you mean flat chested, right?" And before I could waffle even a little bit, Ellen snapped, "Never mind. Anyhow, I don't agree."

I considered myself bound to press on. "Umm, the skirt doesn't quite fall the way it should, either."

"It has to be fitted to me," she countered, getting angrier by the second.

"Look, Ellen," I put to her gently, "I know this isn't what you want to hear, but you asked me to meet you today so I'd tell you what I thought about the dress. Well, the truth is, I just don't feel that it's for you. Listen, give yourself some time. Look around a while longer and—"

"Thanks a lot, Aunt Dez," she retorted with obvious hostility.

I could have cried. I didn't know what to say. So, for a change, I wisely said nothing.

Then very unexpectedly Ellen leaned over and stroked my cheek. "I'm sorry. I *do* appreciate your being honest with me. Besides, I guess I knew all along that the neckline wasn't especially flattering. Maybe I was hoping you'd convince me I was wrong."

And she smiled. And Ellen's smile is positively radiant. Like Audrey's was. "The thing is, I just love those damn little seed pearls," she confessed.

On the way home in the taxi I thought about that gown. Ellen, I was certain, would eventually find something perfect for her. Anyhow, what was much more important was that the man she was marrying was perfect for her. And I'm not just saying that because I was the one who got the two of them together, either. Although I do admit to taking a great deal of satisfaction from this.

Of course, I was very lucky to pass out in the hallway of Mike's apartment building three years ago at a time when Mike—a resident at St. Gregory's Hospital—was around to minister to me. In a way I'm almost—with the accent on *almost*—beholden to that vicious killer whose completely uncalled-for assault on my person was what precipitated the faint.

At any rate, I'm positively ecstatic that it worked out. Mike's a wonderful guy, a really decent human being. And very intelligent. Naturally, his being so attractive is also a nice thing. Plus, let's face it, it doesn't hurt that he's a doctor, either, especially where my sister-in-law Margot—Ellen's mother—is concerned. I mean, she's even willing to overlook that he's still a resident. But what really warms my heart is the fact that you can tell just by seeing the two of them together that Mike positively adores my Ellen. You know what? Now that he was my almost-nephew, I was even able to forgive him for being Ellen's almost-fiancé for so long.

The taxi pulled up in front of my building then, and a couple of minutes afterward I was in the elevator, reluctantly pressing the button for my floor.

I'd soon have my head in the oven again.

Chapter Thirteen

I had finally completed my odious chore. And since I'm not exactly the neatest worker in the world, following this I'd scrubbed myself almost as diligently as I'd scrubbed the oven. It's a wonder there was any skin left on me at all.

It was now a few minutes past five, and I was standing in the middle of the kitchen, trying to make up my mind about supper. I was really tempted to raid the freezer for some leftover eggplant parmigiana, a dish I considered guest-worthy and which I'd kind of been saving for last-minute company (with Ellen being the most likely beneficiary). Then again, why didn't I just whip up one of my constantly varying refrigerator omelets—its name derived (courtesy of my niece) from the fact that just about anything currently on the refrigerator shelf winds up in the omelet. The ringing of the phone terminated the decision-making process.

"Is Missus Shapiro?" said the very recognizable voice.

"Ms. Popov?" I inquired unnecessarily.

"Yes, is Hilda Popov. Is all right I telephone you at house?"

"Of course. I'm very glad you called."

"I telephone because is something maybe I should tell to you. Maybe not important, but . . ." She left it at that.

"Whatever it is, I'd like to hear about it," I responded eagerly. I was about to try and arrange a meeting when Miriam Weiden's cleaning woman spoke again.

"I just finish vorking. Hozband coming for me in car tonight, but not getting to here until seven o'clock."

"You're still at Mrs. Weiden's?"

"No. I vaiting for hozband at Don Restaurant—is not far from Veiden house. You know such place?"

"Don's Restaurant? I don't think I'm familiar with it. What street is it on?"

"You vait, please."

The woman put her hand over the mouthpiece, and I could hear her muffled voice addressing someone nearby. Moments later she was back on the phone with the exact location. "You vill come?"

"I'll get there as soon as I can," I said, already pulling off my clothes. "It shouldn't take me much longer than three-quarters of an hour, okay?"

"Hokay."

Being a regular Mrs. Einstein, it didn't occur to me until I was in the taxi that I hadn't a clue as to what Hilda Popov looked like. And doubtless she was likewise in the dark.

Anyway, my calculations timewise turned out to be on the optimistic side. It was slightly over an hour later that the cab pulled up in front of a large neon sign proclaiming that this was Don's Restaurant. Which, to my way of thinking, it wasn't. Don's establishment was more of a coffee shop than a restaurant. But it was large and bright and had a welcoming feel to it.

The place was fairly crowded, and the majority of booths were occupied. Fortunately, though, only two by solitary females.

Seated directly opposite the door was a heavy-set blonde—almost half of her dyed hair consisting of black roots—who was gnawing on a chicken leg with undisguised enthusiasm. Well, I'd pictured Hilda as large and blond, although my mental image had neglected to include the roots.

Still, I approached the lady confidently. "Ms. Popov?"

"Mmph?" She didn't bother removing the chicken leg from her mouth.

"Uh, sorry."

That narrowed the field considerably. I hurried over to the booth three or four rows behind the blonde where the other solo woman was sitting.

"Ms. Popov?"

She put down her coffee mug, smiling tentatively. "Missus Shapiro?"

"That's right. May I?" I said at the same instant that I squeezed onto the bench opposite her. (I thought it only polite to ask, however.)

Hilda Popov was quite a surprise to me. She was much younger and smaller and darker than I had anticipated. Prettier, too—sort of waiflike.

"I'm sorry I couldn't get here earlier. The traffic," I offered lamely. Actually it was my keys; I hadn't been able to find them anywhere. (I eventually discovered—can you believe this from a New Yorker?—that I'd left them in the door.)

"Is hokay."

"What will you have to eat?"

"Notting, tank you. I going New Chersey tonight to visit sister of hozband. She vill feed me good. Like alvays." And grinning, she patted her stomach.

"You know, Ms. Popov—"

"I am Hilda."

"And I'm Desiree. Listen, Hilda, it might not be a bad idea to have a little something in the meantime to tide you over." She looked perplexed. "Until you get to your sister-in-law's," I clarified.

"Tank you, but not so hongry."

"I hate to have supper alone," I cajoled.

"No, no. I vait."

But by the time the harried waiter finally arrived to take the order, it was for two hot roast beef sandwiches—rare—with French fries—well done, naturally—and coleslaw and pickles. Later, it wouldn't require much persuading to talk Hilda into a slice of

coconut cream pie. And it was, of course, only fair
that this time I keep *her* company.

At any rate, I soon learned the reason for her call.

"Yesterday," she began, "I opstairs in den, packing
in boxes tings from bar. I see vun bottle is all
stickly"—I assumed she meant *sticky*—"and I vould
not put avay no bottle like dat. Never vould I do dis.
Missus Veiden, neider. But I don't tink notting about
it until dis morning, ven I remember someting. Day after
Missus Veiden die, as soon as policemen leave, I clean
room. And I notice on coffee table dere is a—" She
broke off, plainly frustrated. Then a moment later, she
brightened. And raising her hand to the level of her
face, she drew a circle in the air with her forefinger.

Now, it had been a long time since I'd played cha-
rades, and, the truth is, I was never that good at it
anyway. Still, I was having a particularly dumb night,
as evidenced by my next words. "There was a circle
on the coffee table?" (I can be pretty literal.)

Shaking her head impatiently, Hilda tried another
circle, this one on her place mat.

"A ring!" I all but shouted when it dawned on me
at last. "That's what it was—a ring!"

"Yes!" Hilda exclaimed. "From glass. But is not
from big glass. Ring very small. And ven I rub off
from table I say to myself, 'Stickly.'"

"I get it. Like the bottle. And that's what made you
recall the ring."

"I tink so."

"And you're sure the ring wasn't there before that
Wednesday?"

"I am sure. I dust room only day before—Tuesday.
If vas dere, I vould see." A second or two later she
asked earnestly, "Is important—dis vat I am tell to
you?"

"I can't be certain yet; we still have no idea what
caused Mrs. Weiden's death. But it's possible your information will turn out to be extremely helpful, and I
appreciate your coming to me with it. By the way, did
you happen to notice what was in that bottle?"

Looking smug, Hilda reached down and retrieved the handbag lying next to her on the seat. A moment later she took out a small scrap of paper. On it was a brand name printed in neat block letters and underneath this, in the same careful hand, "creme de menthe."

"You know vat is dis?"

"It's a liqueur."

"Yes, green."

"Did you do anything with that bottle?" I said then, although I was already steeling myself for the answer. "Before you packed it away, I mean."

"I vash good. And den I vipe good. I do wrong ting?"

"No, of course not," I told her emphatically.

I was obviously less than convincing, however, because Hilda contradicted softly, "Yes, I do wrong. But is because I forget about ring." And obviously annoyed with herself, she tapped her forehead. "Is vye ven I first see stickly bottle, I don't tink it has notting to do with death of Missus Veiden."

"Well, that's understandable," I was quick to assure her.

"But now I vorrying. Maybe somebody put *poison* in drink of Missus Veiden, and it vas *murderer* put stickly bottle back in bar." She shuddered, then smiled sheepishly. "Or maybe I just vatching too much TV."

"That could be," I said, smiling, too. "Let me ask you about something else, though. When we last spoke you mentioned that there were bad feelings between Mrs. Weiden and Mrs. Hartley. Are you aware of any other people your employer might have had some trouble with?"

"I not know of nobody, but alvays I am busy vorking. Missus Hartley—dis is different. She coming vun day and *screaming* to Missus Veiden. All building hears, I bet you."

"Mrs. Weiden had no problems with *anyone* besides Mrs. Hartley," I pressed. "Not anyone at all?"

Hilda thought this over for a moment. "Vell, some

of times Missus Veiden, she yelling to Harris voman—
I am not listening vat is about. And anyhow, not last-
ing long. And Missus Veiden and daughter also yelling
some of times. But daughter, she is teenager so . . ."
She gave a what-would-you-expect kind of shrug.

"How long have you been with Mrs. Weiden?"

"Almost vun year. In March, I come."

At about this point our food arrived, and except for
a few brief exchanges now and then, we both focused
most of our attention on making it disappear. Hilda,
I noted appreciatively, had quite an appetite for someone of her slight build—although she was hardly in
the same class as Ellen, who can pack it away like a
truck driver. And I'm talking about a truck driver just
going off a twenty-four-hour fast.

Then minutes after we'd finished eating, Hilda's
husband showed up to whisk her away to his sister's
in New Jersey.

I got a refill of my coffee and engaged in a little
pondering.

What had I actually learned from Hilda Popov?

That it was likely the deceased had had a glass of
crème de menthe on the night of her death. Although
this was by no means certain.

After all, in spite of the firmness of her assertion,
it was not inconceivable Hilda had overlooked the telltale ring when she'd dusted Tuesday afternoon. But
even if Miriam *had* imbibed the liqueur that evening,
there was no second ring on the coffee table, no evidence anyone had been with her.

The fact that a sticky bottle had been put back in
the bar? Possibly Miriam, not noticing the stickiness,
had done the honors herself. Also, assuming she did
have the crème de menthe on that fateful Tuesday, I
could see where, for once, she just might not have
given a damn about the condition of the bottle. The
woman *died* that day, for heaven's sake, so I couldn't
discount that she might have been feeling slightly
under the weather by that time.

A few coffee sips later, however, and I admitted that I'd merely been playing devil's advocate. If you want the truth, I didn't believe a word of what I'd just been telling myself.

Miriam had drunk the crème de menthe on Tuesday night, and it had been poisoned; I just knew it. I mean, that stuff is the ideal vehicle for a lethal dose of something or other. It has a very intense flavor—which I can attest to personally. I tasted it once at a friend's insistence, and it was all I could do to keep from gagging. What I'm getting at is that it's doubtful you could detect the introduction of a foreign substance in anything like that.

And as for there only being that single ring—big deal. It could simply be that none of the liqueur had dripped down the killer's glass.

Or better yet, our perpetrator might have been clever enough to wipe away one of the rings in order to make it appear that the victim had been alone. (You know, now that I thought about it, it was very likely the perp who had turned on the TV—and for this same reason.) So if poison should eventually be discovered in Miriam's system—and there was a good chance it would go undetected—well, who's to say she wasn't a suicide? Not the police, evidently.

I nodded in satisfaction. I wasn't claiming Hilda Popov's recollections afforded *evidence* that Miriam had been murdered, you understand. But they did serve to advance this theory.

Or so I chose to look at it.

Chapter Fourteen

It poured all of Sunday.

At about four o'clock Harriet Gould phoned to invite me to have dinner with her and Steve that evening. I had pretty much decided to accept—even if it meant getting myself presentable enough to trek across the hall—when Harriet told me in a voice filled with wifely pride that Steve would be making some of his "special" glogg tonight.

Well, the last time Steve had served me that atrocious preparation of his, it was, thank heavens, in my own apartment. So the moment he turned his back I was able to foist the stuff on my ficus tree—which was dying anyway.

But in the absence of any terminal plants over at the Goulds'—and not feeling up to facing that glogg tonight—I had to decline. Thanking Harriet profusely, I offered the excuse that, as much as I wanted to join them, I was too inundated with paperwork to even consider it.

And then I again devoted myself to the activity I'd been so enthusiastically engaged in prior to Harriet's call: just lazing around.

This was, after all, the perfect day for it.

I called Ernestine Hartley at ten-thirty Monday morning. Last week the butler—or whoever it was I'd spoken to—had informed me that Mrs. Hartley was due back from vacation yesterday. But I'd allowed her some space to get settled. Which, considering that I was waiting on tenterhooks to talk to her, I considered very generous of me.

I gave my name now to that same whoever-it-was, and he said he'd check and see if Mrs. Hartley was at home. And this time he didn't even request that I spell "Shapiro."

She was on the line about half a minute later. And before I had a chance to explain the purpose of my call, *she* explained it to *me*.

"You're the private investigator looking into Miriam's death, and you want to ask me some questions about her," Mrs. Hartley asserted bluntly. She inquired about where my office was located, and I told her it was in the East Thirties.

"Good. My lawyer isn't that far from there, and I have an appointment with him this afternoon. Let me have the address." I gave her the particulars. "I can be over to see you around three." She put down the receiver without so much as an "Is that convenient for you?"

Mrs. Hartley didn't arrive until close to four. And she didn't apologize for it, either. A tall, slim woman with an imperious air, she more or less *swept* into my little cubicle.

I stood up and put out my hand. She took it limply in hers, instantly dropping it. After which she handed me her coat, an obviously expensive fur I couldn't identify. Then pulling a handkerchief from her purse, she proceeded to brush invisible dirt and dust particles from the only available chair before depositing her skinny posterior on the seat.

"You're *certain* you're a private detective?" were practically the first words out of her mouth.

"I'm certain." It took all of my willpower, but I left it at that. And a moment later, reminding myself that this woman could have critical information for me, I even managed a weak little smile.

Mrs. Hartley shrugged. "Oh, well," she said, patting her elegant upswept "do."

I quickly reached the conclusion that Ernestine Hartley was easily the most theatrical woman I'd ever met. With that jet-black hair and the bloodred lipstick and those ridiculously long talons she used for nails— which were, naturally, painted to match her mouth— she was the embodiment of my conception of a forties movie star. Even the chic black wool designer (I'm sure) suit she wore fit right in. And, of course, her entire manner contributed to the effect.

"I heard about Miriam while I was still on vacation," she told me. "And, when I got home yesterday, friends filled me in on the details. Listen, Desiree— I'm going to call you Desiree; I hate formalities— frankly, I'm not surprised that Miriam was murdered. And you *will* find out it was murder, you know."

"Why do you say that?"

"She'd been asking for it for years."

Now, I had expected that Ernestine Hartley would not be exactly flattering in her depiction of the victim, but this assessment—and the matter-of-fact tone in which it was delivered—stunned me.

"I'm not accusing anyone, you understand," she continued. "I have no idea who actually did this worthy deed. But, believe me, Miriam had certainly given enough people reason to want to see dirt shoveled in her face."

"Like?"

"Like me, for openers, darling." She smiled archly. "But no, I wasn't the one."

"I heard that you and Mrs. Weiden had been the best of friends at one time."

"Oh, we were. Until I learned what an amoral, two-faced, lying whore she was."

Well, Mrs. Hartley didn't pull any punches, did she? "When did you make this discovery?" I asked.

"Last June—when she stole the husband right out from under me. And you can take that literally, too. I probably never would have learned about it, either, if the spineless little shit I'm married to—but not for long, fortunately—hadn't gotten a sudden attack of conscience one night after his fourth martini. He swears *she* seduced *him,* of course. But what difference does it make who went after who? They were *both* filthy, flesh-eating maggots.''

I made up my mind then that, for once, I'd get the big one over with right away. "Uh, just for my records, Mrs. Hartley, would you mind telling me where you were the evening Mrs. Weiden died? That was—''

"Oh, I know when it was. I broke open a bottle of Dom Perignon when I got the good news the next day. I'm sorry to disappoint you, Desiree, but I've been in the Dominican Republic for the past month. And, in the event it's crossed your mind, I didn't sneak back to ice her—isn't that the term the cop shows always use? From the second day I was there I spent every glorious night of those four incredible weeks with Juanito, the delicious nineteen-year-old lifeguard who saved me from drowning in the boredom of abstinence. I'll give you the name of the hotel later, if you like. And I'm sure you do like.''

"You mentioned that there were also others Mrs. Weiden hadn't endeared herself to. Can you tell me who you had in mind?''

"Are you acquainted with her *devoted* secretary Erna?''

"I've met Ms. Harris.''

"The truth is, she wasn't. Devoted, that is.'' As if for emphasis, Mrs. Hartley made an elaborate motion of crossing her legs. "Erna couldn't stand Miriam.''

This was definitely the last thing I was expecting. "But she was with her for so many years. Why didn't she ever leave, if that's the case?''

"One reason Erna stayed put was to be near Dan Weiden—Miriam's now-deceased husband. She was in love with the man. Or, at least, that's what they say.''

Well, I've often wondered who this ubiquitous "they'' are, haven't you? But recalling Erna's obvious distress when speaking of Weiden's suicide, I didn't feel I could afford to pooh-pooh this little snippet of gossip. "And Mr. Weiden? Did he reciprocate?" I asked.

"From what I've been told, he had no inkling of Erna's feelings for him."

"Anyway, Dan Weiden died five years ago, and Erna still kept working for Miriam," I pointed out.

And now Ernestine Hartley looked like a cat about to consume a good-sized bowl of cream. She even ran her tongue across her lower lip. "There was, however, a second, still more important reason Erna continued in Miriam's employ."

She waited for me to ask. So I asked. "What reason?"

"You're aware, I assume, that Miriam adopted an infant eighteen years ago. A daughter, who is black— or partially so, at any rate."

"Yes."

"Erna absolutely adored that girl, Desiree—she still does." Her voice became softer, almost seductive. "In fact, there was talk right from the beginning that Erna was actually Deena's birth mother. You see, even though in those days, as you know, there was something of a stigma in having a baby outside of marriage—particularly if the baby was of mixed blood— Erna refused to so much as *consider* an abortion. But being of very limited means, she finally had to accept that it would be best to give up the infant for adoption. Or so they say." *There "they" were again.* "And *that*," Mrs. Hartley declared with a smirk, "is where our Miriam stepped in."

"You're saying that Deena's parents didn't die in a car crash in Switzerland?"

"Oh, *I'm* not saying anything," Mrs. Hartley protested. "But a great many of Miriam's acquaintances— understandably, she has no actual friends—have been telling me this for ages."

I offered a reminder. "It was never really established, though. I mean about Erna being Deena's natural mother."

"Look, I once asked Miriam if it was true."

"And?"

"She didn't confirm it, but she didn't deny it, either. Probably because Erna *was* the mother." Then somewhat reluctantly: "Of course, Miriam being Miriam, it's also possible that, for some devious reason of her own, this is what she wanted me to believe."

"Well, at any rate, if Miriam did adopt Erna's child, that was a very generous thing for her to do," I ventured foolishly.

"Generous, my ass! It was more points for the wonderful, the charitable, the positively *angelic* Miriam." The venom Mrs. Hartley felt was never more apparent than at this moment. "You can't even imagine the kind of gushing PR that adoption bought Miriam. And actually, taking Deena in was no skin off her nose. She hardly gave that little girl any time at all; she was too busy with her *'good works.'* Who do you think raised Deena? For your information, it was Erna, that's who."

"I'm still not clear on why Erna disliked Miriam so much."

"I can't say for certain, but I can make some pretty decent guesses. There was the Deena thing, of course. A black widow spider—aren't they the creatures that eat their young? No, unless I'm mistaken, they're the ones that kill their mates. Anyhow, a *cockroach* is a better mother than Miriam was. Now, I'm not suggesting she was actually *mean* to the child. Primarily, she just wasn't *there* for her, which to my way of thinking is, in some ways, even worse. What I'm trying to make clear is that this couldn't have sat too well with Erna, even if she wasn't the birth mother—which most likely she was. And listen, it's also conceivable that Miriam somehow coerced Erna into agreeing to the adoption in the first place. And—"

"But you said Erna couldn't afford to keep the baby."

"I *said*," Mrs. Hartley corrected, frowning, "that this was the general consensus. Besides, even if she did have to give up her daughter, she still might not have wanted to turn the poor little thing over to Miriam." The woman's mascara-heavy eyes seemed to bore into me now. "There was, however, another reason Erna had no use for her employer."

"This being—?"

"She couldn't stomach the way Miriam treated Dan."

"Would you mind elaborating?"

Mrs. Hartley uncrossed her legs. "Well, if you feel it would be helpful." I came close to laughing out loud. The woman could barely wait to carve up the deceased some more! "Miriam was the most controlling, the most manipulative person I've ever had the misfortune to waste my friendship on," she began. "Dan was in the rag trade—a clothing manufacturer. And Miriam never let him forget that she financed his company and that she was responsible for ninety percent of his important business contacts. While things were going well, she also took credit for his advertising strategies, his marketing plans—everything. Someone told me she even bragged about having a hand in a few of his more popular designs.

"Furthermore, she was constantly reminding the man about what being married to her did for his social standing, although from what I gather, he didn't give a crap about that. Particularly since it meant he had much less time to spend with his own, pre-Miriam friends. She even tried her damnedest to induce him to cut back on getting together with his only brother, and the two were extremely close. Imagine!" Recrossing her legs now, Ernestine Hartley smiled smugly. "There, however, I'm pleased to report, she wasn't successful.

"At any rate, when the company started to go down the toilet, it was suddenly totally Dan's baby. Miriam blamed him for the very things she'd been patting herself on the back for earlier.

"Now, the business troubles occurred soon after Edwin—the brother—died from some illness. Hodgkin's disease, it was. Or it might have been leukemia. No, it was Hodgkin's. And between the loss of his brother and his company's being practically kaput and Miriam's constant carping about what a failure he was, Dan just couldn't take it any longer. So . . ." Mrs. Hartley tilted her head and spread her arms in conclusion.

"I'm surprised Mrs. Weiden's husband remained with her that long if she was so impossible," I remarked.

"Darling, it was Deena. Dan was crazy about Deena; he adopted her, in case you weren't informed. And he was afraid that if he left Miriam she'd find a way to prevent him from seeing the child again. And she would have, too."

"I gather you were fond of Dan."

"I never knew the man," Mrs. Hartley responded as she examined her talons. "I didn't become chummy with Miriam until almost a year after he died. But I did know Miriam—although I admit that it took a while to realize what she was about. At any rate, I don't even doubt that she treated her husband like camel dung."

"The thing I'm having trouble with is why Erna would want to do away with Miriam *now*."

"*You're* the detective, Desiree. I can only supply you with the information I have. The rest, after all . . ." And she smiled. But moments later she was ready with another contribution—as I'd just made a hundred-thousand-dollar bet with myself that she would be. "Of course, I do have a few ideas. Miriam had been giving Deena a very hard time lately, you know. The girl has been seeing this young black man from Jamaica, or maybe it's Nassau. A plumber, no less"—I didn't bother to inform her that Todd was a carpenter—"and the story is that Miriam was threatening to cut her out of the will if she didn't break it off. You see, adopting a black infant who'd supposedly been orphaned by a terrible tragedy was a testimonial to that *dear* woman's boundless altruism. But having a black son-in-law in this day and age wouldn't do a thing for her image one way or another. You can bet your bloomers that when the time came, Miriam expected Deena to marry somebody rich and prestigious, a man who would be a social plus for *her*—Miriam. Besides, she no doubt felt she'd reached her quota when it came to people of color in the family. Anyhow, the point I'm making is that Erna would not have wanted to see that girl disinherited."

And, in spite of her professed disinterest in all things material, I doubted that Deena would, either.

"Naturally," Ernestine Hartley said, sticking her nose right into my head, "that gives Deena a juicy little motive, too, doesn't it?"

"I suppose so," I responded casually.

"And I just remembered someone else who'd have liked to cut out Miriam's gizzard and feed it to the coyotes for breakfast." (Where did this woman come up with these expressions anyway?) "Miriam's former sister-in-law Lynne Weiden—Edwin's wife—had it in for her, too."

"What did Miriam do to this sister-in-law?"

"It's not what Miriam did to *her*, darling; it's what Miriam did to Dan. Dan and Edwin, as I told you before, had been devoted to each other, and Lynne was also *extremely* fond of Dan. There was some speculation about her even having a *thing* for him. At any rate, losing Dan, too—within months of her husband's death—almost drove the poor woman over the edge, from what I understand."

"Lynne blamed Miriam for the suicide?"

"Certainly."

"That was five years back, though. Do you actually think that after all this time she'd murder Miriam to avenge his death?"

"I didn't say that she did anything of the sort," Mrs. Hartley answered testily. "I'm just pointing out that there are plenty of people who'd have been delighted to do the cha-cha on the grave of the dear departed."

I was about to ask if she knew anything about Miriam's being involved with a married man when, once again, Ernestine Hartley intruded into my thoughts.

"Anyhow, here's something more recent for you. Miriam had been seeing some man from New Haven. But I suppose you're already aware of that." There was the hint of a question mark in her tone.

"Well, I did hear something of the sort."

"The fellow has a wife, perhaps a very jealous wife—after all, how many of us *aren't*?—and two children. His name's Philip Chance. Sounds like a movie star, huh? Apparently he resembles one, too—Pierce Brosnan, they say. And the word is that he and Miriam broke up a few weeks prior to her unfortunate demise—with *him* dumping *her*. She wasn't any too happy about it, either. But very possibly to *Mrs.* Chance's unhappiness, it seems likely that the lovers got back together again."

"What makes you think that?"

"A good friend of mine spotted Miriam coming out of a restaurant downtown. She was with someone who fit this Philip Chance's description to a T. Would you like me to tell you when this was?"

"Of course."

Mrs. Hartley smiled enigmatically. "At lunchtime. On the day that she died."

Chapter Fifteen

My head was reeling after my get-together with Ernestine Hartley.

If there was even a smidgen of truth in the revelations of this erstwhile buddy of Miriam's, then the woman whom I had so respected and admired had feet of clay right up to her calves.

It took a few minutes to shake off the immobilizing effect my visitor's words were having on me. But as soon as I was functioning again, I glanced down at the sheet of paper on my desk, which contained the information she'd jotted down before leaving. Then I set about attempting to verify some of what I'd just heard.

The first thing I wanted to establish was whether Mrs. Hartley's own alibi would hold up, so I called the hotel in the Dominican Republic at which she'd been vacationing these past four weeks. I told the manager that I was a New York City detective (well, I *am,* you know) and that I needed to verify a couple of facts. He accepted this vague explanation without question, confirming that Ernestine Hartley had been a guest at the resort that entire month. Then I requested he transfer me to a lifeguard by the name of Juanito. After a short pause the man asked—and with a definite snicker, I might add— "Could you possibly be meaning Juan? Juan Cruz?"

"Yes, that must be it," I said with all the dignity I was able to dredge up.

Fortunately, Juanito or Juan or whatever you want

to tag him with was in his room. As soon as I heard his voice I was struck by how young he sounded. *Leave it to good ole Ernestine!*

He responded to my question in barely accented English. "Oh, yes—Ernie. We became friends." A throaty chuckle. "Very close friends."

Why, you little twerp. I swear, if the kid had a mustache, he was probably twirling it just then.

"Did you and Mrs. Hartley spend much time together?"

"Every night." he responded with obvious pride.

"*Every* night?"

"That's right. Oh, except for her first night at the hotel—which was before we met. But after that . . ." *This* chuckle was positively lascivious.

Well, while Mrs. Hartley's kiddie lover was smarmy enough to inspire me to hop in the shower, he was also believable. I hung up with the advice to myself that I scratch Ernestine Hartley as a suspect.

Actually, though, I hadn't considered her much of one to begin with. Particularly with the way she carried on about the deceased. Of course, there was always the possibility those histrionics of hers were calculated to get me to reach this very conclusion. But somehow I didn't think so. Besides, assuming that the same perpetrator had made all three of the alleged attempts on Miriam's life, it would mean that Mrs. Hartley had flown back and forth from the Dominican Republic twice—the first time in order to commit the attack at the school. And how likely was it that she would know Miriam was going to be there that day? It would also mean—and this was difficult to even imagine—that the admirable Juanito had told me a fib. As for that lake business, I found it a little tough to accept that the victim, who apparently didn't swim much better than a rock, would get into a rowboat with someone she knew to be her sworn enemy. And I certainly didn't see her protecting this enemy if she had even the slightest inkling that the woman had attempted to drown her.

No, as far as I was concerned, Ernestine Hartley was off the hook.

Next . . .

According to Mrs. Hartley, Lynne Weiden lived somewhere in Manhattan.

The telephone book had a number for an L. Weiden, and that seemed like a pretty good bet.

I let the phone ring five times and was just about to hang up when there was a breathless—"Hello."

"Mrs. Weiden? Mrs. *Lynne* Weiden?"

"That's right."

"My name is Desiree Shapiro," I informed her. "I'm a private investigator, and I've been hired by her mother to look into your sister-in-law's death."

"So Miriam *was* murdered, then," she murmured.

"I really can't say for sure. The medical examiner's report still hasn't come in, but there's at least a possibility of that."

"Well, well." And a moment later: "I'm curious, though. Why not wait for the report before you start investigating?"

So I explained—as I'd been required to do before with this case—about time being such a crucial factor in solving a homicide. "The perpetrator's trail gets colder by the second," I told her.

"You haven't been exactly speedy in contacting me, though," she observed with what could be interpreted as a bit of sarcasm.

"Uh, yes, I realize that. But I was wondering if you could spare me a few minutes tonight. I won't keep you long."

"You mean you want to come over or something?"

"We could meet somewhere, if you prefer."

"Look, Ms. Shapiro—you did say *Shapiro,* didn't you?—I'm going to help you conserve some of that precious time you were referring to. I can tell you everything you want to know right now."

"But if—"

"Listen to me. I won't deny that I couldn't stomach

Miriam—your calling me is a pretty good indication that you've already been apprised of this fact. But as for the reason I felt the way I did about her, that's my own business. And even if I did agree to sit down with you, I still wouldn't elaborate on it."

"All right. But there are some other matters we should discuss."

"Those 'some other matters' being primarily where I was the night Miriam died?"

"I suppose it—"

"I was in St. Vincent's, Ms. Shapiro—having my gall bladder out. I had the surgery that Tuesday, and believe me, after that I was in no shape to dash over there and send her off to heaven—or wherever it was she ended up. I'll be happy to furnish you with proof, too. Do you have a fax machine?"

"Yes."

"I'll fax you a copy of the hospital bill as soon as we're through talking."

"Thanks, I'd appreciate it. But that's not the only thing I wanted to speak to you about. Do—"

"You'd also like to ask me whether I know of anyone else who shared my animosity toward my sister-in-law, right? Of course, I haven't even spoken to her in a couple of years, and I haven't been keeping tabs on her, either. But when I *was* a little more involved in her life, I came to realize that there were a lot of people who weren't exactly fans of Miriam's. I can't think of a soul who hated her enough to commit murder, though—myself included. Does that answer all of your questions?"

"I suppose you've pretty much covered things," I conceded. "But if something—"

"Certainly. That goes without saying," Lynne Weiden anticipated maddeningly. "And if anything else occurs to you, feel free to give me a call."

Then we said our good-byes.

Well, I could say one thing for the woman: She'd certainly helped me preserve my vocal cords, hadn't she?

Anyhow, true to her word, she got the fax to me within five minutes. And it confirmed her claim about the surgery.

So Mrs. Weiden, too, was off the hook.

Next . . .

Picking up the receiver again, I dialed information.

There was only one listing for a Philip Chance in New Haven, and it was a residential number. He answered the call himself.

I went through my usual preamble. And then I hit him with "I understand you and Miriam Weiden had been seeing each other."

"Had," the man responded calmly. "That's the operative word here. We *had* been seeing each other. We . . . it was over between us almost a month ago."

"You were spotted having lunch together on the day Mrs. Weiden died."

And now it was as if the phone had gone dead.

"Mr. Chance? Are you still there?"

"I'm here. Look, it's difficult to talk about this on the telephone."

"I could drive up to New Haven whenever you say."

"No," Chance put in hurriedly. "Why don't I come to your office?—tomorrow afternoon, if that's okay. I have some things to take care of in Manhattan anyway."

"Tomorrow would be fine." I gave him the address, and he said he'd stop by around two.

In the cab home that afternoon, I was still trying to come to terms with today's disclosures about Miriam. I attempted to console myself with an adage from Hercule Poirot, the gist of which was that in order to uncover the killer, you had to get to know the victim.

Well, I'd certainly become a lot better acquainted with the victim today. But Hercule notwithstanding, I can't say that I was especially happy about it.

Chapter Sixteen

Not being in the mood to so much as scramble an egg, I decided to have the taxi drop me off at Jerome's, this little coffee shop in my neighborhood.

I was kind of in a BLT frame of mind, so I was hoping that Felix, who most nights is my favorite waiter, would be off today. You see, the first time Felix ever served me I asked for a cheeseburger and fries, and ever since then he's been going under the assumption that I have no desire to vary my menu.

"I know what *you're* going to have, Desiree," he always says, repeating those initial choices to me—right down to the "French fries that gotta be well done" and the "Coke you want with the meal, and I shouldn't bring it before." And then he flashes me that irresistible upper-plate-enhanced grin of his.

Now, since Felix is well into his seventies and takes great pride in his memory, I never have the heart to tell him I'd like a grilled cheese, for a change. Or the turkey with Russian dressing. Or, as at that very moment, a BLT.

But Felix *was* working this evening.

Oh, well, I wasn't really that keen on a BLT anyway.

I finished supper in just over a half hour, and when I walked into the apartment there was a brief message on the answering machine from Norma Davis.

The autopsy report had come in.

*　　*　　*

My hands were shaking as I dialed.

"Those two detectives were here to see me before," Mrs. Davis informed me tremulously.

For an instant I didn't breathe. "What did they tell you?"

"That my daughter was m-murdered. Oh, God! I knew it! In my heart I knew it from the beginning. But it's still a shock."

"Of course it is." I held off a bit before asking gently, "How did she die?"

"Poison. Miriam was poisoned. They found traces of this drug in her tissues. Do you want the name of it?"

"Please."

"I had one of the detectives write it down for me. It's tubocurarine chloride. That's t-u-b-o-c-u-r-a-r-i-n-e. Have you ever heard of it?"

"No, I haven't."

"It's a derivative of curare. *Curare!* The autopsy showed that there was alcohol in Miriam's blood, too. According to the detectives, that's how the drug must have gotten into her system—it was put in her drink. She . . . she expired almost immediately." Mrs. Davis choked up then, and it was close to a minute before she was able to speak again. "The medical examiner estimates the time of death to have been between nine and eleven p.m."

"You said that she . . . that you were certain it happened before ten-thirty. Very likely you were right."

"Uh, Desiree? Now that we know what killed my Miriam, it should be easier to find out who did this to her, shouldn't it?"

"That's what I'm hoping" was as much as I would commit to.

"Anyway, bless my brother-in-law Donald." She said it almost reverently.

"Your brother-in-law?"

"Yes. I mentioned I had a sister living in California, didn't I?"

"She's the one you spent the summer with."

"Yes. Well, her husband is a political consultant out there—and very influential, too. When I told Donald about the police suggesting that Miriam could have had a heart attack or—and this *really* enraged him—that she might even have committed suicide, he said he'd make sure there was a thorough autopsy. I had the idea that because Miriam was . . . you know . . . who she *was*, they'd take special pains to discover the cause of her death. Donald said that we couldn't count on it, but that he'd *see* that they did.

"Apparently he has more powerful connections than I'd ever imagined. The detectives told me there'd been a call about Miriam from someone very high up in the administration—the administration in *Washington*. In fact, there's this rumor that it was from someone close to the *President*."

A thought flashed through my mind. *Suppose your average citizen had been poisoned with the same stuff that had been used on Miriam. Would the medical examiner have expended the extra effort it no doubt required to identify what—to me, at any rate—sounded like a pretty esoteric drug?*

Probably not. The likelihood of its going undetected, I realized then, must have been one of the reasons the killer chose something like that. "Thank God for your brother-in-law," I murmured.

"These detectives working on the case, Mrs. Davis—who are they?" I asked right after this, wondering if I might know the men.

"There's a Sergeant Marino and a younger fellow named Weber—he's the idiot who came up with that suicide thing. Have you ever met them?"

"No, I haven't."

"They left me a card. Do you want to get in touch with them?"

"I don't think so—not at this point. I'll take that information another time, though."

I fully intended to keep a low profile with the NYPD—at least for the present. Experience has taught me that the last thing the police want is some pushy PI like you-know-who poking her nose into one of their investigations. Even if she does wind up uncovering the perpetrator—and very generously allows them to take the credit for it, besides.

And now Mrs. Davis cried out with a sob, "My poor Miriam! My poor, poor Miriam."

A few very long seconds followed, during which I wracked my brain for something comforting to say before the conversation ended. But being such a wizard with words, "I'm so very sorry" was the best I could do.

Getting ready for bed, I suspected that I'd have trouble sleeping that night. So although it was exhausting, it was no big surprise that I spent until dawn throwing myself from one side of the bed to another, while intermittently pounding the bejesus out of my pillow.

For the third time in my career I'd taken on a case that could turn out to be a homicide—or possibly not. Only to eventually discover that I'd been dealing with a crime after all. But unlike those prior instances, I was pretty well convinced from the start that Miriam Weiden *was* a murder victim. However, in view of my having been gifted with an intuition that would be an embarrassment to any woman—much less a professional investigator—this should actually have resulted in her demise being attributed to natural causes. So, in a way, I was astonished to be proven correct. If that makes any sense to you.

Of course, I couldn't even hazard a guess just yet as to who might have administered that poison. The one thing I did know was that it wasn't Miriam Weiden. I mean, what even *semi*rational, suicide-bent human being would go to the trouble of obtaining a substance called tubocurarine chloride when a handful of sleeping pills would do the trick?

At any rate, I didn't expect that finding the perpetrator would be any snap. Particularly in light of all the lies I was being fed about the deceased. I mean, to listen to her secretary and my client, she could have given Mother Teresa a run for her money.

Granted, it wasn't difficult to understand Mrs. Davis's eagerness to protect Miriam's reputation—family is family, I suppose. But didn't she appreciate how that fiction she was promoting could affect my chances of uncovering her daughter's murderer? After all, why hire me to begin with if she was going to obliterate the facts like this?

As for Erna, why the woman would possibly want to shield the reputation of an employer she despised had me completely stumped.

And there were also Miriam's friends the Oxners. They, too, had been almost lyrical in their praise of the victim. After some brief thought, however, I found this somewhat easier to explain to myself. When it came to society gossip, those poor souls had obviously been left out of the loop.

You can see that I was giving quite a bit of credence to Ernestine Hartley's assessment of Miriam. Not that I was accepting it in its entirety. But it was becoming increasingly clear—especially when you also took Willie Johns's input into consideration—that the esteemed, the *venerated* Miriam Weiden was no sweetheart.

And now I reminded myself about tomorrow's meeting with Philip Chance. What would he have to say about his ex-lover? I wondered anxiously. From here my brain took the short leap to something that was perhaps even more important: What, if anything, did *Mrs.* Chance think of our Miriam?

I tossed myself to the other side of the bed again as I spied the first light of morning peeking in under the window shade.

Chapter Seventeen

Considering the kind of night I'd spent, I had to really extend myself to get to the office by 9:45. So Jackie's antics, which I normally try to ignore, were totally unappreciated that Tuesday morning.

The minute I walked in she made a big production out of checking her watch. Which is pretty much par for the course when I'm late (as I sort of always am). Then she gave me the fish eye—also par for the course. Following which she grumbled something unintelligible, but there's a possibility it was merely "good morning," since as a rule I'm spared any withering words if I arrive before ten. (And if she's in an especially generous mood, I'm safe if I show up by ten-thirty.)

Anyway, I was having coffee at my desk a couple of minutes later when it dawned on me that I'd been neglecting something. I hadn't made any attempt to get in touch with Miriam's housekeeper and chauffeur since last Friday.

"The Browns," I muttered as I dialed the number. "I completely forgot about those damn Browns."

Distracted, I must have allowed for almost a dozen rings before hanging up with a shrug.

Now, Erna had only given the couple a few days off, so they must be back on the job by this time. But it never even occurred to me to try them at Miriam's apartment. In fact, I was so intent on questioning Philip Chance this afternoon that instead of the frustration I usually experienced at failing to reach that elusive pair, I was actually philosophical. Sooner or later we would connect.

A short while after this I coerced myself into transcribing some additional pages of notes.

This is always an arduous task for me, being that I'm very possibly the worst typist you've ever come across. I've known people who are a whole lot faster with two fingers than I am with two hands. Plus, I slow myself down even more by making an effort to absorb whatever it is I'm transcribing. At any rate, except for a quick ham-and-brie-with-honey-mustard break around twelve, I kept at it diligently until one-thirty. And in spite of the creepy pace, I did manage to get a fairly decent chunk of work out of the way. Although if I'd come across any clue to Miriam Weiden's murderer during these past few hours, it certainly hadn't registered.

But, uncharacteristically, I wasn't discouraged. Miriam's former lover would be here in half an hour, I informed myself eagerly—and who knows?

Ernestine Hartley was crazy. Philip Chance didn't look any more like Pierce Brosnan than I did. The guy was a dead ringer for a young Cary Grant.

As soon as Chance came through the door I got up and walked out from behind my desk to greet him. We shook hands, and then he smiled. Now, I'd seen handsome men before, but Philip Chance set a brand-new standard. Let me tell you, I probably would have swooned at that moment if I had a penchant for tall, well-built, absolutely gorgeous men—which I don't, being a sucker for the scrawny, needy-looking ones. Still, I thought it wise to plant my tush back in the chair without delay. (Not that there was ever really much likelihood that my knees would buckle and I'd wind up crumpled at this Adonis's feet.)

Once he'd taken a seat alongside the desk, I had to make a conscious effort to avoid focusing on the cleft in that Cary Grantish chin or lingering very long on those blue-green eyes of his. Unless, that is, I wanted

to risk being too tongue-tied to pose even a single
question.

"Uh, you knew Mrs. Weiden quite well, I understand."

"Yes, I did. We were good friends." The voice
wasn't anything special, but who cared? The rest of
him more than made up for it.

"That's all you were—friends?"

Chance colored a little. "No, there was more to it.
But that honestly was the most important part of our
relationship—the friendship. I just got through trying
to convince the police of that."

"You've spoken to the police already?" *Who tipped
them to his existence?* I wondered.

"I got a call from the NYPD this morning, a Detective Weber. He told me he and his partner wanted to
talk to me. I offered to stop by the precinct, since I
was coming into Manhattan today anyway."

"How did they find out about your connection to
Mrs. Weiden?"

"I have no idea. They didn't volunteer the information, and I didn't ask."

"About how long had the two of you been seeing
each other? You and Mrs. Weiden, I mean."

"Three, maybe four months. We met in September." He looked at me with moist eyes. "You know,
it's still hard for me to believe that anyone would
murder that lady. She was such a warm, giving
person."

"You said on the phone that you'd split up about
a month ago."

"I didn't just *say* it—it's true."

"May I ask the cause of the breakup?"

"The sudden infusion of some common sense."
Clearly uncomfortable, Chance drummed his fingers
on the desk before continuing. "I have a wife, a wife
I love, Ms. Shapiro—"

"Desiree."

"And I'm Philip," he responded automatically.
"Nina—my wife—is a very special person, Desiree.

But for a while I was so intrigued by Miriam that I
forgot what was good for me." He was now wearing
the guilty smile of a child caught dipping his hand in
the candy dish too close to dinner time. "That's no
reflection on Miriam," he found it necessary to add.
"But Nina and I have been married for eighteen
years—eighteen years that have, for the most part,
been damn close to perfect. And we also have two
terrific kids. At any rate, I finally straightened out. I
woke up one morning, and it was as if I'd miraculously
acquired some smarts during the night. I realized that
while I enjoyed being with Miriam and admired her
tremendously, I didn't love her. And I couldn't afford
to continue the relationship and gamble on jeopardiz-
ing my marriage."

"You're saying that your wife wasn't aware that
you'd been running around on her?"

Obviously, this was putting things a little less deli-
cately than Philip might have preferred, as evidenced
by the splash of red decorating his cheeks. Nevertheless, he answered levelly, "I'm certain she wasn't." *But
had there been the slightest hesitation before his reply?*

"Just how did you and Mrs. Weiden meet?"

"Nina and I had gone to a cocktail party on Long
Island at the home of some friends—actually, they're
friends of friends. Anyway, this is a very wealthy, well-
connected couple I'm talking about, and there were a
lot of prominent people at the party. About ten minutes after we arrived, though, Nina had to leave. She's
a doctor—a psychiatrist—and she got this urgent call
concerning a patient of hers. But she insisted I stay
because I was eager to speak to someone who was
expected there."

I think I may have raised an eyebrow here. Or
maybe both of them.

"I should probably embellish on that a little," Philip
proposed, most likely in response to the eyebrow(s).
"For ten years I'd been executive vice president of a
small software company—A and J, it was called. But
the company was recently absorbed by a much larger

firm, and the new management instantly concluded that most of the A and J executives were expendable, myself included. So after what I had considered a very secure and successful career, I was shoved back in the job market again." And now hunching his shoulders, Philip Chance pressed his lips together and rolled his eyes heavenward.

After this brief, silent condemnation of his fate, he continued. "Well, I'd heard that there was a fellow invited to the party who might be looking for someone with my kind of experience to head up a new venture he was planning. That's why Nina thought I should stick around." He grinned ruefully. "Fat lot of good that did, though."

"It didn't lead to anything, I gather."

"The guy never showed. But Miriam did. And at one point in the evening I found myself standing next to her, and we got to chatting. Eventually she asked me what I did for a living. 'Nothing,' I told her— mostly for shock value, I suppose. But then I explained about the takeover. She said she had a great many acquaintances and that, if I liked, she could put me in touch with a few people it might be worth my while to talk to. She said she'd make some calls and that I should check with her in a couple of days."

"And apparently you did." I couldn't help it. A bit of snideness had crept into my tone.

Philip Chance didn't seem to pick up on it, maybe because he didn't want to. "Well, naturally. And then after a meeting with one of her contacts, I invited her to lunch. But there was no ulterior motive. It was by way of saying thank you. That day over lunch, however, I felt an electricity between us, even though I refused to acknowledge it to myself. I don't imagine you ever met Miriam, did you?"

"Once, a few years ago."

"Then maybe you can appreciate why I was so taken with her. She was just so witty, so intelligent. I've rarely been with anyone of either sex who was such fantastic company."

"She was also a very attractive woman," I observed wryly.

"That, too," Philip agreed with a smile. And now very soberly: "I'll tell you something else that impressed me about Miriam. She always downplayed the good works she was involved in. The same way she sloughed off my gratitude with regard to all her efforts on my behalf." He shook his head with something akin to awe. "She was really something. It was tough enough to accept her being dead, but learning today that she'd been poisoned . . ."

"Did any of the job leads Mrs. Weiden gave you amount to anything?" I asked a few seconds later, mostly because I'm nosy.

"A couple of things are still pending." His voice grew defensive. "It's not easy finding something at my level, you know."

"I don't imagine it would be," I acknowledged, on the heels of which I reminded him, "Uh, you were telling me how the two of you began your . . . umm . . . relationship."

"Yes. Well, Miriam called me a week or so after our lunch to find out how things were going, and I mentioned that, as a matter of fact, I would be coming into Manhattan late that afternoon to talk to somebody else she had recommended I see. She said she'd be anxious to hear how it went and suggested we get together for cocktails afterward. And, like a fool, I said fine. I had a pretty good inkling by then of where we were headed, but I was too into self-gratification to avoid it. Anyway, following the drinks, we had dinner, and it was a foregone conclusion on both our parts that the evening wouldn't end there."

"And the affair lasted more than three months," I remarked tersely.

Looking miserable at this juncture—and even more appealing, if that's possible—Philip nodded. "I'm not proud of myself for allowing something like that to happen, Desiree. But I can't change what I've already done. I want you to believe this, though: It wasn't only a physical thing between Miriam and me. We developed genuine feelings for each other. That was the hardest part about ending it—knowing that someone I really cared about would no longer be part of my life."

"When you notified her that you wanted out, how did she take it?"

"She was upset, but it seemed to me she was also relieved. Miriam had told me more than once that she wasn't very comfortable in the part of 'the other woman.'"

I was just about to inquire about the reason for their meeting on that fateful Tuesday when Philip broached the subject himself.

"The day before she died, though—on Monday—I received a letter from Miriam. She said that she had to speak to me, as someone she could trust, and pleaded with me to get in touch with her right away."

"Why would she put this in a letter," I interjected, "given that there was this sense of immediacy?"

"Once we'd become er . . . close . . . I was pretty adamant about her never calling me at home. My wife sees patients at the house, and when she's not in session with anyone, she's the one who usually answers the telephone. Even when Arlene, our housekeeper, is there, nine times out of ten it's Nina who picks up. But this aside, it's obvious that Miriam didn't realize quite how imminent the danger was. Still, the letter did sound urgent, so I threw on my coat and hurried over to the luncheonette a couple of blocks away— they have a pay phone there. I didn't want to take the chance of contacting her from the house, especially since Nina was free just then."

"Who brought in the mail that day?" I asked.

"I believe I did." Philip scowled in concentration for a moment. "Yes, now I recall. I spotted the postman through the window, and I went out to the mailbox right after he left. Why?"

"I was thinking that if your wife had seen an envelope with a feminine handwriting, this could also have aroused her suspicions, particularly if she already had some inkling that you'd been cheating on her."

The man actually winced before responding. (Maybe he wasn't too crazy about the word "cheating.") "The envelope was typed, and there was no return address."

And now, his tone bordering on the belligerent, he snapped, "But forget that. As I keep telling you, Nina had no idea about Miriam and me. Listen, knowing Nina, I feel—no, I'm *positive*—she would have confronted me if she'd had even the slightest notion that there might be another woman."

I guess it was all the emotion he packed into this denial that made me put a question to myself then: *Why was Philip Chance so eager to convince me of his wife's ignorance of the affair?*

"You wouldn't still have that letter, would you?" I inquired foolishly.

"Are you kidding? I tore it into shreds as soon as I'd read it."

Why had I bothered to ask? "Tell me about the phone call."

"Miriam wanted me to meet her for lunch at noon the next day. She said it was a matter of life and death and that she meant this literally."

"So you obliged her."

"Of course."

"And?" I prodded.

"She was positive that someone was trying to kill her. She spoke about what happened at the lake last summer—this was the first I'd heard of it—and then she talked about the so-called 'accident' at the school that Friday. I suppose you're aware of those things."

"Yes, I am. Uh, I don't imagine there were any names named."

Philip shook his head. "No. But Miriam did use the pronoun 'she,' as in 'I'm terrified that next time *she'll* get it right.' I did my damnedest to persuade her to open up to me, but she refused to reveal who it was she was so afraid of."

"You believed that somebody *was* out to murder her, though."

"I had no reason to doubt her." There was a prolonged pause, following which Philip put in hesitantly, "This morning, though, I—" But frowning, he broke off abruptly.

"What is it?"

"Nothing, really."

I took a crack at duplicating Jackie's fish eye. "Nothing?"

"Nothing important, that is."

"You can't be sure," I badgered.

"All right. It's just that I'm beginning to have reservations about that first incident's being a bona fide murder attempt. But even assuming it *was,* I have some doubts about whether the woman in the boat with Miriam was the same person who wanted to clobber her with that ladder and later poisoned her."

"Why do you say that?"

"Well, it came to me when I was at the police station before that it had been a long while between attacks number one and two. And then I recalled how Miriam admitted at our lunch that Tuesday that at the time of the occurrence at the lake, she hadn't been sure if the intention had been to drown her or not. It appears that it took the ladder business for her to make up her mind about that."

I mulled this over. "You could be right." A disquieting thought followed. "Naturally, that changes things, though."

"In what way?"

"It would mean the killer wasn't necessarily a woman." Not that this had narrowed the field all that much, but still. . . .

"I don't understand. Didn't Mrs. Davis tell you that whoever went after Miriam at the school was almost definitely female?"

"What are you talking about?" I asked, my jaw just having dropped to the vicinity of my ankles.

"Miriam didn't actually see the person, of course.

But she did say that immediately after she fell to the ground, she caught a quick glimpse of someone in a dark skirt escaping through the open door. You weren't informed about that?"

"No, I wasn't." *What in hell was going on here?* Either the deceased had kept this little nugget from my client, or for reasons of her own, Mrs. Davis had opted not to share it with me.

"Maybe," Philip offered, "Miriam didn't feel it was worthwhile to mention the skirt to anyone else because nobody regarded her as the least bit credible anyway."

"Did you tell the police about the skirt?"

"No. I assumed they'd already heard about it from Miriam herself. It now appears likely I was mistaken, though."

I allowed myself a minute or so for a brief mental recap before remarking, "I'm a little puzzled, Philip."

"About what?"

"Why would Mrs. Weiden want to talk to you—of all people—about fearing for her life?"

"I wish I could make you understand," he responded wearily. "We had been friends, good friends. We still were. And when the police refused to take her seriously, she didn't know who else to turn to. Apparently, even her own mother didn't believe she was in any real jeopardy. At any rate, she wanted my advice."

"What advice did you give her?"

"To get far away from the city for a while, take a trip somewhere. She instantly vetoed the suggestion, insisting she had too many obligations to do anything of the sort. So then I tried to convince her to hire a bodyguard."

"What did she say to that?"

"Just that she'd think about it."

"I finally recommended she call in a private detective to prove out her suspicions. She seemed to respond positively to this. She even promised she'd contact someone right away. I guess she was murdered before she got around to it."

I felt the usual twinge of guilt. "By the way," I asked, quickly changing the subject, "what time did the lunch end?"

"It must have been close to two-thirty."

"What did you do then?"

"I went hunting for an anniversary gift for Nina. Then later I was hungry again—I'd been too upset by what Miriam had to say to eat very much—so I stopped off for a sandwich."

"And you got home—when?"

"Look, you can't possibly believe that *I* killed Miriam," Philip protested, glowering at me. "I wouldn't have harmed her for the world. Besides, she was afraid of a *woman*."

I don't know how often I've given the same response. I gave it now, too. "Honestly, that's a question I have to ask everyone—for my records."

"Well, I was home by eight-thirty or so."

"I suppose your wife and children were there, too."

"Actually, they weren't. The kids were both staying overnight with friends. As for my wife, I had no idea what to expect with Miriam, and I wanted to give myself plenty of leeway—I'm speaking timewise. So I told Nina I had a job interview in Manhattan at five and that I'd grab a bite in the city afterward. She figured it would be a good opportunity to spend a few hours with her mother, who's about a forty-five-minute drive from our place." Philip grinned sheepishly. "I'm afraid I tend to give Nina a bit of grief about going there with her. My mother-in-law was always something of a pill, and lately she's gone a bit dotty, to boot."

"When did she get back to the house?"

"Eleven-thirty, twelve. Something like that."

"Do you recall where you were the previous Friday—the morning of the ladder incident?"

Philip's immediate reaction was to shoot me another black look. But a second later he said offhandedly, "I'm afraid I don't have an alibi for that one, either.

I was shut away in my study, redoing my résumé. In any case, though, I wasn't even aware that Miriam planned to be at the school then." He pulled his chair a little closer to mine. "I wonder if I could ask *you* something now."

"Ask away," I replied in my most gracious and obliging manner.

"Who was it who saw Miriam and me at Andrea's?"

"Andrea's?" I echoed.

"That was where we had lunch."

"I don't even know the name of the person. All I can tell you is that you were spotted walking out together."

"It's funny"—the chuckle that followed, however, was totally devoid of amusement—"we purposely chose a restaurant way downtown in Tribeca because we were certain we wouldn't be recognized there."

"What was it Joe Louis said: 'You can run but you can't hide'?" (I'm not at all sure this response was appropriate here, but it did seem to fit at the moment.) "And anyhow," I continued, "Tribeca's become very cosmopolitan. People from all over visit the shops and restaurants in that area. So it shouldn't be any surprise that someone in Mrs. Weiden's circle— remember, she did know a lot of people—happened to go by Andrea's just as you two were leaving."

Philip took a couple of deep breaths—I had the impression he was recharging himself. His next question, when it came, was posed almost in a whisper. "Does my wife have to find out about Miriam and me?"

"I'm—"

"I doubt if she would ever forgive me. Nina's the best, but if you hurt her, well, she *is* a Scorpio." He accompanied the disclosure with a small, tug-at-your-heart kind of smile.

Being one of those myself—a Scorpio, I mean—I could appreciate the man's concern. Nevertheless, I had to tell him—but gently—that I wasn't able to make a promise like that.

He kept up the pressure. "We have two young boys, Desiree—eight and ten years old. Even the *police* said they might be able to keep Nina out of this."

"I wouldn't count on it. Besides, they don't know anything about Tuesday's lunch, do they?" I pointed out.

"No. At least, not yet. But, I swear to you, that didn't mean a thing. I was trying to help a friend, for God's sake!"

"Let me think about it, okay?"

But the instant I uttered the words I realized that I couldn't possibly go along with Philip Chance's request. Even if he'd had *two* clefts in his chin.

I would definitely be having a talk with his wife. After all, you can't lay your hands on a little tubocurarine chloride by checking the shelves of your local supermarket. Almost certainly it was available only by prescription. And which female connected to this case had a better opportunity of obtaining the drug than a psychiatrist—an MD—who had only to pick up a pen?

Chapter Eighteen

•

Don't get me wrong. I had no designs on Philip Chance. But I was feeling a sort of proprietary pride with regard to the man's striking good looks. It was as if I'd just discovered a superstar.

I met up with Jackie in the ladies' room a few minutes after he'd left my office.

"Well, what did you think of my visitor?" I demanded of her reflection as she ran a comb through her blondish-brown hair.

Turning from the mirror, she looked down at me. (This time I mean that literally—Jackie's not being one of my fellow vertically challenged.) "He's okay."

"*Okay?* You don't think he's *gorgeous*?"

She faced her image again and began applying some blush. "Well, I'd say that was pushing it. He doesn't have such wonderful hair."

Now, with that cleft chin and those great eyes, I really hadn't paid much attention to Philip's hair. The mere fact that he even had some was good enough for me. Come to think of it, though, it was a nice, medium brown shade and kind of straight. "*Hair?*" I squealed at the mirror. "What's *wrong* with his hair?"

"Oh, I don't know. It just isn't anything special, that's all." She removed a lipstick from her cosmetics case. "Take Derwin's hair, for instance," she said, referring to her longtime significant other. "His—"

"Are you out of your *mind*, Jackie?" My voice was at a level where it was irritating my throat. "Derwin wears a toupee, for heaven's sake!"

Jackie could have saved herself the trouble of putting on that blush. She was now coming by a nice, deep pink naturally. Which led me to believe that either she thought I'd forgotten about the toupee or else she didn't remember that I ever knew about it.

"So what?" she countered after an awkward pause. "That's still the sort of hair *I* like to see on a man." And with this, she gathered up her cosmetics, plunked them back in their case, and strode out of the restroom.

I stood there, astonished. Jackie's Derwin didn't sport just any old toupee, but the thickest, most obvious rug you've ever laid eyes on. Part of the reason being that he's too much of a tightwad to spring for anything better. Although this, I suppose, is neither here nor there.

Anyway, Jackie had to be getting a little gaga to make any comparisons between Philip Chance and Derwin, who's lived on this planet a minimum of twenty years longer than Chance has and who, I can say with absolute certainty, couldn't have been anything to leave your happy home for even twenty years ago. And besides—

I interrupted this train of thought. The truth is, I had to be headed for gaga myself to have this to-do with Jackie over something so silly in the first place. It's not as if Philip Chance were my protégé or anything. I mean, who did I think I was—Ed McMahon in his *Star Search* days? And Chance probably couldn't sing a note, besides.

At any rate, I reminded myself, I'd better pay attention to more than the man's looks. After all, it hadn't been positively established that Miriam's killer was a woman—now, had it?

After work that evening I stopped off at my neighborhood pharmacy, where I headed straight for the prescription department at the back of the store. Leaning so far over the low, separating partition that I came close to landing on my head, I looked around for my friend Leon, a pleasant, cheerful man I figured to be somewhere in his late fifties. But Leon was nowhere in sight. Maybe he'd gone out for a sandwich.

A moment or two later I heard a sort of shuffling sound. And immediately afterward a sour-faced, wizened little fellow in a white jacket was standing behind the counter, facing me. "Can I help you?" he inquired tersely.

"Is Leon in tonight?"

"Leon retired last month."

"You're kidding!"

"Why so surprised? If you ask me, it's about time the old geezer packed it in."

He *was* kidding, of course—right? But when I checked for a grin or a tiny twinkle in the eye, there wasn't any.

The nerve of this character! I swear, he looked like he had enough years on Leon to be his father. (Well, maybe his older brother.)

"There was no reason they had to drag me in from the Queens store to replace him, though," the pharmacist went on, grumbling. "I used to work only three blocks from my house; now I have to take two trains." His sour face soured even more. "You got a prescription you wanted Leon to fill—or was this meant to be a personal visit?" He actually leered when he said it.

"Uh, there was a drug I wanted to ask him about."

"Maybe I can give you the answer. By the way, I'm Herman, but everyone calls me Hermie." Hermie attempted an ingratiating smile, but it didn't make the grade. "So what's your question?"

"Umm, would you be able to tell me something about tubocurarine chloride?"

"About what, did you say?"

"Tubocurarine chloride. It's a derivative of curare."

Hermie's already squinty eyes instantly narrowed to slits. "Why would you be interested in a thing like that?" he inquired suspiciously.

"I'm a private investigator, and I'm looking into the death of a woman who was poisoned with that drug."

"How do I *know* you're a private investigator?" he demanded.

"I'll show you my license." Which was a lot more difficult to accomplish than it sounds. I mean, it took forever to dig the thing out of my portable junkyard of a handbag.

When I finally put the license in Hermie's hands, he took his own good time scrutinizing it. I swear, you'd have thought it was a deed to his new house. At last he mumbled, "Well, it looks legitimate enough. But private detective or not, you still might be out to do away with your husband."

"I don't have a husband."

"A mature and elegant lady like you? No kidding?"

I decided to bestow a smile upon him. After all, this was probably the first time in my life that I'd ever been called "elegant." (Although frankly, I could have done without the "mature.")

"Tell you what," Hermie said, "I'll look up tubocurarine chloride in *Facts and Comparisons*—that's this reference we have here."

"Thank you so much, Hermie. That's very kind of you, and I really appreciate it," I gushed. I did stop short of fluttering my eyelashes, however. "When do you suppose you'll have a chance to do that?"

"You don't see a line forming behind you, do you? I can check it out now. Wait here." And he shuffled away.

In less than five minutes he came shuffling back. "Tubocurarine chloride is a neuromuscular blocker."

"What's that?"

"A muscle relaxant. They use it during surgery and electroshock therapy. And also in the diagnosis of myasthenia gravis. Know what that is?"

"I'm not sure." (Actually, I was sure I *didn't*.) "But I'm really anxious to hear about the drug itself."

"Mmm, a single-minded woman. I like that."

Yecch! "Uh, you were saying . . ."

"Yes, well, the stuff is a salt that's mixed with water

and injected. If it's not properly administered it can be lethal."

"Do you suppose the drug could be dissolved in water and then added to someone's drink without that person's detecting it? I'm talking about a liqueur with a pronounced taste. Like crème de menthe, for example."

"I don't see why not."

"And would it take effect right away?"

"If it's given in a high enough concentration, I'm certain it would."

"Thank you, Hermie. You've been extremely helpful." I turned to go.

"Hey, hold it a second." I spun around. "Doesn't this at least deserve a cup of coffee—and maybe a slice of apple pie? Your treat, naturally."

"Absolutely. I'll stop in again, and we'll set something up." Then before he could say boo, I scurried away as fast as a pair of short, stubby, underused legs could manage this.

No sooner was I safely outside the store than I began mulling over which of the other two local pharmacies would be getting my business from now on.

Chapter Nineteen

Walking toward my apartment building, I tried to decide what I could fix for dinner, but the choices were pathetically limited. I would really have to pay a visit to D'Agostino's in the next couple of days. Then I realized I was practically in front of Jerome's—or I would be if I backtracked a block. And a cheeseburger, even if it was for the second night in a row, did a lot more for me at this moment than the alternatives awaiting me in my kitchen.

But hallelujah! I soon discovered that Felix was off that evening. Which meant I could select anything on the coffee shop's extensive menu without worrying about damaging that lovely gentleman's psyche. I felt a little like a kid in a candy store.

My eyes lit up when I saw the full-color photograph accompanying the listing for eggs Benedict, a special favorite of mine. And even without a picture, the fried shrimp sounded pretty appealing to me. Likewise the cheese and onion tart that was served with a nice green salad topped (the copy boasted) with your choice of seven delicious dressings. (I'd have mine with blue cheese.) And then there was always that BLT I'd been salivating for last night. . . .

But by the time the waitress came for my order, I realized that what I really wanted was a cheeseburger again.

Well, how ironic is *that*?

* * *

I had absolutely forbidden myself to think about the investigation during the meal, and for the most part I succeeded.

But once at home I curled up on the sofa and immediately began to ruminate on the beautiful picture of his former lover that Philip Chance had painted for me this afternoon. Which hardly jibed with the other assessments I'd gotten of Mrs. Weiden lately. And now that I'd finally—albeit reluctantly—come to accept these less-than-flattering appraisals of the woman's character, how could I account for Philip's lauding her as he had?

Was it possible she'd had him totally bamboozled during those months they'd been seeing each other? Or was he the one out to bamboozle me? And if so, to what possible advantage?

It seemed that the more I learned, the less I knew. It was so damn frustrating—particularly in view of how personally I took this case.

The thing is, I'd always figured that if the victim hadn't been Saint Miriam the Good, my screwup with regard to her call for help wouldn't prey on me to the extent that it did. But even now that I was finally keyed in to her true nature, it was still no go. I mean, Miriam Weiden may not have been the person I thought she was, but after all, she was still a person.

And speaking of my earlier, misguided conception of the deceased, I was extremely anxious to have a heart-to-heart with Erna—whether she liked it or not. And, of course, she wouldn't like it at all.

Reaching over to the coffee table, I picked up the portable phone.

I got pretty much the reception I expected when I announced myself.

The actual words were "You didn't have to inform me of that; I recognized your voice." But Erna's tone told it like it was: "Oh, no! Not you!"

In response to my request for a meeting, she sniffed, "I can't spare the time for at least a week."

"It would only take a few minutes," I lied.

"I haven't *got* a few minutes. Yesterday it was the police again and now—you. The estate isn't planning to pay for my services forever, you know. And do you have any idea of the amount of work involved in breaking up an apartment like this one? To say nothing of putting all of Miriam's affairs in order."

"I can appreciate how busy you are. I really can." I said this with as much sympathy as I was able to generate, following up with the same type of approach that had already proven successful with the secretary. "But I did think you'd want to help apprehend Mrs. Weiden's murderer."

"That sounds familiar. Seems to me you used this tack with me before." I swear that I could actually hear the smirk in her voice.

"Maybe, but it has now been confirmed that Mrs. Weiden was poisoned, and there are some things we have to talk about." Then before she could trot out any more excuses: "It's extremely important."

"Oh, all right. I guess we can do it Saturday."

"This can't wait," I insisted. "I've been getting a number of conflicting stories, and I need you to clear things up for me."

The sigh was probably heard in LA. "You win," Erna finally agreed. "Be at the apartment by ten tomorrow morning. And try not to be late."

Once again the door to the duplex was opened by a tiny, birdlike woman. But this latest variety wasn't Erna. Quite probably, I speculated, the lady was none other than the phantom Mrs. Brown. I mean, what with her demeanor and that plain dark gray dress and those sensible oxford shoes, she gave every impression of being a housekeeper.

But was she *the* housekeeper?

I didn't get the chance to establish her identity because she was instantly ten steps ahead of me, leading the way down the center hall with remarkably long, purposeful strides. (And she was shorter than I am, for heaven's sake.) At about the midpoint in the corridor the woman stopped abruptly in front of an open door. Stepping aside, she motioned for me to enter the room. I was just over the threshold when she said from the doorway, "Please have a seat; Ms. Harris will be with you soon."

I turned with the question "Mrs. Brown?" poised to leave my lips.

But she was gone.

At any rate, I found myself in a small square space, furnished very simply with a striped wool sofa, a couple of leather chairs, two large metal file cabinets, and a desk piled high with papers.

Settling into the sofa, which was opposite the doorway and several feet behind the desk, I realized I was feeling a bit let down just then. I'm a little ashamed to tell you why—but I will anyway.

I had sort of assumed that my talk with Erna would take place in the kitchen as before, and the masochist in me had been longing for another look at those fantastic appliances. But I convinced myself now that it was probably just as well that I'd been spared the frustration. Besides, it gave me an opportunity to see another room in the victim's apartment (although I was certain that this one, which I immediately figured to be Erna's office, was hardly representative of the rest). I must admit, however, that I wasn't nearly as philosophical about being deprived of the Danish pastries I'd enjoyed so much on my last visit here.

I was thinking longingly of the prune kind when I was joined by Erna, who was wearing faded jeans, an old T-shirt, and an expression that left no doubt as to how pleased she was to meet with me again. Repositioning the desk chair to face the sofa, she sat down with a perfunctory "How are you, Ms. Shapiro?"

Since it was obvious she had zero interest in the answer, I merely offered a reminder. "It's Desiree, remember?"

"Oh, yes, Desiree," she amended indifferently. "Well, what exactly are you here about?"

"Over the past few days I've heard some things about Mrs. Weiden that directly contradict what I was told by you and, in some instances, by my client as well."

It took a few moments for her to ask, "What is it you've heard?"

"For one thing, that your employer had more than her share of enemies."

Erna managed to look totally blank. "Enemies?" *So she's going to play it like this, is she?*

"People like Ernestine Hartley, for example."

"Oh, *that*! Ms. Hartley and Miriam had some stupid argument based on a lie that Mrs. Hartley had been told. I'm not even sure what the whole thing was about."

Of course not. "It was about Mrs. Weiden's sleeping with her good friend Ernestine's husband."

Erna continued to feign ignorance. "I didn't know that. But I can tell you one thing: It never happened. Miriam wasn't that type of person."

"You mean that she wouldn't have betrayed a friend or that she wouldn't have gotten involved with a married man?"

"Both."

"Is that so." I realized instantly that this rejoinder had a confrontational ring to it, and I'd been making every effort to conceal my exasperation. But the comment—and the attitude—had just kind of pushed their way out of my mouth. "Philip Chance came to see me yesterday," I stated more evenly.

"Oh," Erna said.

"Look," I put to her reasonably, "we both know that not very long ago Miriam had a fling with her friend's husband and that even more recently she was carrying on with this fellow Chance—who was similarly married. So why continue to claim there'd been no men at all in Miriam's life? Why not level with me?"

The woman sat there stone-faced for three or four seconds before answering. "I'm not saying Miriam

never made any mistakes—who hasn't? She did so
much for so many people, though, that I'd hate to see
her reputation smeared simply because she had a too-
loving nature."

*A too-loving nature? You mean a runaway, con-
science-free libido, don't you?* But I skipped what I
considered the appropriate retort to Erna's sanitized
version of things and went on to reassure her. "Believe me, I'm not out to trash Mrs. Weiden. My only
interest is in finding out who murdered her. And can't
you see how you've obstructed my investigation by
misleading me the way you have?"

"I didn't want a couple of missteps to cause you to
question Miriam's genuine goodness. Besides, understand something. Until the autopsy report, I really
didn't believe there'd *been* a murder."

"But even this morning, knowing that she'd been
poisoned, you've been attempting to cover up the
facts."

Erna smiled weakly. "Force of habit."

"So it's true about Ernestine Hartley's husband."

The confirmation, a murmured "I . . . yes, it's true,"
was delivered with a great deal of reluctance and instantly followed by a challenge: "But I'll bet even
you've made a mistake or two." (Which remark I considered totally extraneous and not deserving of a
comeback.)

"How long did the affair last?" I asked.

"I wouldn't call it an affair." And now the voice
was so soft that I had to lean forward to catch the
rest. "I don't think they were together more than once
or twice."

"And Philip Chance?"

"That was another story—it went on for months.
Miriam really cared for Chance."

"Still, she took it in good grace when he broke
things off."

"Who told you that?" Erna asked cautiously.

"He did—Chance."

Frowning, she looked down then and began to pluck

at her jeans, absently ridding them of a whole handful of nonexistent lint. It didn't take a mind reader to figure out that she was doing some heavy-duty calculating. At any rate, it was obvious when she raised her eyes that she was about to make a disclosure. "Miriam was so distraught—and understandably, considering her feelings for the man—that she even threatened him after he ended it."

"With what?"

"Probably with telling his wife. But I'm not sure. One morning I walked into the kitchen and overheard her talking to him on the phone. She said something like, 'You'd better think it over, or I'll do what I warned you I would. I promise you that.' Those weren't the exact words, but that's near enough. Anyhow, it was clear to me she was referring to his decision to stop seeing her."

"You're positive it was Philip Chance on the other end of the line?"

Erna's forehead creased. "We-ll, I was under that impression at the time."

"But it might have been someone else?" I pressed.

Again she hesitated. "I suppose so. I'm trying to remember if Miriam actually mentioned the name. It was weeks ago, though—a few days after she and Chance split up—and I wouldn't swear to it. Still, I can't imagine what reason she'd have for saying something like that to anyone besides him."

I moved on. "I wanted to ask you about Lynne Weiden, too."

"What about her?"

"There was some talk that she felt more than just fondness for her brother-in-law."

Erna's curt response was accompanied by a glare. "I wouldn't know."

"I also understand she believed Miriam precipitated Dan's killing himself."

"That's ridiculous," she snapped.

"You weren't aware Lynne blamed Miriam for this?"

"Yes, but she was wrong. I told you when you were

here before: Dan hung himself because he wasn't able to cope. First he lost his only brother—and with the possible exception of Deena, Edwin was the most important person in Dan's life. Then only a couple of months later the company he loved and worked so hard to build up was on the verge of bankruptcy, and he couldn't do a thing to save it. Apparently that put him over the edge."

"So you never thought that Miriam bore any responsibility for the suicide? After all, from what I was told, she was at him constantly once the business started to fail."

"It was Dan's idea to kill himself. No one else's."

The bitterness with which this was uttered all but convinced me that Erna had been in love with Dan Weiden. I mean, whatever she thought to be Miriam's contribution to the tragedy—and I was reasonably sure she didn't absolve her former employer of at least some culpability—it was obvious that the person Erna blamed most was the dead man himself. *Oh, yes,* I concluded, *she'd been in love with him, all right; otherwise, she'd have forgiven him a long time ago for taking his own life.*

I could see from the brightness in her eyes that she was battling tears, so I gave her a minute to compose herself before I said, "You know, I find it hard to believe that you didn't hold Mrs. Weiden at least partially liable for what happened."

"Okay," Erna retorted with a monumental sigh. "For argument's sake, say I had it in for Miriam because of Dan. Can you possibly think that if I'd wanted to avenge his death—and we were just good friends, by the way—I would have waited all this time to do it? Come on!"

"You misunderstood me. I was only wondering why you kept working here after that. I would think you'd have been anxious to put the whole experience behind you, particularly if you did resent Miriam to some extent."

"Which, as I've been telling you, I didn't. And anyway, there was Deena. Miriam was so busy with her charity work that it was impossible for her to spend as much time with her daughter as she wanted to, so I pitched in. It brought out these maternal feelings in me that I never dreamed existed. I wouldn't have left that precious child for twice what I was being paid."

I had the opening. Now all I had to do was work up the courage. I breathed deeply. Then I breathed even more deeply. "Uh, I heard this rumor regarding Deena."

"What rumor?" Erna demanded sharply.

"That she was . . . that is, that she wasn't adopted in Switzerland, but right in this country."

"For crying out loud! Is that garbage still floating around? And I suppose you heard that I was Deena's natural mother, too."

"You're aware people were saying that?"

"Of course. That dopey little tale was making the rounds for years. I thought it had finally worn itself out, though. Not that I wouldn't be proud to have given birth to Deena. But the fact is, she isn't mine. All you have to do is look at the two of us to see that I'm telling the truth, for Christ's sake."

"Uh, I understand that Mrs. Weiden never denied the rumor."

"Probably because she didn't consider it worth responding to."

"Let me ask you about something else. I was informed that you and Mrs. Weiden didn't always get along."

"We got along fine."

"You never argued?"

"Naturally we did," the secretary informed me tartly. "We were together too much not to."

And here—and I must concede she had been showing admirable forbearance—Erna checked her watch, after which, tapping the crystal, she asked pointedly, "Do you know what time it is?"

I decided to treat this as a rhetorical question. "I have just one more matter to cover, okay?"

"Go ahead," she muttered. "But make it snappy."

Now, "snappy" was out of the question. I was about to bring up another very touchy subject, and I wanted to be careful about how I put things.

"I was told that Miriam was . . . well, not overly pleased with her daughter's choice of boyfriend."

"She thought Deena could do better, that's all."

"She wasn't vehemently opposed to the match?"

"No."

"Umm, but she *did* threaten to cut the girl out of her will, didn't she?"

Evidently I hadn't been quite careful enough, because Erna leapt up. "Who the hell told you *that*?" She was standing over me, hands on hips, her eyes shooting poisoned darts at me.

"I can't divulge my source," I declared self-righteously. "But even if it's true—and I have reason to believe that it is—it doesn't mean Deena murdered Miriam." And then I felt I had to include, "Or that you did, either. So please, calm down."

Surprisingly, Erna acceded to my request. "All right. Miriam did make the threat," she admitted, taking her seat again. "She was hoping it would induce Deena to dump Todd—her boyfriend. Which she honestly felt would be best for Deena. She never planned on going through with it, though—even if the two of them got married." And now with obvious pride: "Of course, there was one thing wrong with Miriam's thinking: Her daughter doesn't give a rap about money." It didn't take a millisecond before the secretary added hastily, "I should really have said *two* things. Deena also didn't believe Miriam would ever disinherit her—any more than I did."

"But Mrs. Weiden never actually told you that, did she? I mean that the girl would remain in her will—regardless?"

"She most certainly did."

Well, there was no way I could dispute this claim as to the victim's intentions, so I was primed to go on to another topic—just as Erna got to her feet.

"One more question."

"That's what you said five minutes ago, so save it for the next time." She began to move toward the door.

"It's about that incident with the ladder," I threw in quickly. "Did Miriam tell you that immediately after it occurred she caught a quick glimpse of the perpetrator—and it was someone wearing a dark skirt?"

This put Erna right back in her seat.

"Of course not," she scoffed. "Miriam didn't see who threw that ladder at her—she didn't see *anything*. It all happened too fast. Where did you get this, anyway?"

"Philip Chance. He claims to have heard it from Mrs. Weiden."

"Baloney."

"Why would he make it up?"

Erna glanced at me pityingly. "Because maybe he killed her"—she refrained from tagging on the "stupid" that I suspect was on her mind—"so he wants you to think the murderer was a woman."

I hadn't considered that, and like almost everything else, it was a possibility.

Erna had both palms on either side of the chair seat now, preparatory to rising again.

I stopped her cold with "Are you aware that Miriam met Philip Chance for lunch on the day she died?"

"What?"

"You had no idea of this?"

"No."

"But Mrs. Weiden did go out that afternoon."

"Yes, but she said she had to get a blouse for her new suit. And Bendel's was having a sale."

I must have looked surprised.

"The wealthy are just like the rest of us when it comes to sales," Erna informed me with another of her pitying looks.

"What time did she leave the apartment?"

"About eleven-thirty."

"Did the chauffeur drive her to the store?"

"No, it was Frank's day off—his and Margaret's. Miriam said she'd get a taxi."

"And when did she return?"

"I think it was around three. She mentioned that after Bendel's she'd checked out Bergdorf's and Bloomingdale's. She said she stopped off for lunch somewhere, too."

"I don't imagine she was carrying any packages when she came home," I observed wryly.

"No. She told me none of the stores had had what she wanted."

"And you accepted that this is where she was—shopping?"

"Why wouldn't I?" The woman had a point there. "I suppose it was Philip Chance who told you about the lunch."

"After I informed him that somebody had spotted them walking out of the restaurant together."

"And the reason for that lunch?" she put to me. "What did he have to say about that?"

"According to Mr. Chance, Miriam had been very anxious to talk to him about the attempt on her life. He told me she wanted his advice."

"That'd be the day," Erna mumbled sarcastically.

"You don't believe it?"

"Do you?" she shot back.

I honestly had no idea.

Now, the fact that it was a pretty exotic substance that killed Miriam had eliminated the possibility of suicide for me right from the beginning. I mean, it was highly unlikely the deceased would have had some of that stuff hanging around in her medicine cabinet. And later everyone-calls-me-Hermie's description of the drug had pretty much verified my conclusion. But being positively anal, I seemed to require still further corroboration.

So at the risk of inducing a conniption fit in my hostess, I ventured bravely, "Uh, there's one more thing I have to know."

Well, I've been on the receiving end of dark looks

before, but the one Erna aimed my way was pure ebony. "Forget it," she retorted. As predicted, she was fuming.

She shot out of her seat just as I said the words. "Tubocurarine chloride—the drug that killed Mrs. Weiden."

Stopping in her tracks, she glowered at me. "What about it?"

"Is there any possibility Mrs. Weiden might have kept some in the house? What I mean is, could she have maybe had a prescription for it at one time?"

"Miriam never took *any* medication," Erna snapped. "You couldn't even get an aspirin in this place; I always had to keep some here—in my desk." She turned and opened the left-hand middle drawer.

Then reaching in and rummaging around, she spat out, "And I've never needed a couple more than after this god-awful session with you."

Chapter Twenty

Close up like this, Margaret Brown won the bird-woman contest hands down. She was even shorter and thinner than the secretary, with a beakier nose, a smaller mouth, and rounder, darker eyes.

Her husband Frank was a squat, heavy-set man with regular features and an affable smile. He was dressed in a pair of old denim overalls that were covered with dirt. "Been fixing something on the terrace," he'd explained. I hadn't even known there *was* a terrace.

We were sitting in Erna's office, which she had agreed to let me continue to occupy so that I could question the Browns. (I think she would have given in to almost any request of mine at that point just so she could make her escape.) Margaret and I were on the sofa, while Frank was leaning back in the desk chair, facing us.

"I'd like to talk to you about Mrs. Weiden for a few minutes," I began. Then I threw in—with a smile, naturally—"I spent most of my free time last week trying to reach you two people."

"Oh, that's too bad," Frank commiserated. "I keep telling Maggie we should spring for an answering machine one of these years. The reason you probably had trouble getting us is I was in the hospital for a couple of days. They thought I was having a heart attack at first, but it turned out it was indigestion—I just ate too much. That's what happens, I guess, when your wife is such a good cook." But after quickly ascertaining that the aforementioned wife wasn't looking in his direction, he shook his head and winked at me.

Margaret turned toward him then. "No, that's what happens when you're past sixty and you keep shoveling food in your mouth—and without bothering to chew it, too." And to me: "But what is it you'd like to ask us?"

"Do either of you know of anyone who might have wanted to harm Mrs. Weiden?"

"Lord, no!" Frank exclaimed. "You couldn't find a better person. We were very fond of her, weren't we, Maggie?" Her answer obviously wasn't required, because the chauffeur/handyman went on without taking a breath. "It must have been some nut. Who else would do a thing like that to someone like Mrs. Weiden?"

"You were with her a long time, I understand."

"Going on twenty-six years," he proclaimed proudly.

I focused on Mrs. Brown now. "Had you ever heard Mrs. Weiden exchange harsh words with anyone?"

Frank beat his wife to the punch. "Not Mrs. Weiden. Am I right, Maggie?" But before the woman had time to so much as nod he embellished this with "She was a real lady, wasn't she, Maggie?"

His spouse eyed him expectantly. But it seemed that for once he was allowing her to respond. Which she did—but only after taking a couple of seconds to verify that she actually had the floor. "Yes, she was," she agreed with a sad smile. "She certainly was."

"Were *you* ever privy to any disagreements Mrs. Weiden might have been involved in?" I put to Margaret.

"No, she hardly ever even raised her voice."

"Uh, how did Mrs. Weiden get along with the other members of the household—her daughter, for example?"

Frank was back to being spokesman. "Well, when it comes to family, there's nobody who doesn't get a little agitated now and then. Years ago Mrs. Weiden and Deena got along good. Real good. Lately, though, they'd have their little arguments every so often. But, a course, they *would,* with Deena being a teenager and all. Still, it was nothing compared to the way it used to be between Maggie and our girls. Especially Frannie—she's our youngest. I'm surprised her and Maggie never got to the point of slugging each other." He chuckled at the idea, then noting his wife's withering glare hastily tagged on, "They're really terrific kids, though, all three of our gals."

"Did you ever hear what any of those arguments between Mrs. Weiden and Deena were about?"

"Mostly it was about how Deena dressed—the kids these days wear the weirdest clothes—and how Deena'd better be home by such and such a time. It was never anything much. Wait a minute. This one day I heard something that really upset me." My heartbeat quickened in anticipation.

"Yes?" I asked eagerly.

"It seemed Deena wanted—" He broke off, hunching his shoulders. "But maybe I was mistaken, since it's such an ugly thing, and besides, my hearing's not the best. To me, though, it sounded like she was trying to get permission to have her *body* pierced."

I couldn't have been more deflated. Nevertheless, I asked, mostly to be polite, "Did she have it done?"

"Not to my knowledge. Mrs. Weiden wouldn't hear of it—she hit the ceiling, she did. But I'll tell you, the way I see it, most girls wouldn't have bothered to ask their mother's permission, right?" But as he did with his wife, the garrulous Mr. Brown spared me the effort of a reply. "They would not," he asserted.

I reached over and touched Margaret's shoulder. "Were you aware of any of these little altercations between mother and daughter?"

"Not really. Once in a great while I'd hear them bickering some, maybe. But I don't pay attention to that type of silliness—it's normal."

Well, that had led absolutely nowhere. "How about Mrs. Weiden and Ms. Harris? How did they get along?"

"Like sisters," Frank responded.

"Funny. I understood that they had their share of arguments."

"I said like sisters, didn't I?" There was a *gotcha* twinkle in his eyes. "Do you know of any sisters who *don't* go digging at each other at times?"

"I see what you mean," I told him, acknowledging the little joke with a polite smile. "Did you ever hear what they were fighting about?"

"Oh, I never said they had a *fight*. Sometimes Mrs. Weiden would be kinda ticked off at Ms. Harris. Like if Ms. Harris was late when they had to go somewhere or if she'd neglected to invite a particular person to this or that function. That sort of stuff."

"Mrs. Brown?"

Her voice was tight. "It seemed to me Mrs. Weiden and Ms. Harris had a very nice relationship."

"You never witnessed Mrs. Weiden's being the least bit irritated with her secretary—or vice versa?"

Unmistakably ill at ease now, the housekeeper was slow to reply. "All right. I can't say they *never* got on each other's nerves. But it didn't happen often."

"These . . . uh . . . infrequent disagreements they did get into, though, would you have an idea what any of them were about?"

"Listen, I do my job, and I mind my own business." She threw a quick, but meaningful glance at her husband when she made this declaration.

"I admire your discretion, Mrs. Brown, I really do. Also your loyalty. But in this instance you may have information crucial to the investigation without being aware of its significance."

She was looking at me doubtfully.

"You can never tell about those things, honestly," I entreated. "They can lead somewhere totally unexpected."

It took a few seconds before Margaret was willing to feed me even the tiniest crumbs. "Well, I do recall Mrs. Weiden's being angry with Ms. Harris once for not giving her a phone message. From a board member of one of the charities, I believe it was."

"Anything else?"

"Mrs. Weiden was also slightly miffed when she visited the children's ward of this hospital—somewhere in the Bronx, I think—and Ms. Harris forgot to call the story in to the newspapers. Mrs. Weiden always wanted to make the public aware of the misfortunes of others." *Yeah, sure she did.* "That was at least a year ago, though. Oh, and on occasion it would be the other way around; Ms. Harris would give Mrs. Weiden what for. Like when Mrs. Weiden had a bad cold and refused to stay home and rest it up. 'You have no more sense than a baby,' Ms. Harris said to her."

"There must have been other instances where they didn't see eye to eye. Maybe," I added hopefully, "concerning something that even surprised you a little."

"I don't like to carry tales," Margaret pronounced virtuously.

"I'm not asking you to divulge that kind of thing because I'm being nosy. It's just that if I'm going to solve Mrs. Weiden's murder, I have to find out all that I can about her, particularly when it comes to her dealings with other people."

This appeared to satisfy the woman—somewhat, anyhow. "All right," she conceded unhappily. "There *was* this incident a couple of months ago. But it was Ms. Harris who lost her temper that time. 'He's a married man,' she yelled at Mrs. Weiden. 'Why can't you leave him alone?' "

"What did Mrs. Weiden say to this?"

"I didn't stay around for that part. By then I was through dusting the table outside Mrs. Weiden's office. But from the little I did catch when I was walking away, she didn't appear to be that angry. Her tone was a lot calmer than Ms. Harris's."

"Please, try hard to remember. Did you hear them quarrel at any other time?" (No one can ever accuse me of not being persistent.)

Margaret Brown cupped her chin in her hand, and I had the feeling she was giving a great deal of thought to her response. Then her lips parted—and promptly came together again. A moment later she said firmly, "Not that I can remember."

What had she been about to tell me? "Are you sure of that?"

"I'm positive."

I didn't believe her for a second. "But if something does occur to you, you'll contact me, won't you?"

"Yes, of course," the housekeeper readily agreed.

Now, for the past few minutes Frank had been just sitting there, looking dejected. Which was understandable. After all, he had more or less been forced into silence for what to him must have seemed an eternity. I was about to put him out of his misery. "Let me ask you another question, Mr. Brown. Did you ever drive Mrs. Weiden to meet a man, someone you suspected she might be romantically involved with?"

"Can't say that I did. Every so often when I'd take her over to a restaurant or wherever, there'd be some gentleman waiting outside for her. But, a course, whoever it was could have been connected with one of her charities."

"Did any of these men resemble"—I hesitated for an instant before making the choice—"Pierce Brosnan?"

"Who?"

"Cary Grant, I meant to say."

"Yes, come to think of it." *(So there, Ernestine Hartley!)* "A couple of months back Mrs. Weiden had a dinner appointment at . . . at . . . darn!" He scratched his head. "What *is* the name of that place? It's over on Fifty-second and Park—real famous."

"The Four Seasons?"

"That's it. Anyhow, when I pulled up in front of the building this handsome fella—he was the spittin' image of Cary Grant, only much younger—got out of a cab just as I was opening the car door for Mrs. Weiden. She kissed him on the cheek, but I didn't take that to mean they were . . . you know, lovers."

He actually blushed. "It was just how she was: a very warm, friendly person."

"Did you drive her back to the apartment that evening?"

"No, she said the gentleman would be seeing her home."

I left my card with the Browns.

"Don't forget," I told them, "if you think of something—*anything*—give me a call. You can never predict what sort of information could help nail Mrs. Weiden's killer. So please."

"Don't worry," Frank assured me, "we'll get in touch with you."

But I'd been looking at his wife when I said this.

Chapter Twenty-one

Well, being the champion busybody that I am, I still hadn't quite forgiven myself for not seeing something more of the apartment the last time I came. So this morning, before making my unlamented departure, I pleaded the necessity to use the powder room.

En route, I passed only one open door. I stuck my head in—naturally—and came face-to-face with a startled Hilda wielding a feather duster. Looking anxious, she put a finger to her lips. I nodded and withdrew the head.

Now, I'd only had a brief glimpse inside, but it was enough time for it to register that this was the formal dining room, an extremely large, multiwindowed space, strikingly decorated in navy blue, wine, and gold. Of course, beautiful as it was, I didn't imagine that it could measure up to what the Oxner dining room must be like, that apartment, in my mind, having started to take on the opulence of the Taj Mahal.

And by the way, in case you're interested (although you probably aren't), the powder room here turned out to be very pretty. But again, not quite of the same caliber as the one I'd slavered over at the Oxners'.

Anyhow, a short while later I was downstairs in the lobby introducing myself to Harry, the doorman who'd been on duty when Miriam went out to meet her former lover on the last day of her life.

"I'll bet nobody ever calls you Speedy," the skinny little man remarked.

"Huh?"

"The woman's been rotting in her grave for weeks, and you just get around to coming to see me now?"

I mean, talk about *attitude*!

"It was only very recently that I learned Mrs. Weiden had had a lunch date that Tuesday." Hearing myself make excuses to this jerk, I could have kicked my backside all the way to New Jersey!

"I wouldn't know what she had or didn't have. All I can tell you is the woman left the building that morning around eleven-thirty, twelve."

"Were you still on the door when she got back?"

"Yep. She came in right before three—that's when my shift ends."

"Uh, would you know if anyone brought her home?"

"Yeah. Now that I think of it, they did."

"Really?" I was surprised.

Harry smirked. "Sure. A guy from the Yellow Cab Company."

I didn't thank him with a tip when I left. As a matter of fact, I didn't thank him at all.

After a fast stop at Little Angie's for a couple of slices of the most scrumptious pizza in the entire world, I went to the office.

With nothing of a really pressing nature to occupy me, I immediately sat down at the computer to transcribe my latest batch of notes. As usual, I tried to prevail upon myself not to attempt to absorb them. But having just gone into my stubborn mode, I refused to listen.

Then at two o'clock I made an effort to get in touch with Nina Chance.

I should probably mention here that the night before, once I'd wrapped up the arrangements with Erna, I'd phoned Mrs. Davis to set something up with her for today, too. But her Wednesday, she advised me, was packed—two doctor visits, a dental checkup, and an exercise class. Plus, her women's group was meeting in the evening. Of course, she'd be only too happy to cancel everything, she added hopefully, if I had something of significance to tell her.

Well, I didn't feel that the questions I was planning to put to her could legitimately qualify. So it was agreed that I'd stop by on Thursday.

At any rate, my original intention had been to postpone satisfying my itch to have a talk with Nina Chance until I'd cleared up some loose ends with both Erna and my client. But with Erna already out of the way and Mrs. Davis slated for tomorrow morning, I figured it was now okay to make plans to see the good doctor.

I dialed the listing for her office. The machine picked up, instructing me to leave a message and informing me that Dr. Chance would return my call as soon as possible. Ignoring the dictate, I hung up. I'd take another stab at this later.

Going back to my transcribing, I began to intermittently curse out loud at the progress I wasn't making. But it was no wonder things were proceeding at such a creepy pace; I was constantly pausing to dissect virtually every paragraph.

At three-thirty I phoned the psychiatrist again, ditto at around four-fifteen, and another ditto at a few minutes before five. Each time the answering machine went through its drill.

It began to seem very likely that I'd have to give in to this insistent electronic pain-in-the-you-know-where after all. But before I did, I'd take a final shot at reaching Dr. Chance directly.

I walked into my apartment just before six and went straight to the telephone.

"Dr. Chance." I was so astonished that a real, bona fide person had picked up that I came close to dropping the receiver.

Before I relate the conversation that followed, though, let me clue you in to my thinking. My feeling was that if the police were living up to what they'd told Philip Chance about trying to keep his wife out of this, and if the woman hadn't had prior knowledge of her husband's involvement with Miriam, it would be pretty damn callous to lay that on her over the phone. But on the other hand, I was concerned that if I didn't go into any explanations and just said that I was investigating the murder of Miriam Weiden—a rival whose existence Dr. Chance might be genuinely unaware of or else could *claim* to be unaware of—she would refuse to see me. So I had concluded that in this instance dishonesty was by far and away the best policy.

"Uh, my name is Adele Plotkin." Until I said this I had no idea that I'd be using an alias—I'm still not sure what prompted me to do it. (And don't ask why *Adele Plotkin,* either—I mean, who knows?) "I've . . . umm . . . been very depressed lately, and my internist suggested I get in touch with you. He thinks you might be able to help me."

"Who is your internist, Ms. Plotkin?"

I provided the name of the doctor who'd been my primary caregiver for more than twenty years. "Dr. John Riccardi." Not being familiar with the procedure regarding something like this, I had my fingers crossed Nina Chance wouldn't ask for his phone number.

She didn't.

"I don't believe I know him," she murmured.

"He seems to know *you.* By reputation, at least."

"Oh? That's very flattering."

"Umm, I'd like to make an appointment with you."

"Is this an emergency?"

"I don't suppose you could really call it that. But I *am* in a lot of emotional pain."

"I'm afraid I won't be able to see you until Monday. Do you think you could wait until then?"

"We-ll," I answered in this tremulous voice, "I—" And now with an extremely audible sigh: "Of course, doctor . . . I can manage. I'm sure I can." I was *feigning* feigned bravery—if you get what I mean—and, I must say, giving a performance that could have prompted Meryl Streep to start looking over her shoulder.

As it turned out, though, my act was *too* good.

"Listen, I'm going out of town tomorrow, and I won't be returning until late Sunday evening," the psychiatrist told me. "I think it might be advisable, though, for you to schedule something sooner. I can refer you to a colleague of mine and recommend that she arrange a session for you in the next day or so."

"I'd rather wait for you to get back—Dr. Riccardi spoke so highly of you. Don't worry. I'm not suicidal or anything."

"Oh, I wasn't suggesting that you were." I doubt she was absolutely convinced of this, however, because her tone was hesitant when she inquired, "But are you certain you'd be . . . er . . . comfortable putting this off until next week?"

I assured her there was no problem, finally wheedling an appointment for Monday morning.

"Please use the side entrance," the doctor said after supplying the address. "It leads directly to my office."

Which was a major relief.

I mean, I didn't particularly relish running into Philip Chance—and alerting him to the fact that I was there to interrogate his wife.

Chapter Twenty-two

It was Thursday morning.

Glancing around Mrs. Davis's comfortable living room, I was suddenly reminded of a package of Life-savers—you know, the assorted kind. I could almost taste the lime-green throw pillows that contributed to the cheerful hodgepodge of colors here.

Naturally, though, there was nothing cheerful about my client's expression. "You told me yesterday it wasn't anything earth-shattering—the news you have for me?" Her voice rose just enough at the end to turn this into a question.

"I wouldn't call it news. There are a few points I'd appreciate your clearing up."

"Oh. I thought maybe— But you *are* making progress, aren't you?"

Now, how do you answer something like that? I had no idea whether I was getting anywhere or not. And what's more, I wouldn't until I (hopefully) actually got there. "Things are moving along," I said. This being as close to truthful as I could come without discouraging the woman.

"You have no idea *at all* yet who poisoned Miriam?"

"Nothing definite. Not so far, that is."

She wasn't about to let go. "But you *will* find her killer?"

Almost of its own volition, an unequivocal "I will" popped out. It was the abridged version of my actual thoughts, however, the full text being "I hope to God I will."

"Well, that puts my mind at ease a little, anyway." She shifted in her chair. "So exactly what is it you'd like me to clarify?"

"For starters, I'm interested in knowing whether Miriam saw anything of the person who threw the ladder at her."

Mrs. Davis's voice was testy. "I thought we'd already discussed that. She didn't see a thing."

"According to Philip Chance, she caught a peek of someone wearing a dark skirt."

"She *what*? That's absurd!" Then looking puzzled: "And this was according to Philip who?"

Mrs. Davis definitely did not seem familiar with the name. But could be I wasn't the only one walking around with some high-school-drama-club-type skills. "Philip Chance," I answered.

She was thoughtful for a moment. "Uh-uh, it doesn't ring a bell."

"Chance was a friend of Miriam's."

"The only explanation I can think of is that he misunderstood whatever it was she said to him. If Miriam had gotten even the tiniest glimpse at whoever it was, she'd have told me—me *and* the police." But a second or two later she added with somewhat less certainty, "Don't you agree?"

"You're probably right. Uh, Mrs. Davis, there are a couple of other matters I have to ask you about, too. I . . . umm . . . for years I had been under the impression that your daughter was a truly exemplary human being, close to saintly even. And my conversations with you and her secretary only served to reinforce that initial impression. But—"

Mrs. Davis cut me off. "Miriam *was* a very special person. You can't imagine how many worthwhile causes that girl was involved with, how many sick and needy people she helped."

"Please understand. I'm aware that Mrs. Weiden was extremely generous—with both her time and her money. And I don't doubt that she had many other fine qualities as well. But like the rest of us, she did have some character flaws, flaws that could conceivably have earned her her share of enemies. And by withholding this information from me, you've made it that much more difficult to identify her murderer."

"I don't know what you mean by 'flaws.'"

I offered up a few examples that spotlighted the less-than-admirable side of the victim's nature.

"From what I was told, Mrs. Weiden was very keen on publicity," I began, hoping I could avoid putting things too harshly. "Supposedly she wanted her good works well documented by the media."

My client pretty much echoed Margaret Brown. "If that was the case—and I have no knowledge of it—the purpose was undoubtedly to familiarize people with what her various charities were accomplishing. Which is, of course, how you induce the public to contribute."

I left it at that, cautiously proceeding to a still more sensitive area. "I understand Mrs. Weiden was rather, well, rough on her husband. Particularly with regard to that company of his."

"Look, I liked Dan a lot, but he wasn't much of a businessman. Maybe Miriam did push him a little too hard, but it was with the best of intentions—she was hoping to motivate him. How could she know he was so emotionally fragile?"

Was Mrs. Davis's knowledge of her daughter really that limited? Or was it possible she was in denial? Or, *I wondered,* was she still determined to whitewash Miriam's character—even at the expense of apprehending her killer?

I tried again. "I was also informed that Mrs. Weiden betrayed one of her closest friends by sleeping with the friend's husband."

"Are you referring to that Hartley fellow? I heard that same rumor, and I questioned Miriam about it. She swore to me she'd never even been alone with the man. You should have seen how she cried because she wasn't able to convince Ernestine Hartley of that."

Oh, brother! "You're confident she was being honest with you?"

"Yes, I am."

I had pretty much concluded by then that no matter what I confronted her with, Norma Davis would never be up front with me. Nonetheless, I decided to make one final attempt. "Uh, there was some talk, too, that Mrs. Weiden wasn't the most . . . caring of mothers."

"That is a rotten lie," she seethed. "When Deena was growing up, my daughter's one regret was that she couldn't be with her little girl as often as she'd have liked to be. But as I'm sure you can appreciate, there were a great many demands on her time. And being the humanitarian she was, Miriam couldn't bring herself to abandon her commitment to those in need. She did cut back on some of the committees and things, though. And she was very careful, very particular about the people she brought in to look after the child. Besides, Erna was always there for Deena when Miriam wasn't able to make herself available. And Erna positively adored my granddaughter. She still does."

"Did you—"

But Mrs. Davis wasn't listening. "Unfortunately, right up until last year I had a full-time job, and I couldn't afford to leave it." She glanced at me sharply. "Don't look so surprised, Desiree; I'm a very independent person. At any rate, if not for my work, I'd have liked nothing better than to fill in for Miriam myself with Deena."

"Are you aware that Mrs. Weiden spoke about disinheriting Deena if she married the young man she's been seeing?"

"I don't believe it! Miriam wouldn't have done a thing like that to that sweet girl. Not in a million years."

"You're very attached to your granddaughter," I observed.

"You can't imagine how much I love that child. I didn't even love my husband like that. Or Miriam. Or—" She didn't finish.

"Who else were you going to say?" I prodded gently.

The woman's tone was hushed now. "Ruth. I was going to say Ruth. But I realized that wouldn't have been the truth. She's been gone a long time, but my daughter Ruth was my heart. Even my feelings for Deena can't touch what I felt for her. They come close, maybe, but still, it's not the same." And now she looked directly into my eyes. "You know, sometimes Deena reminds me a little of Ruth, but probably that's because they both mean so much to me."

"I'm so very sorry," I mumbled awkwardly.

A few moments passed before Mrs. Davis acknowledged the words of sympathy. "Thank you. But as I told you, it was a long time ago. Ruth—she was my firstborn—died of a cerebral hemorrhage at eighteen. She was two years older than Miriam."

It was then that Mrs. Davis said a very strange thing. "If Miriam did have any failings, Desiree, I'm convinced that it was because of me—and Ruth."

"I don't understand."

"From the time she was a baby Miriam seemed to pick up on how much more devoted I was to her sister—and later to the memory of her sister. I did try to hide it—I promise you I did—but apparently I wasn't successful. I think that's why her entire life Miriam kept trying to win love—at first, I'm afraid, mainly from me. Then when she came into that inheritance from her first husband, well, it was an opportunity for her to accomplish something truly important. Lord knows I'm no psychiatrist, but I would swear that she looked at this as a way of gaining the love of the entire world. Does this make any sense to you?"

"Yes, of course it does."

"One night, after she'd been instrumental in raising a great deal of money for one of her charities—I think it was muscular dystrophy—Miriam even asked if I was proud of her now. I assured her that I'd always been proud of her. I can see her face this very minute, though, and I'll tell you something. This funny little smile she gave me. . . . well, I realized she didn't accept that."

Mrs. Davis lifted her eyes to the ceiling then, and it was a good four or five seconds before she spoke again. "Listen, I suppose it's time I was completely honest with you. And with myself, too."

Finally! I screamed inside.

"I'm not at all certain Miriam had an affair with Ernestine Hartley's husband—and that's the truth. But if she did, I'd say it was because she was so eager for affection. And by the same token, you could also be right about the media coverage. But if she *was* anxious for the recognition—and I don't know this for a fact, either—it was to make up for all the attention, all the praise she never received from me."

"Uh, Mrs. Weiden's father? He also showed this preference for your older daughter?"

"Unfortunately he wasn't around long enough to make a difference. Ben died when Miriam was three. No, Desiree," Mrs. Davis asserted, "any character defects Miriam may have had, I helped her develop." Her voice suddenly broke. "Maybe it's what I did to my poor Miriam that got her killed. God forgive me, though, I just couldn't love her. Not the way she needed me to."

And now, for the first time, I watched real tears flow freely down my client's cheeks.

Chapter Twenty-three

On Friday I managed to prod myself into getting to the office by an ungodly 9:18.

Jackie glanced at her watch when I came in, looked at me, then rechecked the watch. "What's the matter?" she said. "They painting the apartment again?"

Now, I couldn't be totally certain whether she was being facetious or if this was meant as a legitimate question. But while I was leaning heavily toward facetious, I decided to opt for legitimate. Mostly because it was much too early to try to think up a clever comeback. "I have a lot of paperwork to catch up on," I told her.

"That philanthropist murder?"

"Uh-huh."

"How's it going?"

"I only wish I knew."

"Give it time. You'll find the killer."

"Thanks, I hope you're right." I started to walk away.

"Any chance we could have lunch later?" I backtracked a few steps. "There's this new Italian place over by First Avenue," Jackie informed me. "It's supposed to be terrif—"

"Don't tempt me. I made up my mind to bring my notes up-to-date today, so I'd better just have something at my desk. We'll go out next week, okay?"

"Sure, suit yourself. I understand they make the best veal piccata, though," she needled, zeroing in on one of my major weaknesses in the dining department.

"Very tender and with an excellent sauce. But listen, if you want to wait . . ." She bent her head and began pushing some papers around her desk, an evil little smile turning up the corners of her mouth.

"Bitch," I muttered before making for my cubbyhole.

I was unusually disciplined that morning, actually putting my mind on hold and allowing my fingers to do their stuff. So I was going at a fairly decent (for me) clip when Elliot Gilbert looked in on me at a couple of minutes after eleven. (I've mentioned, haven't I, that Elliot is one half of Gilbert and Sullivan, the law firm that rents me my office space?)

"I see that you're busy," he said, an apologetic expression on his round, pleasant face. "Why don't I come by later?"

"Don't be silly. I can use a break," I lied.

"Well, if you're sure . . ." Entering the office, he sat down tentatively, positioning his short, stocky torso on the edge of the chair. He cleared his throat. "I'll try to be brief. The matter I wanted to discuss with you concerns a missing person. . . ."

As it turned out, "brief" wasn't the word I'd have used, since Elliot's recitation took close to a half hour. But to boil it down, it seems the son of a longtime business associate of his had disappeared the week before. The son's former wife suspected that her ex had skipped to avoid making any further alimony and child-support payments, while the business associate was insisting that this Mark was a devoted father and that he'd never willingly have abandoned his two little girls.

When Elliot had finished laying everything out in minuscule detail, he peered at me expectantly. "So?"

"So?" I repeated, confused. (I'm really not at my sharpest when I get up before my usual time. Maybe the early-morning air adversely affects my brain or something.)

"Are you available to handle this for me?"

I was tempted to give him a yes. After all, not only didn't prospective clients grow on trees, but they weren't exactly tying up my phone lines, either. Besides, if this guy did run out on his kids, it would have given me no end of satisfaction to nail the shit. But common sense instantly forced me to reconsider. "Unfortunately I'm not," I answered regretfully. "I'm tied up with a murder investigation right now, and it wouldn't be fair to accept this case and not be able to devote the time I should to it."

"I understand, Dez, although I can't say I'm not disappointed. Frankly, the situation has me very concerned. I'm actually hoping the ex-wife has it right—that Mark *is* trying to escape his responsibilities—because I can't close my eyes to the possibility it could be something far worse."

And then Elliot stood up. "I have to go and line up another investigator," he advised me. "But I'd feel a lot better if you were free to help with this one."

After he'd left the office, I replayed those parting words: "I'd feel a lot better if you were free to help with this one."

Well, how do you like that? All along I'd suspected that the principal reason Elliot and his partner Pat Sullivan tossed so much work my way was because they were being nice—which is what, by nature, they both are. But now it was apparent that Elliot actually considered me the best man/woman for the job.

I went back to my typing with a much-appreciated infusion of confidence.

As soon as I got up on Saturday I resolved to spend the day poring over my notes, which as of four-thirty yesterday had been brought current. I'd managed to piddle away the entire morning, however, and I was just reaching into my attaché case for Miriam Weiden's file when Ellen called.

"Oh, I'm so glad you're home," she said. "I didn't wake you or anything, did I?"

Well, I can't claim that I've never slept past noon—

although I swear it had been I-don't-know-how-long since I'd indulged myself like that. Still, I'm not crazy about having this very occasional slothfulness of mine acknowledged. Besides, hadn't Ellen asked me this same question at pretty much this same time only last week?

"Ellen," I told her in my most acerbic tone, "the little hand of the clock is presently on the twelve, and the big hand is on the four. So the answer is no, you did not wake me."

Ellen ignored my little temper tantrum. "Good. Listen, I have today off, and Mike lent me his car. I was hoping you could take a ride into Englewood with me."

"Englewood?"

"It's in New Jersey."

"I'm aware of *that*." Much as I love my niece, she was really getting under my skin right now. I decided to blame my sour disposition on the lousy dream I'd had last night. I can't recall the whole thing, only the part where I was chased by a flock of wild geese and then, as I was running away, fell into a lake and was attacked by an extremely evil crocodile (or it could have been an alligator), who without any provocation at all, swam over and bit off one of my ears. It was really pretty terrifying. In fact, do you know the first thing I did on opening my eyes that morning? I checked for missing facial features.

At any rate, Ellen was going into an explanation now. "You remember Ginger in my building, don't you? Well, I was talking to her yesterday evening, and she said that her friend Hannah has this friend Moira whose sister Michelle—they're twins, Moira and Michelle—is getting married in June. And Moira told Hannah who told Ginger about this bridal shop in Englewood that's supposed to carry the most *exquisite* gowns—that's where Michelle got hers. Brides by Genevieve it's called. Anyway, they're having a sale this week, and it ends today. Can you drive out there with me?"

Although I'd stopped trying to follow all this right after "her friend Hannah has this friend Moira," it wasn't hard to get the gist of it anyway. "Oh, Ellen, I'd love to—"

"I'm s-o-o relieved. I was worried you might have an appointment or something."

Now, I'd been just about to add a "but," this being: "—but I really have too much work to do today." It was okay, though; there's no doubt I'd have backed down. I mean, it's tough keeping my nose out of Ellen's business—especially when she invites it there.

Brides by Genevieve was on the first floor of a weathered two-family, white-shingled house on a street of very similar houses. A large sign that dangled from the roof of the porch alerted people to the shop's existence.

As we walked into the vestibule, three young women were exiting the bridal establishment. And seeing them out was an enormous woman—and I'm talking enormous in both directions—wearing an almost blindingly gaudy Hawaiian muumuu and close to half a pound of makeup. She had sparse, tightly curled blond hair, more than a half dozen bangle bracelets clinking together on each arm, and on her bare feet were sandals the length of snowshoes. Her toenails were painted purple.

The entrance opened directly into the showroom—or whatever they called it—which was now, except for Ellen and me, empty of customers. A very large space, it was furnished only with a beige tweed carpet, a dozen faux-suede rust armchairs—mostly sitting together in pairs—and, as part of each chair grouping, a tiny glass-topped table holding a selection of bridal magazines. In one corner was a three-way floor mirror and in front of this, a short, low platform. On the walls, in neat acrylic box frames, were photographs of radiant models in splendiferous wedding gowns.

It was an understated, tastefully decorated room—in

sharp contrast to this outlandishly turned out woman I took to be the proprietress.

"Genevieve?" Ellen inquired tentatively.

"Genevieve's away on vacation," the woman informed her. "I'm Minnie, her sister." She directed her attention to me. "What's the matter, Mom? I admit Minnie's not that fancy, but Genevieve's name isn't really Genevieve, you know. It's Gertie."

Well, I can't imagine what kind of expression she thought she'd seen on my face—but she hadn't. Listen, it wouldn't have bothered me if this dame's name were Petunia. "If Minnie's okay with you, it's okay with me," I retorted, trying not to sound *too* snide. "And by the way, I'm not Mom. I'm Auntie."

Minnie laughed heartily—it was more of a cackle, actually. "Touché."

Once Ellen and I had shed our coats and were settled in our seats, Minnie had a brief chat with the bride-to-be regarding preferences. Then requesting she stand again, Minnie appraised her from head to toe. After which she began trotting out gowns for her inspection.

"Too froufrou for me" was Ellen's reaction to the first.

Minnie was unruffled. "I thought it might be, but I wanted to be sure."

Selections number two, three, and four, however, also received a thumb down for various reasons.

"Oh, I like that," Ellen finally said of number five, an ivory silk A-line. And then she and a beaming Minnie retreated to the try-on room. When they returned Ellen had on the A-line.

Now, there was nothing at all wrong with the dress. But that was really the most I could say for it.

"What do you think, Aunt Dez?" my niece demanded.

"Umm, it's nice," I answered. I mean, far be it from me to influence her—unless, of course, it should turn out to be absolutely necessary.

"Don't sound so enthusiastic," she muttered. My

mouth was open to respond, although I have no idea what would have come out of it, but Ellen preempted me. "That's okay. I feel the same way." She turned to Minnie, sounding contrite. "The dress is very pretty, but it looks better on the hanger than it does on me."

Minnie tried to convince her that she'd be a knockout in that gown. All it required was a little tuck here and the *tiniest* bit of restyling there. "And it's a terrific buy, too," she said. "Fifty-percent off."

The "terrific buy" was upward of three thousand dollars—even at half price. But Ellen wasn't overly concerned about costs. Her parents, with a little assistance from Mike's, were footing the bill for the entire wedding. And Ellen had chosen to regard her dress as her contribution to the festivities. (Well, I suppose you *could* call it that, although I can't think of anyone besides my niece who actually would.)

And now over Ellen's too-meek protests, Minnie propelled her over to the mirror and coaxed her onto the platform. "See what a couple of darts would do?" she said, pinching in the fabric at the bustline. They'd—" But in the middle of the sales pitch she stopped, took a few steps backward, and, folding her arms across her triple-D chest, examined Ellen with narrowed eyes. "Never mind. Come with me," she ordered.

A few minutes later Ellen was modeling once again. "Well?" Minnie asked me, a wide smile parting the purple lips that matched her toenails. "Does she look gorgeous—or what?"

I was so overcome I actually had tears in my eyes. A choked "Ohh, Ellen," was all I could manage.

The gown—a white lace, mock-turtleneck sheath with long, narrow sleeves—was exquisitely understated. And it was perfect.

"You'd think it was made for her, wouldn't you?" Minnie enthused. "But the truth is, we altered it for another young woman—that's why the price is marked down so much. Anyhow, the poor thing's fiancé—the no-good son of a bitch—up and left her two months before the wedding, so . . ." Minnie hunched her shoulders and spread her arms. "She was a skinny little nothing, too, just like Ellen here. Good thing I remembered about that dress."

Minnie waited patiently for what she regarded as a reasonable amount of time while Ellen, back on the platform now, admired herself in the three-way mirror. After which the saleswoman bustled off to summon a seamstress from somewhere in the bowels of the house. In two or three minutes Ellen was having her hem measured.

Minnie's work, however, was not yet done.

First she attempted to induce Ellen to select a headpiece. Then, with Ellen electing to wait until another time, she strode purposefully in my direction. Perching her formidable cheeks precariously on the arm of the chair alongside mine, she inquired sweetly, "So, Auntie, will you be in the wedding party?"

"I'm the matron of honor," I answered proudly— and foolishly.

"Ah, how nice. Listen, I have a dress in mind that would be just the thing for you—a pale pink chiffon with little bugle beads. Absolutely stunning, with the *most* slenderizing lines. And do I have to tell you how gorgeous that color is with your red hair?"

For Minnie to accept that I couldn't possibly look at anything for myself right now required my fabricating an almost-immediate appointment, coupled with the assurance that I'd be returning soon.

"Make certain you come in on a Saturday or on a Thursday evening—I help out here then. And not exactly being another Olive Oyl myself"—she fixed her eyes on my thigh area—"*I* know what kind of gown would look good on someone carrying around all those extra pounds."

Thanks a heap, lady.

Minnie got to her feet at this point. Then smoothing the skirt of her garish muumuu, she said with a straight face, "After all, we full-figured gals *do* have to watch what we wear."

                          *   *   *

Following Brides by Genevieve, a hyper Ellen and
I stopped off at a diner, Ellen insisting she was too
excited for a "major meal." (She was able, however,
to precede her open hot-turkey sandwich with a crab-
meat cocktail and top it off with apple pie à la mode.)

"Now all Mike and I have to do is decide on the
kind of wedding we want and then find a place," Ellen
got out between mouthfuls of the crab-meat cocktail.

I reminded her that not much more than a week
ago she'd left it that the color of her gown would
determine the size of the wedding. "You remember,
don't you? White dress, big affair. Off-white, more
intimate type of reception."

"Did I say *that*? Honestly, Aunt Dez, sometimes I
come out with such junk."

It was well after nine when Ellen dropped me off
at the apartment. And I was too tired to really accomplish anything workwise, so my notes remained sitting
in my attaché case.

They didn't get an airing on Sunday, either. I was
on the phone almost continuously that day, all of the
conversations being of the extended variety. I heard
from two of my neighbors—Barbara Gleason and
Harriet Gould—both of whom where in extremely
chatty moods. After that, Christie Wright, my old college buddy from Minnesota, checked in, and we hadn't
spoken in over a month so there was a lot to talk
about. Finally Ellen was on the line, wanting to know
if I really, *really* loved her gown.

And then it was time to start getting dressed for
that birthday party my friend Pat Martucci was throwing that evening.

Chapter Twenty-four

Pat had told me eight o'clock.

Not wanting to be the first to arrive but also not into fashionably late, I got there at eight-twenty.

I was amazed to find the party already in full swing.

There must have been close to seventy-five people crammed into Pat and Burton's small living room. I didn't see either of them when I walked in, so I grappled my way through the crowd and finally made it to the bedroom. My intention had been to toss my coat on the brass four-poster that extended almost from wall to wall in this tiny space. Naturally, everyone here had had the same idea—and sprawled on top of all of that outerwear was a red-faced, basketball-player-sized gentleman, who was snoring at decibels that made my teeth ache. Anyhow, not having an alternative, I opened the door to the closet, found an empty hanger, and hung my ten-year-old trench coat next to the beautiful shearling Pat had recently treated herself to in order, she said, to look especially nice when Burton's boss invited them for dinner. (Although why she should be concerned about this baffled me, since Burton had been working for that man for four years now, and he had yet to have them over even once.)

When I returned to the living room I spotted the birthday guy across the room, next to the windows. He was in conversation with a tall, thin fellow with a salt-and-pepper ponytail—which, come to think of it, pretty well describes Burton himself. Now that he's shaved off his mustache, that is.

Anyhow, it was a real struggle getting over there. Above that din, you couldn't even hear my *excuse me*'s—either that, or no one found them particularly motivating. So I had to resort to a whole lot of pushing and poking. But when I finally reached the spot last occupied by Burton and his friend, there'd been a change in the cast of characters. Stretching my neck as far as I was able to, I looked around. No Burton. Also, no sign of Pat. But I did notice all these people who kept pouring out of the kitchen carrying plates. Well, not being able to locate my hosts, I knew where I was headed.

If I had thought the living room was packed, it was only because I hadn't yet been in the kitchen. And this is a decent-size kitchen I'm talking about, too. Believe me, never before have my elbows gotten such a workout. But eventually I made it over to the food table, which offered up all kinds of delicious-looking edibles. I picked up a paper plate, a napkin, and some utensils from the counter behind the table and then proceeded to wait my turn for some nourishment. I estimated that I was about twelfth on what was a very raggedy line—that is, if no one barged in ahead of me.

But one person after another infiltrated the line up front. So it was at least ten minutes before I got the chance to put anything on my plate. And by then I was all but salivating. I'll say this, though, Pat had really outdone herself. There was a huge ham, a giant roast turkey, four large platters of southern fried chicken, and all sorts of salads. Also, two types of cranberry sauce and a couple of jello molds. I was engaged in the serious task of making my choices when I received a sharp jab in the ribs. I turned around. My accoster was a short, skinny woman with enormous tinted, pink-framed glasses and clunky platform shoes. "Get to it, will ya?" she said in this incongruous close-to-baritone voice. "The rest of us would like to have a little something to eat, too. And before tomorrow, if you don't mind."

Intimidated (coward that I am), I hurriedly plunked

a couple of slices of ham on my plate, along with a single chicken breast, a spoonful of cranberry sauce, and some coleslaw. After which I squeezed between countless bodies—making protecting my plate my first priority—and at last found myself in the living room again.

There was a small, makeshift bar set up to the right of the entrance to the kitchen, and as I was inching my way past it someone called out, "Hey, you with the red hair! Want a glass of white wine?"

"Sure." An elderly man shoved a plastic cup in my hand.

And now having immediately upon arrival given up on finding somewhere to sit, my goal was to locate somewhere to stand. I finally maneuvered my way into a corner that appeared to be slightly less congested than the rest of the room. I mean, I could actually exhale without bumping into anyone. Nevertheless, I had a problem: There was no place to set anything down. And no way I could continue to hold my plate *and* my cup *and* my utensils and still manage to eat. I was verging on despair.

A small group of people had congregated just to my left. "Would you like a glass of wine?" I asked the man facing in my direction.

"No thanks." He looked at me oddly, I thought.

By this time, though, I could practically *taste* that fried chicken, so I tried the woman next to him— whose only response was to raise an artistically penciled eyebrow.

But at that moment a thin, aesthetic-looking fellow, dressed entirely in black, was approaching the little gathering. In an attempt to restore my courage, I told myself that this one looked thirsty. "I have an extra glass of white wine," I said as soon as he was within arm's reach of me.

He was at least interested enough to ask, "Did you drink any of it?"

"No, of course not."

He wasn't very trusting. "Is that the truth?"

"I swear."

"Okay, then. Thanks. I was just debating whether it was worth the effort to try and make it over to the bar." He held out his hand for the cup.

And now I could devote myself to the food. So leaning against the wall, that's exactly what I did.

Once I had thoroughly cleaned my plate though, I had another dilemma: what to do with it. I was standing there mulling this over when a very slight, very young man in a tweed sports coat—which was so big for him I suspected it might be his father's—sidled over to me. "How's everything?" he said.

"Fine." I tried to smile, but I was still wondering how to dispose of that damn plate.

"You a friend of Burton's?"

"Yes. And of Pat's. Have you seen her, by the way?"

"Yeah. She was near the front door a couple of minutes ago. But I don't know where she is now. I'm Herbie."

He held out his hand, and I shook it briefly. His palms were sweaty. "Desiree," I informed him.

"I like that name." In the same breath he then said of my newish pale green suit, "That's a nice outfit."

"Thank you."

"I work with Burton. You know, at the university. I'm an archaeologist, too." *I'd have bet he was in junior high.*

"I imagine that's a very interesting profession."

"Yeah, I guess so. Listen, you wanna cut out of here and go for a drink someplace?"

"Thanks, but I don't think so."

"Whatsa matter?" he demanded, shoving his face closer to mine. He was, I realized then, definitely in his cups. "I'm not good-looking enough for you?"

"It's not that at all. I—"

"Hey, anyone with an ass the size of yours has no right to be fussy." And with this, he stormed off.

Good. Now, if it were only as easy to get rid of this plate. . . .

It was then that a miracle occurred. A few yards away from me a man was actually vacating his chair. Moving more quickly than I'd have thought myself capable of, I scrambled over, just managing to beat out that woman with the pink-framed glasses I'd encountered in the kitchen, who was bearing down on this same seat from the opposite direction. She glared at me malevolently before retreating in defeat. She also mumbled something under her breath, which I felt fortunate not to hear.

What did I care, anyway? I was sitting at last. And even more important, next to me was a small table cluttered with used dinnerware—but with just enough room to accommodate one more burdensome plate.

I had barely gotten myself comfortable for the first time since I'd walked in tonight when I attracted a second admirer: a large black poodle, of all things.

I have no idea who invited this guy (girl?); he/she certainly wasn't a resident here. At any rate, initially he just deposited his head in my lap to induce me to pet it, and as a dog lover, I was happy to accommodate him. But when a couple of minutes later he staked out a propriety claim to me by planting that weighty body across my feet, I felt that he was really stretching the bounds of our newly emerging friendship.

And the trouble was, I couldn't budge him. I don't know how long I sat pinned to the floor like that. But matters reached the near-critical stage when I began to feel an urge to visit the bathroom.

I was really at a loss as to how to deal with this latest predicament (I wasn't even able to cross my legs, for heaven's sake!), when from somewhere across the room there was—mercifully—a long, low whistle.

The poodle jumped up as if he'd been shot out of a cannon and took off through the crowd, knocking a drink out of at least one person's hand in the process.

Instantly relinquishing my hard-won seat, I determinedly shoved my way to the bathroom. I was just reaching for the knob when it was grabbed by another hand. You'll never guess whose—or maybe you will. But I'll give you a hint, anyway: It wasn't the poodle's.

Pink-framed Glasses favored me with a truly sadistic smile before slamming the door in my face.

She finally emerged after taking her own sweet time in there. "It's all yours, dear," she shouted above the racket, another truly sadistic smile decorating her lips.

I hurried into the bathroom—and got the shock of my life. There, stretched out in the tub, was a man playing a harmonica. And he was stark naked!

My only option was to get back to my own apartment—and as quickly as possible.

Later that evening I realized that I hadn't even said good-bye to Pat and Burton before my hasty departure—or hello, either, for that matter.

All in all, I decided then, Burton's fortieth had been the party to end all parties. For me, at any rate.

Chapter Twenty-five

As I drove out to New Haven on Monday morning I kept nervously rehearsing ways that I—Adele Plotkin—could make the transition to me—Desiree Shapiro. The fact that I'd given Dr. Chance an alias, and would now have to admit to it, was going to leave me looking pretty much like a horse's patootie. Particularly since I could think of no good reason why I'd even used that little ploy. Certainly I wasn't egotist enough to believe that my own name would occasion instant recognition. (Even among my fellow PIs, I suspect that more often than not I'm referred to as Desiree Somebody-or-other.) Maybe, I speculated, it had flashed across my mind that Philip Chance might decide to leaf through his wife's appointment book, or . . . But I couldn't conjure up an *or*.

Well, it didn't make any difference. I mean, it seemed fairly likely that the doctor would discuss my visit with her husband later. There was also the possibility she might ask to see my investigator's license. So whatever had triggered that silly impulse, I was now stuck with trying to explain it—along with, of course, my showing up under false pretenses to begin with.

I pulled up in front of the psychiatrist's office/home a quarter of an hour early for my eleven o'clock appointment. I'd sit in the car for another five or ten minutes before going inside.

Nina and Philip Chance lived not far from Yale, on a quiet block of stately old houses set far back from

the street on wide, sloping lawns. I surmised that most
of the residents here had to be at least quite comfortable, if not actually wealthy. I was just remarking to
myself on the trees there—they were positively massive—when suddenly the Chances' front door flew
open, and Philip came barreling down the stairs.
Quickly reaching the walkway, he turned in my direction. I scrunched down in my seat, but he hurried by
me. When I lifted my head a couple of seconds later,
he was rushing around to the driver's side of the styl-
ish beige car (I'm not very good on cars, but I think
it was a Lexus) that was parked about five feet behind
my Chevy. His tires let out a loud screech as he
sped away.

Dr. Chance was a rather tall woman of forty-
something, with a lovely olive-toned complexion and
almond-shaped hazel eyes. Her thick dark hair was
parted in the middle, pulled tightly back, and coiled
into a bun at the nape of the neck. As you can appreciate, it isn't easy to carry off a hairdo that severe,
but Nina Chance did it admirably. While not what I'd
consider beautiful—her face was too narrow and her
lips too thin—the lady was extremely attractive. With
a figure that bordered on the sensational—both slender and womanly. She even managed to look sexy in
that tailored pin-striped suit, for heaven's sake. For
an instant I pictured her standing beside her movie
starish husband. What an unbelievable couple they
made!

She was now seated behind her desk in the comfortable inner office, her ballpoint pen poised to record
my history. I was in the chair opposite her, squirming.

"All right, Ms. Plotkin, just let me get some particulars before we talk." She smiled encouragingly. "Full
name?"

"Umm, Desiree Shapiro." My mouth was so dry the
words were accompanied by this little clicking sound.

"What did you say?" she asked, perplexed.

"Look, Dr. Chance," I told her, "it was urgent that

I speak to you, and I was concerned that if you knew who I was, you'd refuse to see me."

"And just who are you?"

"Uh, I'm a private investigator. I've—"

I didn't get to finish. "This is outrageous!" the psychiatrist exclaimed, the veins at her temples bulging. She threw down the pen. "You'd better leave, Ms. Whatever-your-name-is." (Apparently all that angst I'd expended on how to explain away Adele Plotkin had been wasted. Nina Chance was far too angry about my having tricked her into this meeting to zero in on any specifics.)

"Shapiro. Desiree Shapiro. But please, give me a few minutes. I—"

"Not even a second." Keeping her voice low, most likely the better to contain her fury, she pushed her chair back.

"Don't you even want to know what this is about?"

"Just get out of here," she commanded, rising, "and let me take care of the people who need my help."

"It's about your husband," I put in hurriedly.

"Philip? You're investigating *Philip*?" It appeared the NYPD hadn't been here, after all—at least, not so far.

"No, not specifically. A . . . a friend of his was murdered, and I'm looking into it."

She sat down slowly. "Which friend are you talking about?"

"Miriam Weiden. You may have heard of her; she was a philanthropist. Her name was frequently mentioned in the newspapers."

The doctor's forehead pleated up like an accordion. "Miriam Weiden, Miriam Weiden," she murmured. "No, it doesn't sound familiar. You say she was a friend of Philip's?"

"Yes, they were lovers for a time," I replied unhappily, wincing at my own words.

"You know this for a fact?" She sounded controlled, but the veins at the woman's temples were bulging again.

"I'm afraid so," I had to admit. And then I thought it might be nice to stick in something a bit more positive here—so I did. "But Mr. Chance broke it off when he realized how foolish he'd been to jeopardize his marriage like that."

"And how did *you* become privy to his thoughts?"

"This was what he told me."

"Just like that? He called you up and said, 'I was foolish to jeopardize my marriage, Ms. Shapiro'?"

"No, of course not. I phoned *him*. He was seen leaving a restaurant with the victim on the day of her death, so I wanted to question him. And, well, that's when he informed me that he'd ended it with Mrs. Weiden weeks before she was killed. Which, by the way, has been more or less confirmed by others."

"Then why were they together again?"

Now, as you may have noticed, this was another instance where I was the one being interrogated. But I didn't imagine Philip's infidelity could have been too easy for his wife to swallow, and I felt that she was entitled to some answers. Sooner or later it would be my turn (I hoped). "According to Mr. Chance, the victim still considered him a good friend, and she had a serious problem that she wanted to discuss with him."

"This affair—when did it begin?"

"Not long after they met. This was at a party on Long Island back in September. I understand you received a call about a patient that evening and had to leave early."

"That'll teach me to uphold my Hippocratic oath," the doctor responded with obvious sarcasm.

"Uh, listen, I don't want you to get the idea that I'm defending your husband. I assure you, I don't condone adultery. But I think you should know that the relationship started innocently enough. Miriam Weiden had a great many contacts, and she offered to pave the way for Mr. Chance with some people who might be helpful to his career. He was really grateful for her efforts, and . . . er . . . the affair just evolved from there."

She clucked her tongue. "Ms. Shapiro, those things don't just *evolve*. My husband made a conscious decision to express his gratitude—if that's what you care to call it—by pulling down his pants and employing his Johnson."

I was a little taken aback by the way she put it. I suppose I had expected a member of the medical profession to couch the act in more scientific terms.

"Well, at least Philip had the good sense to screw someone with clout. Incidentally, how did she die?"

"She was poisoned. Tubocurarine chloride."

"Really," was all the psychiatrist said.

"Dr. Chance, I'd appreciate it very much if you could answer one or two questions for me."

Making a sour face, she checked her wrist. *Why is everyone I come in contact with such a damn clock-watcher?* "I don't see how I can help you," she muttered, "but all right. I'm expecting a patient—a genuine patient—at noon, though. So keep it short."

"I will. Mrs. Weiden died on Tuesday, January twenty-first—that was three weeks ago tomorrow—sometime between the hours of nine and eleven p.m. Mr. Chance claims he stayed in the city after their lunch together and that he returned home about eight-thirty."

"And you're interested in finding out if I have an alibi for that night—correct? Listen, I wasn't even aware that Mrs. Weiden *existed,* much less that she and my husband were playing house together."

"I don't doubt that. It's just that I need the information for my records." (Sound familiar?)

"But you can't seriously expect me to account for my whereabouts weeks back," she scoffed.

"I think your husband mentioned something about your going to see your mother."

"I did have dinner over there around that time, and it *was* on an evening when Philip wasn't at home, but whether it was that *particular* evening, I have no idea."

I attempted to jostle her memory. "If I recall correctly, Mr. Chance said that your children were both staying overnight with friends."

The doctor's expression was bemused. "Please! Do you know how often kids sleep over at each other's houses?"

I took another crack at it. "They'd been off from school the day before—Martin Luther King Day."

"Doesn't help. All I can tell you is that I only work two evenings a week, and Tuesday isn't one of them. So it's possible I did drive over to my mother's then."

"Maybe she would remember the date."

"Forget it. I can assure you, she would not. Besides, my mother isn't too well"—Dr. Chance's voice dropped to a lethal-sounding low—"so under no circumstances are you to question her." And now she moved toward the edge of her seat. "I believe we're finished here."

"Please, just one thing more. I'll make it fast."

Plainly irritated, she hesitated for a moment, then said curtly, "I'll give you two minutes."

"Miriam Weiden was also attacked on the Friday preceding her death. Around ten a.m. It seems a heavy steel ladder missed her by inches, and—"

"—and you want me to tell you where I was at the time. I can't. The two patients I'd been seeing on Friday mornings were both feeling well enough by the beginning of January to discontinue treatment. And I didn't take on anyone else until two weeks ago. So I was free until one o'clock that day. Which means I was probably available to try and flatten Mrs. Weiden with that ladder. Only—again—I didn't even know there *was* a Mrs. Weiden." And with this, she got to her feet.

I stood, too, and thanked her for taking the time to speak to me. Suddenly I felt compelled to add, "Uh, I realize this doesn't concern me, but I hope that—" I started over. "I wish I hadn't had to tell you about your husband and Mrs. Weiden, but I didn't see how I could avoid it. In spite of his . . . behavior, though, Mr. Chance seems to love you very much."

"He said that to you?"

"Yes."

And here Nina Chance did something totally unexpected: She laughed. So hard that she actually had to wipe her eyes. After which she apologized. "I'm sorry, but this is all very, very funny. You know, Ms. Shapiro, I am the *last* person you should suspect of this murder." She put her palms flat on her desktop and leaned so far across the desk that we were practically nose to nose.

"I shouldn't be telling you this—it's absolutely none of your business—but it really tickles me, and I just can't keep it in any longer.

"It's a lie about my husband's loving me very much—I seriously doubt that he loves me at all. And long ago the feeling became mutual. Lately it's a struggle to even carry on a conversation at the dinner table. In public, however, Philip has this compulsion to always put things in the best possible light. You see, he doesn't only want to be liked; he wants to be envied. So it's essential for him to convince everyone that he has the nicest home, the smartest kids, the most perfect marriage. Which is the reason he fed you all that bilge about how marvelous things were between us. And his confiding that he'd made a terrible mistake by carrying on with another woman? That, Ms. Shapiro, was to reinforce the myth and possibly to make the infidelity a bit more palatable to you."

"Why haven't you divorced him?" I surprised *myself* with the chutzpah of that one. But sometimes I just can't seem to keep seemliness and a little restraint from taking a backseat to curiosity.

"Oh, I thought about it—briefly," the doctor responded. "The truth is, though, that I like having Philip around to fix a leaky faucet and escort me to social functions, and, yes—and I trust this won't embarrass you—to satisfy my sexual urges. Fortunately, that's the one part of our marriage that's still damn good, because frankly, I'm just too busy to start seeking out other bed partners. I suppose another reason I'm still with Philip is that I don't have to depend on him for emotional fulfillment. I've got two lovely sons and a very rewarding career, Ms. Shapiro, as well as some wonderful friends."

"And now that you know about Mrs. Weiden?" Honestly, I had no inkling I was going to ask her that until I'd asked it.

"As long as he used protection during their . . . ahh . . . get-togethers—and I'm sure he did; Philip isn't stupid—it isn't that big a deal to me. Of course, I won't pretend that I'm delighted about his cheating," she admitted. "Would you like to know the primary reason, though? It's because I'd look like a fool if it ever came out. But my husband is a discreet person, so . . ." And she let it go at that.

"Mr. Chance wants to remain in the marriage, too?"

"I'd say so. First of all, he positively dotes on our boys, and if we ever divorced, he would probably like sole custody—which I'd never consent to. And he's well aware of it. Also, unlike a great many other men, Philip enjoys having a successful woman—a psychiatrist—for a wife." At this juncture we heard the tinkling of the door chimes in the outer office, indicating the arrival of the doctor's next appointment. But caught up in her narrative, she went on, disregarding her patient as she had my two-minute time allotment, now long past. "My profession is a prestige thing with Philip, part of that desire to be envied. To hear him talk, Freud is second to *me*."

"Losing his job must have been especially difficult for someone like your husband," I commented.

"He's been able to handle it. He's confident that eventually he'll find something suitable. You see, Philip's ego being what it is, the alternative would be absolutely unthinkable. Naturally—"

Cutting herself off abruptly, Nina Chance scowled. "I've allowed myself to get way off the track here.

What I originally started to tell you—and I think it will enable you to appreciate the absurdity of my being regarded a suspect—is that if I'd wanted to kill off my husband's bimbo, I would have done it fifteen years ago."

I'm certain the woman got a kick out of the confusion that must have been registered on my face, because she grinned.

"That's when Philip embarked on the first of his little escapades," she informed me. "And back in those days it almost tore my heart out. But after a while I learned to accept it."

"Does Mr. Chance realize that you're aware of . . . umm . . . those little escapades?"

"Yes, although we don't discuss the subject anymore. I just pretend to believe his elaborate lies, and he knows that's what I'm doing: pretending. Let me tell you something, Ms. Shapiro. They should give my husband's Johnson a medal for all the action it's seen. He treats himself to a change of women regularly, too, so there's no danger—God forbid—of his becoming bored.

"In fact, I'd be willing to make you a sizable wager that the reason Philip dumped Mrs. Weiden was because he already had another Mrs. Weiden in reserve, waiting for her next."

Chapter Twenty-six

I do some of my best thinking when I'm behind the wheel. And I had plenty to think about on today's drive back to Manhattan.

Was Philip really the satyr his wife made him out to be?

It was possible.

Or had this merely been a clever machination of that lady's in order to divest herself of a motive for murder?

Also possible. Although if the man *was* a devoted and loving husband—for the most part, at any rate—would his spouse have smeared him like this?

Sure, I decided, if she was bent on self-preservation—*and* had been the one to slip the tubocurarine chloride in Miriam's drink.

But anyhow, whatever her reason for labeling the guy a four-star cheater, I had every intention of keeping Nina Chance on my suspect list. I mean, suppose she'd even been telling me the truth about Philip's long-playing mattress action. How could I be certain she hadn't somehow gotten wind of his latest fling and that it—and Miriam Weiden—hadn't simply proved to be the last straw? And after all, I reminded myself, who would have had easier access to a nice, unhealthy dose of tubocurarine chloride than a physician?

Okay, now Philip. Let's say he'd misrepresented the state of his marriage and feigned all that contrition regarding his faithlessness. The big question was: For what purpose?

Was it, as his wife contended—that he habitually tried to put a positive spin on things?

Maybe.

Or was it something far more sinister? Had he made himself out to be a choirboy—or as near to one as he could, considering the adultery—in order to obscure the fact that he was a lowlife bastard who'd poisoned his discarded lover because she'd threatened to reveal their relationship?

This was feasible, too.

But wait. There was the deceased's use of the pronoun "she" to consider, which obviously grew out of what had transpired at the lake. That incident, however, may have been totally unrelated to the poisoning, in which event Miriam's killer might not have been a woman at all.

Still, if Philip Chance was telling the truth about that mention of a skirt, I was back to a "she" again. Unless . . .

Oh, hell!

Now, normally, when I'm into some heavy-duty analyzing, I wind up reaching for the Extra-Strength Tylenol. But in this instance all of that brain-taxing seemed to have gone straight to my stomach, so what I really could have used was a good swig of Pepto-Bismol. One of the few things that my packed-to-bulging handbag couldn't provide.

Forcing myself to abandon the Chances, I switched on the radio. Before long, though—in fact, right in the middle of Whitney Houston's goose-bump-evoking rendition of "I'll Always Love You"—I was grappling with the investigation again. This time planting my other suspects in the hot seat.

I began with young Deena. *Had* Miriam been bluffing when she stated her intention to disinherit her daughter if she married Todd? I mean, I only had Erna's word for this. Similarly, I only had Deena's word—echoed by Erna, naturally—about how all those millions didn't mean ca-ca to her.

As for Erna's own relationship with the deceased, I

just couldn't dope it out. Mostly, I had trouble accepting that the secretary had actually liked her employer. I figured that it was her love for Miriam's child (who was in reality *Erna's* child?) that kept the woman at her job all these years. And now that Deena was grown, my guess was that Erna had continued to hang in there to look after the girl's interests. In fact, given the depth of Erna's attachment to Deena, if Miriam was serious about altering her will, it didn't require a particularly lively imagination to picture Erna dumping a little something lethal into that glass of crème de menthe—you know, as a preventive measure.

Suddenly I was struck by a horrifying idea. Miriam may have been murdered for a reason I didn't even suspect. *Or,* God forbid, the perpetrator might be someone I wasn't considering at all.

In either case, I could only pray that I'd see the light.

After depositing my car at the garage near the office, I stopped off at the coffee shop down the block for a sandwich. (By then my stomach was no longer giving me fits. But not caring to tempt whatever fates are in charge of that kind of thing, I made myself forego Little Angie's.)

Anyhow, when I walked into work, Jackie greeted me with a positively perky, "Hi, Dez. Oh, I *love* your hair that way." Now, the last time I'd checked the mirror, my coiffeur was definitely exhibiting its displeasure with the humidity. So this could only mean that Jackie was making an effort to let me know that I was currently being regarded with favor. (Which proves what sort of good will can be generated when you notify her that you won't be in until such and such a time and then show up in the vicinity of the estimated hour.) "How did the morning go?" she asked.

"I'm still no closer to finding out who killed Mrs. Weiden. At least, I don't think I am. But Nina Chance did present me with some very interesting information about her husband—interesting if true, that is."

Jackie didn't have to inquire who Nina Chance was. When I'd reported to her on Friday that I had an appointment today, she made sure, as usual, to get all the particulars. "Well, don't hold out on me."

"It's too long a story. We'll talk when we sit down and have lunch—maybe tomorrow."

"Okay," Jackie responded affably. "And we really should try that new Italian place. Everyone I know who's eaten there just loves it." She slapped her palm across her forehead then. "Oh, I almost forgot. Your friend telephoned—you know, the one who's been married all those times."

"Pat?"

"Right. And she sounds pretty ticked off." She handed me the message slip. "If I were you, I'd call her back ten minutes ago."

Pat Martucci formerly Altmann formerly Green formerly Anderson was very pleasant when she got on the line—until she realized who was on the other end of it.

"You could have phoned," she informed me testily.

It was obvious she was about to lace into me for the second time in two weeks. Only now I wasn't even nominally guilty. I'd planned to get in touch with her this very evening to tell her what a great party it had been (the truth, really, if you're referring strictly to the fare). But she hadn't given me much of a chance, had she? At that moment the temperature of my blood would very likely have registered a hundred degrees Celsius. "I was going to, Pat," I snarled, "tonight, in fact."

"*Going* to? If you couldn't make it, it would have been nice to let me know in advance. Listen, I can understand that something urgent might have cropped up, but your not having the courtesy to—"

"What are you *talking* about? I was at the party."

She sounded skeptical. "I asked Burton, and he told me he didn't see you, either."

"The place was so jammed that I couldn't find you. I did spot Burton at one point, but by the time I got to where he was, he wasn't there anymore."

"You really came?" Pat asked meekly. She was clearly embarrassed now—as she deserved to be.

"I really did." I hit her with the proof. "And so did a very large, affectionate poodle; a naked guy who played the harmonica in the bathtub; some snoring giant who usurped practically your entire bed; a skinny, extremely nasty woman with pink-framed glasses and a voice like a foghorn—"

"Candace," Pat put in meekly. "That's her name, Candace. She works with Burton, and she's a bitch." And then, her voice actually quivering: "Ohh, Dez, I'm so-o-o sorry. It's just that you're such a good friend that I felt terrible thinking you'd miss Burton's birthday celebration without even bothering to phone and—" She broke off. "God! Am I a jerk!"

I let her off the hook. "We all are sometimes. I'm sure that if you strain your memory you'll recall that I've run off at the mouth myself on occasion."

Pat produced a pitifully weak laugh. Then she apologized again, and I assured her that all was forgiven. After which I said how terrific everything had been last night, pretty much restricting my specific comments to the food.

"You enjoyed yourself, then—honestly?" she inquired anxiously.

I answered her honestly, too. "Believe me, Pat, I can't even *tell* you how much I enjoyed myself."

Chapter Twenty-seven

I was at the office until after seven Monday evening, transcribing my notes on Nina Chance.

Once at home I had a quick supper. Then after straightening up after myself, I sat down at the kitchen table with the entire case file and, to assure that I retained my edge, a second cup of coffee. (Which tonight was so much worse than my usual atrocious brew as to be close to gag producing.)

I was just opening the folder when the telephone rang.

"This is Margaret Brown," the woman announced in response to my hello. "I . . . well, I have something to tell you." Promptly following that was a qualifier. "I don't see how it can help you any in finding the one who murdered Mrs. Weiden. But this past Thursday, right after those detectives were here asking us some more questions, I finally confided in Frank about . . . about a conversation I overheard months ago. And he's been pestering me to call you. 'You never know' is what he keeps on saying to me."

I had a strong sense that Mrs. Brown was about to reveal something significant, and a shiver of anticipation raced down my spine. "How soon can we get together?"

"Oh, there's no need for that. This will only take a couple of minutes."

I was actually relieved. I mean, although I normally press for face-to-face communication, I was so anxious for her revelation that I probably would have pulled out every strand of hair on my head prior to any meeting. "Fine. Please go on."

"All right. Yes, I'll do that." There was what seemed to me like an interminable silence before Margaret's next words. "On this particular morning—the one I'm referring to—I'd just come downstairs after spending quite a bit of time on the second floor, attending to some chores. I was a few feet from Mrs. Weiden's office—I was on my way there to ask when I should fix lunch—when I heard Ms. Harris shouting from behind the closed door. She was so angry I was worried she might have a stroke.

"'God, Miriam, what kind of a person are you!' she yelled. Then Mrs. Weiden said something back to Ms. Harris that I couldn't make out. I got the feeling she was asking her to lower her voice, but maybe not. Well, this certainly didn't seem to be anything I should be listening to, so I had every intention of turning around and going upstairs again. But what was said after that, it . . . it froze me right in my tracks."

Now, obviously reluctant to tell her story, Margaret had been speaking slowly from the very beginning—to give you an idea of *how* slowly, I type faster than that woman talked. Anyway, I'd kept my teeth clamped on my tongue to prevent an attempt to hurry her along, but at this point I just couldn't contain myself. "And what *was* said after that?"

Even with the prompting, the reply was none too speedy. "I can't give you the exact words," she eventually got out. "This was five or six months ago, you realize. As near as I can remember, though, Ms. Harris said, 'Why didn't you tell me? But never mind telling *me*. Why didn't you at least tell Deena? All these years that poor girl's been thinking she was an orphan.'" And now Margaret Brown's voice took on considerable volume, either in imitation of Erna or simply to give the statement the emphasis it merited. "'*And here she's your own natural child!*'"

For a few seconds my mind had difficulty absorbing what I'd heard.

"—and I hope you understand that I wasn't trying to eavesdrop," the housekeeper was maintaining.

Admirably concealing my impatience, I murmured reassuringly, "Of course I do." I even waited close to a full minute before asking, "What was Mrs. Weiden's response to this?"

"I don't know. I snapped out of my . . . *trance,* I imagine you could call it, and got out of there as fast as this sixty-three-year-old body could carry me." A moment later she inquired hesitantly, "Ms. Shapiro? Do you really believe this—what I've just related to you—could have anything to do with Mrs. Weiden's murder?"

"I have no idea, but it's conceivable that it might."

"Then I suppose I did right." It was apparent that she wasn't at all convinced of this, however.

"You really did. Honestly. And thanks for contacting me. I can appreciate that it was a difficult decision for you to make."

"It's just that I was afraid to repeat a thing like that because of what it might do to Mrs. Weiden's reputation," Margaret explained. "And it's not even as though I know for a fact that it's true—what Ms. Harris was accusing her of. But Frank, he was pretty insistent about my telling you about it anyway. Besides, it's not like you'd go on the TV news with this." I thought I heard a gulp here.

"I'll keep it as quiet as I possibly can," I promised.

"Frank was sure you would. Uh, you won't say this came from me?"

"I'm almost certain that won't be necessary."

Margaret considered the answer briefly before concluding with a sigh of resignation, "Well, if there's any chance I've helped you with your investigation, that's what's important, isn't it?"

The instant we hung up I tried reaching Erna at the Weiden apartment.

"I can't talk to you," she informed me. "I'm leaving for home, and there's a car waiting downstairs."

"I have to see you tomorrow," I said tersely.

"Tell me you're kidding."

"I'm not. I just learned something that we should definitely discuss."

"Oh, no you don't. I've wasted enough time trying to answer your million-and-one questions."

"This concerns Deena."

For three or four seconds—nothing. And then: "All right." Her voice sounded strange—I think she must have had her teeth clenched. "Be here in the morning at ten. I'll give you fifteen minutes."

I just hate it when somebody slams down the receiver in my ear, don't you?

Chapter Twenty-eight

There were all sorts of cartons piled up in the foyer, just inside the door to the apartment. "The Salvation Army is supposed to be picking up this stuff later today," Erna explained, nimbly maneuvering her way around the stumbling blocks. I, being not the most graceful of God's creatures, immediately banged my knee on one of the larger boxes. "Be careful," she admonished too late.

To my disappointment, I soon found that this morning's meeting was to be held in Erna's office. Which, I grumbled to myself, undoubtedly meant no Danish. Probably not even a cup of coffee.

We took the seats we'd occupied last week—Erna, the desk chair and me, the sofa.

Now, you'll probably think I'm saying this to be mean—particularly since I was feeling deprived of my breakfast goodies—but I swear it's an honest observation. Anyway, it suddenly occurred to me that in her brown corduroy pants and brown cotton shirt, Erna Harris looked exactly like a sparrow. In fact, she even out-bird-ladied Margaret today. "Go ahead. Your fifteen minutes start now," she notified me. I anticipated that in a second she'd check her watch, and she didn't disappoint me.

Well, I'd rehearsed precisely how I intended to proceed with this, but instead I ended up just blurting out, "Miriam was Deena's mother."

"Of course she was," Erna responded crossly.

"I'm talking about her *natural* mother."

"You're crazy. Where did you get an idea like that?"

"That's not important. The point is, it's true, isn't it?"

"No."

"My source is impeccable," I pronounced.

And then, no doubt recognizing the possibility that she and Miriam might have been overheard, Erna demanded, "Was it Margaret? Frank? Sometimes they—"

"The Browns knew about this, too?" I broke in, all innocence.

"No one knew. Because it's a lie."

"You can do all the denying you want to, Erna, but you're wasting your time. This won't be that difficult to verify." (I wasn't the least bit sure of that. However, I was not about to be inhibited by facts.) "And keep in mind that in the course of my looking into Deena's birth, it's almost unavoidable that other people would also find out about her parentage."

"Is that a threat?"

"No, I just want you to have some idea of what you can look forward to."

I could have knitted a sweater (if I knew how to knit) in the time it took the secretary to respond. And when she did, it was in a tone positively seething with hostility. "All right. But Deena is not to hear about this—understood?"

"I won't say anything to her unless I absolutely have to."

"What does that mean?" The sparrow eyes were ablaze.

"It means that I won't breathe a word to her unless there's a very good reason for it." And then I quickly threw in, "Which I don't anticipate." Belatedly, it dawned on me. "You mean that girl still hasn't been informed that Miriam was her birth mother?"

"No. I kept after Miriam to tell her," Erna amplified somewhat grudgingly, "but all I'd get was that she'd talk to her about it when the time was right."

"When did you discover this, anyway?"

"I hope you don't expect me to give you the precise date," was the snippy reply. "All I know is that it was sometime toward the end of July."

"So then after you confronted her, Mrs. Weiden stalled for about six months?"

"That's right."

"Didn't *you* ever consider going to Deena?"

"Of course. But I thought it would be a lot easier for her to accept her mother's deception if it came from Miriam herself."

"Was Mrs. Davis also aware that Deena was Miriam's natural child?"

"I'm certain she wasn't. In fact, Miriam made me swear I wouldn't say anything to Norma."

And now I asked the question I'd been wondering about since Margaret's phone call last night. "Who was Deena's father?"

"I'm not a hundred percent sure, but I have a pretty fair inkling that it was this young fellow upstate, at Coral Lake—this *very* young fellow. He was a nice-looking kid of maybe eighteen or so. His mother was black, and his father was either white or Hispanic. Anyway, the summer before Deena was born Miriam and I were at the lake for an entire month, and she hired this Billy—wait, I'm wrong; his name was Bobby—to do some work around the place. Almost from the beginning I suspected that they had something going. Every so often I'd notice these intimate looks passing between them."

"Did she ever see him again? After that summer, I mean."

"Not that I'm aware of. I'm not even certain he continued to live up there. I remember that he was planning to go away to college in the fall. At least, I think I do—it was so long ago." She smiled almost apologetically here—to my complete astonishment. Her good nature lasted for about six seconds, too.

"So," I mused, "Miriam actually went to Switzerland in order to conceal her pregnancy and have her baby in secret."

"Give this woman a big cigar," the secretary remarked snidely.

I decided I hadn't heard that. "And her excuse for being away from home all that time was that she was arranging for the adoption," I mumbled, continuing to ruminate aloud. Then to Erna: "Did Bobby know about the baby?"

"Miriam never told him."

"How did you finally happen to uncover the truth, anyway?"

Once again it felt like Erna was taking forever to answer. "Well, all these years," she said at last, "Miriam had been sending an annual contribution to a hospital in Switzerland. She claimed they'd treated her for some gastrointestinal problem when she was over there and that they'd been just wonderful to her. At any rate, following every contribution she'd get a letter marked 'personal and confidential' from this Dr. Eric Bauer. I wondered about that 'personal and confidential' business, but knowing Miriam, I figured that she'd probably had an affair with Dr. Bauer after she left the hospital. Of course, I couldn't be certain of this, and I have to admit that I'd always been somewhat curious, only—" And now Erna stopped abruptly. "Listen, would you like some coffee?"

I made the mistake of giving her an honest answer. "I'd love some."

"Margaret's off today, so I'll have to make it myself. I'll be back shortly, though."

And before I had the presence to say, "No, no! Don't bother!" she was out the door.

Damn! I lamented. *Why did my tongue always have to precede my brain like that?*

Apparently Erna had been as anxious to postpone the rest of her story as I'd been to hear it, because it was more than fifteen minutes before she reappeared. She was carrying a tray containing two mugs of coffee and the necessary accompaniments, along with a plate of store-bought cookies. I consoled myself with the fact that the cookies were at least Pepperidge Farm.

(With all these years of indulging under my belt—and feel free to take that literally—naturally I recognized my old friends at once.)

Setting the tray on the desktop, she took her seat again. Then after fixing my coffee for me and passing me the plate of cookies, she very deliberately stirred two teaspoons of sugar into her own cup. Following which she reached for a cookie and had a few delicate nibbles. Next came a couple of sips of coffee, and a second later another bite of cookie—with everything seeming to proceed in slow motion. I tell you, I was frustrated enough to strangle the woman!

But, well, since she'd gone to the trouble of providing the refreshments . . . As I watched her continue to nibble and sip, I did the same.

It was a good two or three minutes longer before Erna deigned to resume her explanation.

She kicked off with "I'm not very proud of myself." And now she raised the mug to her lips again. I still wonder if she heard my teeth gnashing together at this juncture. "I'd stopped into Miriam's office that morning with an invitation I needed her response to," Erna eventually went on. "But she wasn't there at the moment—I could hear her down the hall, talking to Frank about a number of matters. So I scribbled a note for her and clipped it to the invitation. But as I went to put these things on her desk, I knocked the box of paper clips into the wastebasket. When I bent to retrieve the box I saw the letter from Dr. Bauer in the trash—I was aware that it had come in that morning, since I'd handed it to Miriam myself."

There was a short pause here for another swallow of coffee. "Anyway, Miriam had ripped the letter into pieces, but they were *large* pieces. Maybe she'd become a little careless after all this time. Or maybe she'd finally gotten around to trusting that I'd respect her privacy. Of course, she didn't trust enough not to tear the letter at all." Erna gave me a small, guilty smile. "And she was right.

"At any rate, Miriam and Frank were still deep in

conversation. And I don't know what possessed me, but I took those scraps of paper out of the wastebasket and fitted them together.

"The letter was pretty brief. Bauer thanked Miriam for her contribution to the hospital and went on to say that he hoped she and Deena were well and that he couldn't believe Deena was already in college. Then he wrote how it seemed like only a couple of years had passed since he'd delivered that darling baby girl of Miriam's."

"But he might have been referring to Miriam's *adopted* baby girl," I pointed out. "Maybe he actually *delivered* Deena to some woman killed in a car crash."

Erna glowered at me. "You didn't let me finish. Bauer also said something about what a beautiful young lady Deena must be. 'After all, though,'—and this is verbatim—'with your genes, how could she not be?'"

"So then you knew," I murmured.

Erna's tone was matter-of-fact. "That's right; I knew."

"It's hard to believe anyone would go through that much subterfuge."

"Keep in mind that this was almost two decades ago. If she'd admitted to Deena's being the product of an affair—and a short-lived, interracial one, at that— Miriam would have been regarded as a bimbo by a great many of her so-called friends. But by claiming to have adopted a poor, motherless infant, she was a much-admired humanitarian." Erna shook her head slowly from side to side. "The machinations of Miriam Weiden's mind always amazed me," she muttered bitterly. "But *this*—this was her crowning achievement."

"Yet even after learning what she'd done, you remained in the job."

I suppose I sounded somewhat accusatory, because Erna retorted testily, "Do you really think I had much choice? What kind of a reference do you imagine I'd have gotten if I quit?"

"You honestly believe—"

"You bet I do! Miriam had occasion to set me straight about that once, a couple of years back." But an instant later, evidently regretting that she'd revealed so much hostility toward the deceased these last few minutes, Erna attempted some damage control. "I suppose it's flattering in a way. A day or two after I'd given her my notice that time, she insisted that she *had* to threaten me because she'd have been lost if I left her. And listen," Erna added defensively, "it's not as though I wasn't extremely well paid. Besides, as a rule—I'm talking about on a day-to-day basis—I was fairly content working for Miriam."

Something occurred to me at this moment. "What do you intend doing about Deena—assuming she hasn't somehow already found out about her mother's denying her her birthright?"

"She hasn't. And I don't know yet what I intend doing," Erna snapped.

"I have a suggestion."

"Go on." The permission, I want you to know, was accompanied by a scowl.

"Not now, but after the investigation is concluded, I suggest you let my client in on this. I think that if she were the one to break the news to Deena, she could present it in a positive light."

"Oh, really?" Erna responded sarcastically. "And just how does she manage to accomplish this?"

"First, by putting it that Miriam didn't want her child to have to bear the stigma of illegitimacy, which, Mrs. Davis could make clear, is what would have happened back then. In other words, the thrust of the explanation would be that Miriam did this to protect *her*—Deena. Maybe even more important, though, my client is almost as crazy about that girl as you are. So I have a feeling she'd be very glad to know that Deena is her natural granddaughter—once she adjusted to her own daughter's Machiavellian mentality, that is. And I'm certain she'd be able to convey her happiness to Deena, which should help soften the facts."

"And you honestly feel Deena would buy into that—about Miriam's doing this for *her*?"

"My guess is that Deena would want to believe it. So, yes, I would say that it's very possible."

For one fleeting moment Miriam's longtime secretary looked at me with an expression approximating respect. "I'm still not sure, but you may have something there."

"Well, think about it, anyway."

It was less than five minutes later. Erna and I had both gotten to our feet preparatory to my leaving when, almost pleadingly, she demanded reassurance. "I have your word that you won't say anything to Deena yourself, correct?"

"Only if circumstances make it impossible for me to avoid it. And I'm hoping that won't happen."

"Well, see that it doesn't," she grumbled. "Uh, you do think it's for the best that I uncovered the truth, don't you?"

"Yes, of course."

"The thing is, you see, I have a guilty conscience."

"*You* do?"

Her "yes" was almost inaudible. "For years I wanted to know what could be so 'personal and confidential.' I used to tell myself it wasn't any of my business, but I was so damn curious."

I could relate to this.

"And, well, that accident with the box of paper clips?" Erna was peering at me unhappily. "I'm just not certain it really *was* an accident."

Chapter Twenty-nine

It was close to noon when I walked out of the Weiden apartment—Erna's mandated fifteen minutes had been more like two hours. And all that talk about Miriam's colossal deception had left me slightly numb.

No wonder Mrs. Davis saw something of her dead daughter Ruth in Deena!

It was a nice, sunny day, and for once I ignored the available taxis in favor of a short stroll, hoping to clear my mind. I headed east for a block and then continued south. On Lexington and East Fifty-something I spotted a promising-looking coffee shop and thought I'd stop off for some lunch before taking a taxi the rest of the way to the office.

The office!

There was a pay phone a few yards past the coffee shop, and I placed a hasty call to Jackie.

She practically pounced. "Oh, Dez! Are you all right?"

The tone of voice was so unexpected that I came *this* close to dropping the receiver.

"I'm fine. What's the matter?"

"I've been *so-o* worried. After all, you said that you'd found out something important last night and that you were interrogating a suspect this morning." (I hadn't been either foolhardy or brave enough to set off for my meeting without first notifying Jackie of my plans.) "You're going to think this is silly," she went on, "but as soon as you hung up I got this terrible feeling—it was almost like a premonition—that

you could be in danger. That it wasn't healthy for you
to know whatever it was you'd learned. And when
you didn't show up by eleven—and you told me you'd
be in by then at the latest—I started to have visions of
someone slipping you some of that tubercular stuff."

"Tubocurarine chloride. And are you sure that
wasn't just wishful thinking?"

"Don't be such a smart-ass. Anyhow, I'm very relieved you're okay."

I was touched. It had been a while since Jackie ex-
pressed this kind of concern for my well-being. And
she can be so infuriating sometimes that, too often, I
lose sight of what a dear friend she is. This was a
poignant reminder.

At any rate, I told her of my intention to have
something to eat before coming in to work, but an
instant later I recalled that we had a semitentative
lunch date for today. "Damn! We talked about going
to that new Italian place of yours this afternoon,
didn't we?"

"Oh, don't worry about it. We can do it another
time," said Jackie the (suddenly) Benevolent.

I retraced my steps to the coffee shop. There was a
single available table, and a fortyish man in a black
raincoat was striding purposefully toward it. But being
a veteran at this sort of thing, I managed to maneuver
myself into position and plunk my bottom on one of
the chairs just before the poor guy—who was unaware
he had such awesome competition—could do the
same.

Now, as you know, normally I scrupulously avoid
mixing my meals with murder. But the conversation
with Erna was already beginning to replay itself, un-
bidden, in my head. So right after ordering a grilled
cheese and bacon, I gave in and allowed myself some
serious contemplation.

*Was the true nature of Deena's birth of major sig-
nificance with regard to my investigation?* I put to
myself.

Not really, I immediately determined. While Deena might have been infuriated—and who could blame her?—to learn that her own natural mother had been passing her off as an adopted child, it was very likely the girl was completely unaware of what Erna's penchant for jigsaw puzzles had turned up.

What about Erna herself, though? This recent—and certainly most disturbing—revelation concerning the victim's egregious behavior could conceivably have been the one to finally enrage the secretary enough to do the deed. Although I still felt pretty strongly that if Erna was, in fact, my poisoner, in all probability her motivation was to prevent Miriam from monkeying around with that will of hers.

So actually, I concluded, while the news had been a shocker, it hadn't gotten me any closer to unmasking the killer than I'd been the day before. Or the day before that. I mean, it appeared, from here anyway, to merely be further proof of what a singularly self-centered and devious woman Miriam Weiden had been—and how cleverly she'd concealed it from so many people.

That phony humility of hers! That— The sound of throat clearing aborted my thoughts.

I looked up to see a small blonde girl of about twenty standing over me. "Excuse me, Miss, but would it be all right if I sat here? There aren't any empty tables, and I have to be back at my desk in twenty-five minutes."

Well, I wasn't exactly delighted by the interruption, but what could I say?

I mumbled my permission, and the girl placed her tiny little rump on the chair across from mine. "My name is Brenda," she informed me. "What's your—" She was staring at me, her eyes wide. "Oh, what *gorgeous* earrings."

Now, one of the quickest routes to my heart is via my earlobes; earrings, as I've already mentioned, being among my very favorite things. And I was particularly enamored of today's pair of silver-and-turquoise dangles. "Thank you," I simpered, inordinately pleased. I noted then, almost with pity, that the girl's own auditory appendages were totally naked.

At that moment the waitress appeared at my elbow with lunch. And while she was in the neighborhood, she took Brenda's order—for a shrimp cocktail, a steak sandwich with sautéed onions, a double portion of fries, and a milk shake.

As I bit into my grilled cheese and bacon, Brenda inquired, "Do you work in this area?"

My mother had trained me well, so I swallowed hurriedly before answering. "No, I work in the East Thirties."

"Don't tell me. Bloomingdale's, right?" She inclined her head in the direction of the store, which was about two blocks north.

I laughed. "Not today. I had some business to take care of not far from here."

"What do you do?" Her cheeks immediately turned bright pink. "Oh, I hope it's all right for me to ask."

"Sure. I'm a PI—a private investigator."

"Really? No kidding! You're the first one I've ever met." She inched her chair a bit closer to mine. "Do you carry a gun?" she whispered.

"Not usually."

"What about now?" There was a sudden eagerness in her tone.

I chuckled. "No. And don't be so bloodthirsty, Brenda."

Her meal arrived soon afterward, and she managed to vacuum it up with surprising speed, in spite of continuing to pepper me with questions. What was my name, by the way? What sort of cases was I currently working on? What had been my most interesting case? Was I ever afraid I'd be killed? And then, her cheeks bright pink again: "Geez, what a stupid thing to say!"

By the time Brenda looked up at the clock some twenty minutes later and announced that she had to leave for the office—she was a secretary at an insurance company, she'd apprised me—I admit that I was

a little sorry. Maybe it was because I was flattered—
she had seemed positively fascinated by every sentence I uttered. Or maybe it was because there was
this childlike quality about her. But whatever the reason, I had really been enjoying her company. Well,
I'd just have to get through this second cup of coffee
on my own.

The waitress promptly brought Brenda her check,
and the girl dug into her humongous pocketbook. And
dug. And dug. Then she emptied the bag's entire contents on the table, many of her belongings rolling onto
the floor. Scooping these up, she began to sift through
a sizable pile that included such unexpected treasures
as a jump rope, a cracked glass globe of the Empire
State Building, and a book on kung fu.

Finally, her eyes filling up, she murmured, "Oh,
God. I must have left my wallet in my other handbag."
And then fearfully: "You don't suppose they'll ar-
rest me?"

"No, of course not. And please don't cry. I'll take
care of that." Before she could protest, I snatched the
check off her place mat.

Brenda tried to grab it from my hand, but I moved
my arm out of reach. "Okay," she eventually agreed,
getting up and slipping on her too-large navy wind-
breaker. "You have to let me pay you back, though."

"Oh, it's not nec—"

"You *have* to. It'll make me feel better. Can I have
your address?"

I gave her one of my business cards, and she came
over to hug me. "Thank you so much, Desiree. I'll
send you the money tonight. I promise." She hurried
away then, almost bumping into a couple of women
who'd entered the coffee shop moments before. The
smaller of the two ladies paused at my table.

"So how *is* Carol?" she demanded.

"Carol?"

By way of explanation, she jerked her thumb toward
the door.

"Oh, you mean Brenda," I corrected.

"Maybe today. But three weeks ago she was Carol. How much did she get you for?"

"You mean—?" It wasn't the least bit necessary to say more.

"Uh-huh," the woman confirmed. "Quite a little actress, that one. But listen, honey, you're lucky. The day she finagled me into picking up her check, she'd brought her little sister along."

Somewhere between Brenda's (Carol's?) departure and my own, I'd made up my mind to skip the office entirely today. I would go home, splash cold water on my face (my eyelids were beginning to droop on me), and study my notes—and I mean *really* study them.

Stopping off at the same pay phone I'd utilized previously—which, miraculously, was not only still intact but had retained its all-important dial tone as well—I contacted Jackie again.

"I've changed my plans," I updated her. "I'm going to be working at the apartment this afternoon."

"*Now* what do I do?" she responded petulantly. "I told everyone who tried to reach you to try again after two. I'll be bombarded with calls for the rest of the day."

It required some gentle probing, but I discovered that this concern about bombardment could be attributed to a grand total of two messages Jackie had had to take for me earlier. One from Ellen and one from Pat Martucci.

Well, this was the Jackie I knew and loved.

Chapter Thirty

I'm embarrassed to admit it. But the truth is, in spite of the many, *many* times I'd gone over my notes, I'd consistently neglected to look at this one particular circumstance while taking into account the character of the deceased.

Until today.

Today, however, as soon as I reviewed what my client had told me about the boating episode, I realized that something just wasn't right there. Of course, I should have been aware of this more than a week ago—when I'd gotten my first glimpse of the kind of woman Miriam Weiden *really* was.

At any rate, follow my thinking.

Miriam strongly suspected that someone had tried to drown her. And even if this impression didn't actually take root until she was almost crowned with the ladder, at that point she became fairly certain that what had transpired at the lake had also been a bona fide attempt to do away with her.

So why hadn't she identified her alleged attacker at this juncture?

I could no longer accept the baloney that the victim's refusal to name names stemmed from her concern about maligning an innocent human being. The Miriam I'd come to know wouldn't have cared beans about a thing like that—even if it meant there was still a possibility that whoever it was had actually been trying to rescue her. This became even more apparent to me when I considered that she was beside herself by then, frantic that her assailant would take another crack at her.

And the way I looked at it, there could be only one reason Miriam had stayed mum: *She didn't feel she'd be able to persuade anyone that the person with her at the lake had intended to murder her.*

Now, for my present purposes I opted to disregard everything I'd heard from those I'd interrogated during the course of my investigation. After all, people— especially suspects—are not unfailing sticklers for the truth. For the time being anyhow, I was going to rely strictly on the word of the victim herself. And what had Miriam said in her phone call to me? To quote her verbatim: "I'm terrified there'll be a third try— and that this time she'll succeed."

Well, the deceased may or may not have glimpsed any dark skirt at the high school, depending on who it was you believed, but the one thing not open to question was that Miriam saw who was in the boat with her that day. And *that* person, at least, was definitely a woman.

This being the case, I had only two candidates: Erna and Deena. (In August, Miriam hadn't even met Philip Chance yet, which put his wife in the clear.)

Okay, suppose Miriam had specified to my client that it was Erna who'd planned to drown her. However skeptical Mrs. Davis might have been, I didn't see Miriam as being that positive she'd dismiss this charge out of hand.

Conversely, however, consider that it was Deena the victim had named. In light of my client's feelings for the girl, any suggestion that Deena had made a deliberate effort to push Miriam's head underwater would almost certainly have been rejected. I mean, as it was, until that lethal dose of tubocurarine chloride, Norma Davis had difficulty in accepting that anyone was out to purposely harm her daughter. No. She'd sooner have attributed such an allegation to Miriam's state of anxiety. *And Miriam knew it.*

And can you imagine Erna's reaction if the deceased had accused Deena to *her*? Listen, when I'd asked who had spent time with her employer at Coral Lake that week, Erna hadn't even mentioned Deena. And I didn't buy that she wasn't aware her little friend had been up there, either.

Just then another thought sprang into my head. But this new idea certainly didn't negate my conclusion. If anything, it made me more confident than ever that I was on the right track with Deena.

What I'm referring to is the additional possibility—although I considered it fairly remote—that one of these women, or maybe both, was a bald-faced liar. I'll explain. For argument's sake, let's say that when the deceased finally spoke about that lake business she *had* implicated Deena to Erna and/or Mrs. Davis. I'm willing to bet they would have insisted that the teenager's actions were nothing less than heroic. It wouldn't have surprised me to learn that even after the murder they refused to connect the dots. So it hardly required much of an effort to imagine these ladies being so anxious to shield an innocent (in their minds) young girl that they'd elect not to apprise me of the victim's disclosure. But as I said, I didn't regard this scenario as very likely; I remained pretty much convinced that Miriam had remained silent.

It was right after this that I hit a stumbling block in my ruminations. Why hadn't the deceased pointed the finger at Deena during that lunch with Philip Chance? Certainly he had no special affection for the girl—it was highly improbable that he'd ever met her.

I eventually decided that—who knows?—perhaps Miriam had been concerned that identifying her own daughter as the culprit might in some way reflect badly on *her*.

Anyhow, the important thing was that Deena was the "she" Miriam had been referring to—this, I didn't doubt. That little egghead Hercule was right about how crucial it is to know the victim.

After all, it was only after becoming acquainted with

the *genuine* Miriam Weiden that I was able to look at that initial attempt on her life and appreciate the significance of what she'd done about it. Or more correctly, *had not* done about it.

Chapter Thirty-one

I wasn't too hopeful when I tried Deena's apartment at a little after nine o'clock that night. Almost certainly she'd be at Todd's—whose last name, idiot that I am, I'd neglected to find out.

The phone rang four times. I had already removed the receiver from my ear, resigned to getting a message to the girl via my client—although I wasn't particularly pleased to go that route—when just then I thought I heard a voice. I quickly put the receiver to my ear again. Well, what do you know? Deena had finally gotten around to acquiring another answering machine.

I left word that I had to talk to her about something important and asked that she contact me as soon as possible.

After this I returned that morning's calls. All two of them.

Pat was first. Burton would be out of town for the rest of the week, she said, and she wanted to know if I was free for dinner any night. As it happened, I was free for dinner *every* night. I mean, it was hardly as if I'd been wearing out my dancing shoes lately. We settled on Friday.

I got back to Ellen next. "I just wanted to tell you we're going to start looking at places," she notified me.

My niece is often under the misconception that since *she* has an idea of what she's talking about, so will I. In this instance, though, I probably should have

been able to read her. But I suppose all that strain
I'd imposed on my brain earlier had had its effect.
"What kind of places?"

"For the reception," she clarified. "Oh, Aunt Dez,
I'm so excited. I did tell you it's going to be a big
affair, didn't I? Mike's parents are just thrilled about
that—they have an awful lot of people they'd like to
invite."

"How do your folks feel about a large wedding?"

"Great. Especially since the Lyntons will be picking
up part of the bill. And incidentally, you know how
my mother's been pushing for us to get married in
Florida?" As a matter of fact, I didn't. "Well, Mom
and I finally compromised."

"Compromised?"

"I told her that if she'd agree to hold the thing in
New York, I'd give in and wear a white gown."

"But you already—"

"I'm aware of that," Ellen broke in, giggling. "But
my mother isn't."

"Why you clever little witch, you," I murmured appreciatively, starting to giggle, too. Anytime someone
manages to outwit my sister-in-law (which happens far
too rarely to suit me), my spirits positively soar.
(Granted, this is not nice. But I've had more than a
couple of run-ins with Margot over the years, and I
am a Scorpio.) Besides, I was delighted that Ellen and
Mike would be having the wedding around here.

As I slathered on the cleansing cream that night, I
reflected that it had turned out to be a truly fine day.
I was very happy about Ellen's news—every aspect of
it. And, of course, I'd had a major breakthrough with
the case. I was even encouraged enough to believe I
might at last be on the verge of wrapping it up.

Wednesday seemed to go on forever.

That entire morning I waited anxiously at my desk
to hear from Deena. Nothing. I'd made tentative plans
to have that lunch with Jackie today, but fearful of
missing Deena's call, I postponed it once again, order-

ing in instead. Really, I all but glued myself to the chair. I even delayed a trip to the ladies' room until I couldn't put it off another second.

Finally, at four-thirty Deena phoned.

I thought I detected an uneasiness in her voice. "I just now checked my messages. You said there was something important you wanted to speak to me about?"

"That's right."

"Is it . . . have you found out who poisoned my mother?"

"I think this had better wait until we get together."

"Oh, then can you make it tonight?"

"I certainly can," I agreed. "Where?"

"I have to pick up some books at my place, so we could meet there."

Our get-together was scheduled for six-thirty.

In the cab that evening I went over what I would say to the girl. And what she was likely to say to me. And how I should respond. And how she'd probably react to my response. By the time the taxi pulled up in front of Deena's building, I'd scripted practically an entire miniseries.

Although making it up the four flights to the apartment still left me wrung out and breathless, at least I was less apprehensive than I'd been during my previous climb. The reason being that I had simply made up my mind not to allow myself to suffer a coronary when it was possible I was could be on the very brink of uncovering Miriam's killer.

It was Todd who opened the door. Damn! I should have realized there was a good chance he'd be here tonight. I immediately began to rethink a decision I'd made earlier in the day.

You see, in the course of my investigations there were occasions where I'd barely escaped being a victim myself. In fact, it was getting to be almost habitual. So before leaving for work this morning, I had considered removing my thirty-two from its resting place in my panty drawer and tossing it into my handbag—just in case. But I'd immediately dismissed the idea, since to begin with, I didn't feel that the "evidence" I'd be presenting to Deena was weighty enough to put me in any real jeopardy. Plus, the truth is, I'd never so much as pointed that thing at anyone.

At this moment, however, it occurred to me that if Todd had also been involved in Miriam's death, I'd have the two of them to contend with. And that made me a little edgy. I mean, who knew how his presence could affect the dynamics of the situation?

Oh, hell. It's doubtful the gun would have done me any good, anyway. Somehow I'd probably have wound up shooting off a couple of my toes.

Deena was on the sofa. A quick glance at my face, and she was all apology. "Are you okay, Desiree?" Jumping up, she patted one of the cushions. "Here." Then, as soon as I made contact with the seat she said, "I'm really sorry. I forgot the trouble you have with my stairs. We should have done this at Todd's— he lives on the first floor. Listen, can I get you something? How about a cup of coffee?"

I shuddered inwardly, recalling the last cup she'd prepared for me. "No, thanks. I'm fine. I just need a second or two to catch my breath, that's all."

"Of course." She sat down next to me.

Todd was standing in the middle of the tiny room now, looking uncomfortable. "Are you sure you don't want me to wait in the kitchen, Deenie?"

Deena turned to me. "Okay with you if Todd stays?"

"No problem," I answered, not being able to come up with a decent excuse for vetoing this.

He sat down on the hard wooden floor, his knees drawn up to his chin. After which two sets of eyes focused on me in anticipation.

Wriggling out of my coat, I said to Deena, "It's about Coral Lake. Contrary to what you claimed last time, you *did* know your mother almost drowned that day." I spoke more slowly here, for effect. "Because you were the one who was with her."

"How can you accuse me of a thing like that?" Deena retorted. "Besides, the boat was out of commission, so we *couldn't* go rowing that weekend."

I shook my head. "That delivery man who came along? I've managed to locate him. He gave me a very good description of you." (One thing I'll tell you: When I lie, I'm so convincing that I almost believe myself.)

"I don't know about any description. It wasn't me, though," the girl maintained. "Whatever took place on the lake didn't happen when Todd and I were up there." But her tone had lost much of its firmness.

"I faxed the man your picture, and he identified you."

"Evidently there's something wrong with his eyes. Or his brain." But Deena's lower lip had begun to quiver.

And then, very softly, Todd said, "Level with her, Deenie." *Well, how do you like that? Todd's presence might actually turn out to be a positive.*

She glared at him. "Level with her about what?"

"Please," he urged. "I always knew someone would find out. Let's just get it over with."

"I have no idea what—"

"Please," he repeated.

It took a long time for Deena to reach her decision. But finally she shrugged. "All right. I *was* in the boat with my mother that day."

"Why have you been denying it?"

"Erna advised me to. She was afraid that if it came out, it might make me a suspect in the murder."

And now, because I had nothing to lose, I threw in, "I imagine I should level with you, too. The delivery man was pretty disturbed after the incident. He told me that at first he wouldn't even allow himself to think it, but later he had to admit that it did appear more like you were trying to drown your mother than to save her."

I was hardly prepared for what happened next. Suddenly Deena burst into tears. And I mean *tears*. It was as if she'd been storing them up for all of her eighteen years. She covered her face with her hands, and I patted her back once or twice. Then not knowing what else to do, I squeezed her shoulder every so often. Meanwhile, Todd rushed from the room, returning with a large wad of tissues. Deena quickly went through these, and he was called upon to furnish her with a fistful of replacements less than a minute later.

When the crying jag was over at last, the girl raised her still-damp face and met my eyes. "What the delivery man told you? Well, he might be right."

"No, he's not," Todd interjected forcefully.

Deena held up her hand to him. "I want to get it off my chest, Todd. Look, Desiree, I loved my mother. I honestly did," the girl insisted, turning her entire body toward me now. "But lately we had a lot of . . . *stuff* to resolve. That's why I suggested to her that we take the boat on the lake. I wanted to be alone with her, to really hash things out. What's been bothering me, though, is that we were arguing like crazy, and I was even thinking how much I hated her when just then we realized that that decrepit old rowboat was filling up with water. I didn't *actually* hate her, of course. It's only that at that moment I was so angry, so totally frustrated. Have you ever felt that way toward someone you cared about?"

"More than once."

"And then when we were in the water and I had my arm across her neck, I'm afraid that for an instant there I *might* have had it in my mind to . . . to do something terrible. Only it all happened so fast that I'll never know for sure."

Shades of Erna and her box of paper clips! Here was Deena, too, questioning her own intentions. I wanted to say something that was encouraging—if not necessarily true. "If you'd really had the idea of drowning your mother, you probably *would* know for sure. So stop beating up on yourself for no reason. Would you care to hear what I think your trouble is?"

"What?"

"Now that your mother is gone, you're trying to heap all this blame on yourself for experiencing that hostility, however temporary, toward her."

"I'd like to believe that."

"I'm not exactly a licensed therapist," I conceded, "but it makes sense, doesn't it? Tell me, though, exactly what sort of problems were the two of you having?"

"Mostly my mother didn't approve of my going with Todd, and she was always harping on me about it. She even threatened to disinherit me if we got married. I wasn't interested in the money, I swear. But if she really loved me, I didn't see why she wouldn't just let me be happy. I still don't."

"She probably had the notion that you'd be better off with somebody rich and prestigious." I cast an apologetic glance at Todd, who was sitting there immobile, looking grim. So attempting to take the sting out of the words, I added, "Apparently a lot of women mistakenly imagine that motherhood in itself gives them all the tools they need to figure out what's best for their children." But Todd was looking no less grim.

"This summer," Deena resumed, "my mother had also stared lobbying for me to finish college in California, at Berkeley—my great-aunt and -uncle live near there. Anything to separate Todd and me. Listen, I realize I told you last time that my mother and I got along pretty well. And I'm sorry I lied, but I just didn't want to wind up being accused of poisoning her."

"I can understand that," I responded with a wry grin. "You certainly fooled people, though—you and your mother. Everyone seems to think the two of you had a fairly smooth relationship."

"My mother was very strict about never airing private matters in front of other people. When I was living at home, I had to save everything up for at night, when we were alone. I don't think even Margaret and Frank—they were my mother's housekeeper and chauffeur—had any idea of how much friction there'd been between us recently. Only Erna knew what was going on, and that was because I told her. And, of course, Todd knew, because I tell him everything." She smiled at her handsome young boyfriend, and he flashed her an ear-to-ear smile in return.

"Well, I guess we've pretty much covered things," I said at this point. "I really appreciate your honesty." And with a quick glance at Todd: "Both of you." Then I rose and struggled into the trench coat I'd been sitting on all this time. It now looked like a rummage sale reject.

Deena and Todd got up, too. She was the one to walk me to the door.

I was already out in the hall when there was a tug on my sleeve. I turned around, and Deena was standing alongside me. She peered at me earnestly, her hand still on my sleeve. "My mother adopted me and brought me to this country, and thanks to her, I have a wonderful life. You were right, Desiree. I *couldn't* have killed her. No matter what."

While schlepping myself down those hundreds of stairs (well, that's how it seemed to me), I made an effort—just as I had after my last meeting here—to sort things out in my mind.

Had Deena been about to push Miriam under when that delivery man came along? And I'm not referring to her having some sudden, transitory impulse, either. What I'm suggesting is that these self-doubts of hers could have been the creation of a very clever perpetrator seeking to counteract what the witness I'd supposedly tracked down had supposedly observed. It was equally possible, though, that Deena Weiden was completely innocent of any attempt to harm her mother—regardless of Miriam's perception and the girl's own misgivings.

But even if Deena was culpable that afternoon at Coral Lake, I cautioned myself, this didn't necessarily

make her the poisoner. After all, as Philip Chance
had reminded me, it was months between that alleged
murder attempt and the next suspicious incident. In
fact, the more I reflected on things, the more conceivable I found it that I was contending with two different perps here. I mean, just consider the character of
the victim.

By the time I made it down to the street floor I was
forced to admit that, notwithstanding what I chose to
regard as some absolutely brilliant deducing on my
part, Miriam's killer remained a giant question mark.

Chapter Thirty-two

There were a couple of interesting developments on Thursday. Unfortunately, none of them had a thing to do with the investigation.

I had just gotten settled in my cubbyhole that morning when Elliot Gilbert stopped by, his face wearing an uncharacteristic frown. "Thought you'd like to hear about Mark."

Mark? Mark who? "Yes, of course I would," I answered, frantically attempting to place the name. "Come sit down."

"They found him," he announced, depositing himself on the visitor's chair.

Found him? And now the cobwebs cleared. This was the case Elliot had wanted me to handle. You know, the one concerning the man who'd disappeared—intentionally or not—abandoning his two little girls and his support payments.

Well, Elliot's expression left no question as to his feelings with regard to the outcome of this matter. In fact, my extremely kind and compassionate landlord appeared to be taking the bad news, whatever it was, even more to heart than he usually did. Then I remembered: This Mark was the son of Elliot's longtime business associate. Under the circumstances, I wasn't anxious to say the next words. But I realized it was expected of me, so I forced them out. "What happened?"

Elliot shook his head sadly. "His father's devastated. And Mark senior—he's the father—tells me his wife—Mark's mother—had to be placed under a doc-tor's care." There were two more shakes of the head before Elliot got around to parting with any of the particulars. "The detectives located the fellow in Flor-ida," he finally revealed. "Fort Lauderdale. He'd run off with his boss's wife—and apparently with a nice chunk of the company funds as well."

I tried to offer something positive. "At least he's all right though. Physically, I mean."

"You know, Dez, I thought at first that this was the only thing that really mattered—his safety. But I was wrong. The amount of suffering this young man has caused? I'm not too certain his family would be expe-riencing that much more pain if he'd turned up dead.

"At any rate, I figured I'd fill you in. He's back in town now, by the way, and I expect that he'll be ar-rested any minute." Elliot got to his feet. "Which is fine with me—except for one thing."

"What's that?"

For the first time since entering the office, he man-aged a grin—albeit a rueful one. "His father wants this firm to represent him."

"Are you going to?"

"I imagine so. We've had plenty of other distin-guished clients, of course—pimps, rapists, murderers, you name it. Yet I'm reluctant to take on Mark Sloane. Why is that, do you suppose?" He answered the question himself. "I think it's because from almost everything I'd heard about his character, I was antici-pating that Mark junior would prove to be one of the good guys."

And with this, Elliot picked up and left.

Instantly my thoughts turned to Miriam—and the good guy that once upon a time I'd presumed *her* to be. Well, I'd gotten past my disillusionment in order to perform my job. And I had no doubt that Elliot—whose appraisal of the fugitive hadn't even been based on personal contact—would do the same. *Still,* I asked myself, *wouldn't life be simpler if more people were what they seemed to be?*

*   *   *

That afternoon Jackie and I had our much-postponed lunch date. Now, I don't know what I expected of this new restaurant she'd been hyping, but it definitely wasn't this.

The single room was small and dark. And so noisy I was certain we'd both wind up hoarse after an hour or so of attempting to communicate with each other. What's more—and you may have trouble believing this—the seating was so cramped that I swear I could smell the garlic on the breath of the woman at the next table.

But the veal piccata *was* supposed to be sensational here. And I was willing to close my eyes—and nasal passages—to a lot of things for that.

Anyway, Jackie had just ordered that very entree, and "Make that two" was poised to leap off my lips when, I have no idea why—maybe it was the first evidence of a sixth sense I've ever displayed—I asked for the linguini with mussels instead.

Jackie didn't comment on the choice, although she did look at me quizzically. The thing is, though, I was every bit as surprised as she was.

As it turned out, Jackie pronounced the veal "superb." "It has a really special flavor," she told me, pushing the dish toward me for a taste. I hadn't yet tried my own food at that point, so I said I'd sample it later. But by the time later came around, Jackie had consumed every last morsel on her plate.

When we left the restaurant, she asked how I'd enjoyed the meal. The truth is, I hadn't. The mussels were on the fishy side. The linguini was limp. And the sauce was Bland with a capital B. But I knew Jackie would be disappointed to hear that, so I answered with what I regard as a kindness lie. "It was very nice."

Thursday's mail was delivered shortly after I got back to my desk. I leafed through it. Along with the usual flood of bills and solicitations was a small white envelope, neatly handprinted in bright blue ink. There was no return address.

Curious, I opened the envelope and unfolded the sheet of paper inside. A ten-dollar bill fluttered onto the desk. The letter itself consisted of two brief sentences explaining that I was being repaid for Tuesday's lunch. The signature read, "With thanks from Brenda."

I was floored. After what I'd been told by that woman in the coffee shop (whom I now labeled a mean-spirited busybody), I had said a firm good-bye to my twenty-three dollars and fifty-two cents, plus tip.

Well, that goes to show how wrong you can be. I felt guilty about my lack of faith in the girl and, at the same time, vindicated for having formed a favorable opinion of her to begin with. I didn't even let myself consider that I'd been short-changed here—Brenda probably had no idea what the meal came to. The important thing was that she'd attempted to honor her debt. And if it flashed through my mind that she might have been a little leery of stiffing a private investigator—particularly one who owned a gun—I quickly banished the thought, preferring to give both Brenda and my judgment the benefit of the doubt.

Later, at home, I began to regret the hours I hadn't devoted to work that afternoon. Instead, to fill up my time, I'd paid every bill marked "second notice," chatted on the phone for close to an hour with my neighbor Harriet, and then dragged out my old standby the nail-polish bottle. I vowed to make up for my dereliction by picking over every word of my notes tomorrow.

Still, it wasn't as if I'd committed a capital offense, I decided. I mean, even you-know-Who gave Himself a day off.

Chapter Thirty-three

I was awakened by the phone on Friday. I opened one eye to check the clock: six-thirty. *Six-thirty?*

"Dez?" She sounded so unlike herself that it was a second or two before I recognized that this was Jackie. "I just wanted to know how you feel," she said in this weak little voice.

"I'm fine." And now fully conscious and alarmed, I demanded, "Why? What's wrong?"

"I've got food poisoning."

"Oh, no! You're sure it's not just an upset stomach?"

"You can *tell* the difference." Even in this debilitated state Jackie managed to get her irritation across.

"You're right. What do you think caused it?"

"Since you seem to be okay, that eliminates the zabaglione." (Which had been the dessert of choice for us both.) "So it could only be that damn veal."

"Are you sure? What did you have for dinner last night?"

"Only a salad," she croaked.

"Listen, can I get you anything? I could come over and—"

"Thanks, but I don't need a thing. *Uh-oh.* I can't talk anymore."

"I hope you—"

But Jackie was gone, leaving me to be grateful to the Fates—or whatever it was that had prompted me to order those delicious mussels.

* * *

True to the promise I'd made myself yesterday, practically the instant I got to the office that morning I took out Miriam Weiden's file. I then spent so many hours going through it that by the end of the day I was bleary-eyed. Either Miriam's murderer had been too clever to leave a clue of any kind, or I was too obtuse to appreciate it.

At seven-thirty Pat Martucci and I met at a Chinese restaurant in the East Thirties. We arrived at the entrance at precisely the same time. In order to accomplish a little mutual cheek bussing, I stood on tiptoe while Pat bent way, *way* down. "One of these days you're going to give me a broken back," she remarked, grinning. She was, I noted, looking particularly attractive tonight—maybe it was the haircut. Anyway I've always thought that Pat, who's big and blonde and robust, would make the perfect Wagnerian heroine. Provided, of course, you could find the right person to dub over her froglike singing voice.

It was while we were gorging ourselves on dim sum that Pat dropped her bombshell. "Burton and I have been talking about getting married."

Now, every one of Pat's legal mates had eventually revealed himself to be an A-One louse. Ditto her significant others, of which she'd had many, since she was constantly falling instantly, passionately, and very temporarily in love. (Pre-Burton, of course.) To give you an idea of the caliber of the men who used to slither in and out of her life, there was a phony baron; a convicted forger; a widower whose wife, it turned out, was still living—*and* with the "bereaved" husband; even a fellow we began to suspect could be a serial killer (but who was more likely just a run-of-the-mill sicko). At any rate, Pat finally came to recognize that it was far less traumatic to terminate a soured relationship in an apartment or even the backseat of a car than in a divorce court. And considering her track record, I had to agree that her decision not to tie the knot again was probably a sound one.

Nevertheless, on hearing her news, I impulsively shot out of my chair. "O-h-h, Pat!" I exclaimed, rushing over to hug her.

"I'll bet you're surprised, huh?" she said as soon as I was back in seat.

"I don't know. Maybe a little."

"I'd never consider it if Burton weren't such a prince. And, don't forget, it's not as if we just met, either. We've been together for over two years." She looked at me beseechingly then. "So? Do you approve?"

Well, Burton Wizniak was a very nice person—as far as I could determine, anyway. And he really did appear to be crazy about Pat. In fact, from the time they met, I'd pegged him as being in a different league than his predecessors. Still, while I was truly excited for my friend, in the minute or so since the announcement, my reservations about her making anything permanent had resurfaced. I mean, maybe that black cloud that once seemed to hover over Pat's head—as far as men were concerned, that is—might not have entirely dissipated. Which is why I hedged a bit. "I think it's likely you have yourself a winner here."

This was good enough for Pat. "I'm very glad you feel that way. My mother's coming to visit in April, and I said to Burton that I thought it might be a good idea if we got married before then. It would ease my conscience a little."

"I don't follow you."

"Two years ago I told my mother that we'd eloped. So this way it wouldn't be as though I lied. I was just, you know, slightly premature."

I do like the way Pat thinks, don't you?

On Saturday I turned down a bowling invitation from Ellen, preferring to clean the apartment. Which is a pretty fair indication of how keen I am on bowling. Sometime after that I called to check on Jackie, who sounded about ready to pick out a burial plot.

She rejected my latest offer to come over and minister to her. All she wanted was to sleep, she said.

On Sunday I spoke to Jackie again, who was now feeling well enough to recognize that her present condition might not prove fatal after all. Then I proceeded to go through the Weiden file for what felt like the hundredth time—with the usual success. I was beginning to regard it as a form of self-punishment.

Monday was Presidents' Day. And I had made up my mind to do nothing whatsoever. I treated myself to a few extra hours of sleep that morning, and at around twelve-thirty I went down for the mail.

Harriet and Steve Gould were just about to enter the elevator when I stepped out into the lobby.

"Was the mailman here yet?" I asked.

Steve was the one who responded. "No mail today, Dez. It's a federal holiday, remember?"

I turned around and rode back upstairs with the Goulds, never dreaming I was now only minutes away from solving Miriam Weiden's murder.

Chapter Thirty-four

All I can say is, thank God for Presidents' Day.

Now, I might eventually have arrived at the truth without any help from George and Abe. But I can never be certain of that.

At any rate, as soon as I was back in the apartment I thought I'd fix myself some lunch. I had just opened the refrigerator to check on the possibilities when, at long last, the light went on. And I'm not talking about the one in the refrigerator.

The thing is, I'd been aware all along about the birthday of Martin Luther King, Jr. being celebrated the day before Miriam died. (Hadn't Deena groused that it had been impossible to study for her test because the kids who lived above Todd were making such a racket? And hadn't she explained that they were home from school because of the holiday?)

But what had I done with this vital piece of information? Nothing, that's what.

At that moment I seriously considered slamming my head against the wall. How could I have failed to realize that there would have been no regular mail delivery that Monday?

You see what I'm getting at, don't you?

Philip Chance had lied through his teeth about receiving that letter from Miriam.

And in a flash I understood why.

I reached for a chair. And if I were a drinking woman, I'd have reached for a scotch or a bourbon as well. The impact of suddenly identifying Miriam's killer after all these weeks actually stunned me.

I sat there at the kitchen table for maybe five, ten minutes, reflecting on my new-found knowledge. The problem was that while I was now firmly convinced that Chance was my guy, persuading the authorities of this was a whole other story. I could just picture going to those two detectives assigned to the case and accusing him of the murder—with my only proof against the man being that he'd told me a fib about some letter. Pu-leeze. The cops would have laughed themselves silly.

But I had to do *something*.

I went to the phone.

Philip sounded sincere in his regret that he wasn't able to see me today. He hoped I'd forgive him, but he was busy getting together this income-tax material for his accountant. He could, however, stop in at my office tomorrow.

"What I need to speak to you about can't wait, Philip. Really," I informed him. Which it couldn't. By then I was positively bursting to hear what he'd have to say when I confronted him.

"We-ell . . ." He was on the brink of weakening— curiosity, I've discovered, can be a powerful persuader—so I closed in for the kill. "I think you'll find it to your advantage to talk to me. I can drive up to Connecticut this afternoon."

He barely hesitated. "All right. But I'd rather not do this in my home."

That made two of us. I certainly preferred a public place, even though it wasn't too likely that the man would want my blood messing up his nice carpeting. (I was reasonably sure that the Chances had nothing *but* nice carpeting.) "Fine. Just tell me where you'd like to meet."

"There's this restaurant here in town—Shorty's. I'll give you the directions. Four o'clock okay?"

"Perfect."

As soon as we finished talking, I dug out my tape

recorder. It was, of course, doubtful that I could manipulate Philip into incriminating himself. And it was equally improbable that he'd reveal something that might lead to the gathering of further evidence—*hard* evidence—against him. Still, you never know, do you? I shoved the tape recorder into my handbag.

Then I went into the bedroom and got my thirty-two out of my panty drawer. I tensed up just looking at the thing. But it was a precaution I felt I should take. (Either I was starting to get smarter or more cowardly.) The gun went into my handbag, too—along with the silent prayer that I wouldn't have cause to use it.

During the drive out to Connecticut I aimed a few sweet little expletives at myself for not having spotted a clue that practically stood up and saluted me. But a short while afterward I decided to be charitable. Okay, so it took me a while to arrive at the truth. But I was there now, wasn't I?

I suppose I should explain here that on some level I recognized that Philip might have invented that story about being summoned by Miriam simply because it made him appear less guilty—and not because he'd actually killed her. After all, it was possible he'd wanted to see her for a reason he didn't care to share with me. That's not what my gut told me, though. And I refused to acknowledge that my gut had, on occasion, proved to be less than reliable.

Which turned out okay, since it was about to receive a little help.

Immersing myself in some heavy-duty thinking, I began to recall these vague notions I'd had the day I questioned Philip, thoughts that were only now starting to come together. (It's funny how once you're convinced you're on the right track, so many odd bits and pieces fall into place.)

The first thing that occurred to me was that when I'd asked Philip if his wife knew anything about his fling with Miriam, there was a pronounced hesitation before he came out with his denial. And later on in our conversation he'd been absolutely adamant in his insistence that Nina had no inkling of the affair—almost as if he was protesting *too* much. In retrospect, I had the strong feeling that both these responses had been carefully calculated to make me suspect that he feared Nina *had* disposed of her rival.

And wasn't it Philip who brought up the alternative theories that the incident at the lake last summer—which, of course, took place before he'd so much as laid eyes on Miriam—was (a) the handiwork of someone other than the eventual murderer or (b) not really a bona fide attempt on the victim's life at all? And didn't either concept open up the possibility that he or Nina might have been the one to flavor Miriam's crème de menthe with a dash or two of tubocurarine chloride? But then after this Philip had engaged in some very fancy footwork by injecting that skirt business—this "revelation" only serving to take *him* off the hook. Listen, the man had even managed to undermine his wife's alibi for that Tuesday evening by referring to her mother as "nutty"—something like that, anyway.

Also, maybe you'll accuse me of total paranoia, but I seriously doubted that Chance's mention of Nina's being a Scorpio had been that casual. And I have to say that I resented this sneaky attempt to make use of my sign in that manner. I mean, we Scorpios may not choose to turn the other cheek after we've been kicked in the teeth (and I would put fooling around with one's husband in this category, wouldn't you?), but this doesn't mean we go around poisoning everyone who's done us dirty. Take me, for example. Although it's true that when somebody's treated me like garbage, I'm not apt to forgive—and less likely to forget—I've never, not once, extracted vengeance. (Unless you regard fervently praying that a building falls on the despicable creature as a form of payback.)

At any rate, I was by this point all but certain that during our little go-round, Philip Chance hadn't been restricting his efforts to exonerating himself. While he was at it, he also seemed to have taken some pains to frame his spouse.

As to the why, I chewed that over for quite some time. And I finally remembered what Nina had told me about Philip's attachment to his sons. Naturally, what I'm about to propose is sheer speculation. But when you consider it for a bit, it *does* make sense.

Okay. Suppose that Philip, for one reason or another, decided he wanted out of the marriage. Being an unregenerate "player," it's not improbable he'd even found himself another sweetie—only this lady was someone with whom he was actually thinking of making things permanent. Well, a divorce would mean that, at best, he'd be awarded only partial custody of the boys. However, if their mother should wind up in Bedford Hills Correctional Facility . . .

Now, I believe I know what's on your mind. If it was Philip's intention to pin the crime on Nina, he hadn't done a very thorough job of it. But it was conceivable he was providing the police with something more convincing than anything he'd given me. Plus, there was also the possibility that his best stuff was being held in abeyance.

Anyhow, I said to myself, *No matter how anxious Philip was to split with his wife, if he were an innocent man would he have plotted against her like this?*

"Uh-uh, I just don't see it," I answered out loud as I pulled up in front of Shorty's.

A large uninviting restaurant-cum-gin mill, Shorty's was located in the part of New Haven known as "over the hill," a far less affluent section of the city than the one in which Philip and Nina Chance hung their hats.

The instant I opened the door I was assaulted by the intermingling aromas of grease and stale beer. And to make it still more appetizing, the place was practically pleading for a makeover. The furniture was decrepit, the wood floors were creaky and scarred, and the paint was peeling off the grungy pale gray walls (which I suspected had actually been white maybe twenty years back).

Sitting on the torn vinyl stools at the long bar just inside the entrance were a couple of elderly men in overalls, both displaying two or three days' worth of facial stubble. The only other occupied stool had been laid claim to by a chunky frizzed-out blonde in black stockings and red four-inch heels. If this was a sampling of Shorty's patrons, I figured it was highly unlikely Philip Chance would run into anyone he knew here—and that he'd figured the same thing. In fact, I wondered at his being familiar with an establishment like this to begin with.

The dining room beyond the bar area was deserted, except for a man with a newspaper plastered up against his face and Philip, who was seated at a table in the rear. He was wearing a Harris tweed jacket, a white shirt, and a brown-and-beige striped tie—along with that almost irresistible Cary Grantish face. *What a shame to waste all that gorgeousness on such murdering scum!*

Politely getting to his feet, Chance helped me off with my coat, after which he pulled out one of the wooden chairs for me. (I hoped the damn thing wouldn't give me splinters.) When he went to hang the coat on the hook behind him, I reached into my handbag and turned on my tape recorder.

We spent a couple of minutes pretending to be interested in each other's health and general well-being. And following this—as I feared he would—Philip asked what I'd have to eat.

Now that we were so much closer to the kitchen, the grease odor was stronger than ever. My stomach was starting to feel a little queasy, but I forced myself to ignore it. After all, I couldn't just sit there, could I? I settled on a ham and Swiss on rye and a ginger ale. I mean, what could they do to ham and Swiss?

Obviously more adventurous—or foolhardy—than I am, Philip ordered a hot roast beef sandwich—with French fries, yet—and coffee.

And then it was time. Dropping most of the civility from my tone, I said, "Let's just get down to it, okay?"

Philip responded with an affable, "Please."

"I'll tell you what I know. Which is that you didn't receive any correspondence from Miriam the day before she died."

If he was taken aback it didn't show. "Of course I did."

"You couldn't have. It was a federal holiday—Martin Luther King Day."

Well, I couldn't be certain if Philip had been unaware of the holiday itself when he'd fed me that baloney about the letter, or if he just hadn't realized there were no mail deliveries that Monday. But with his two kids off from school, odds are it was the latter. In any event this, at least, caught him off guard.

But I'll say one thing for the man: He recovered quickly. "There may not have been any regular mail, but there *was* express mail."

"Sorry, but that won't work. You mentioned seeing the postman leave the letter in the box. In case you're not aware of it, you have to sign for express mail."

Philip was instantly ready with an explanation—although hardly a convincing one. Not as far as I was concerned, anyway. "I suppose I must have been a little confused, Desiree," he said apologetically. "When we last spoke, you and I, Miriam hadn't been dead for very long, and I was still pretty shaken up. Frankly, I don't recall discussing how her note came to me, but if you say I mentioned a mailbox, then I probably did. Now that I think about it, though, it was the *previous* time Miriam wrote to me that I went outside to pick up the mail. On the day before she died, the postman came to the door."

At this moment the waiter presented us with our food. He didn't *exactly* slam everything down, but about a third of my ginger ale sloshed onto the table, while a sizable portion of Philip's coffee wound up in his saucer.

Once the fellow was out of earshot, Philip put to

me, "Look, why would I lie to you about a thing like that?"

"You wanted me to think it was Miriam who initiated that meeting."

"Wouldn't it have been simpler to tell you that she *called* me?"

"That could be verified by the telephone records." *As you, you weasel, well know,* I stuck in silently. "Most likely you even concocted that story about warning her never to call you at the house. Anyhow, *you* were the one who got in touch with *Miriam,* and I have no doubt it was from an outside phone. She had no qualms about seeing you for lunch, of course, because you weren't the person she feared. At any rate, I know she was determined to resume your relationship. And my sense is that your purpose in arranging for this get-together was to dissuade her from carrying out a threat to cause trouble if you refused to start playing house again. But then, when you couldn't make any headway . . ." I concluded with an elaborate shrug.

"Threat? There was never any threat. Besides, I wasn't vulnerable to anything like that." And now Philip attempted to eliminate any possible motive he might have had for the crime by completely dismantling the perfect marriage he'd so painstakingly constructed for himself. "Listen, Desiree, I have to confess that I wasn't entirely honest with you that last time. The truth is, the involvement with Miriam—well, I hate like hell to admit it, but I'd cheated on Nina before. Apparently I can't seem to help myself, although I realize that's no excuse." He flashed that guilty-little-boy smile he evidently dragged out whenever he found himself in an indefensible position. "I've even considered consulting a professional about my problem. But never mind about that. What's important is that Nina's always known about my, uh, weakness. And this being the case, why in heaven's name would I commit murder to prevent Miriam from tattling to her?"

"Look, when Erna—Miriam's secretary—told me she'd overheard the victim on the phone attempting to strongarm you into getting back with her, I initially figured Miriam must have threatened to reveal this sole indiscretion of yours to your wife. Then later, when I learned about your penchant for bedhopping—*and* that your spouse was well aware of it—I considered that you might have been afraid this affair with Miriam could turn out to be one affair too many for Nina to swallow. It's finally dawned on me, though, that it probably wasn't your marriage that was in jeopardy at all; it was your career. You yourself said that some of the leads you'd gotten from Miriam were still pending. Well, with a few words to those potential employers, she could have closed the door on whatever opportunities she'd made available to you. Not only that, but it would have been simple enough for someone like Miriam to see to it her message got around. So," I concluded, "we're talking about the possibility of Miriam Weiden's putting the kibosh on your entire professional future."

"You've got the wrong lady," Philip protested. "Miriam wasn't like that—not with me, anyway. I told you. She was one of the finest women I'd ever known. I have no idea what it was that Erna heard—or thought she heard. But if Miriam *was* threatening someone, for whatever reason, I can assure you that it wasn't me."

I was becoming increasingly frustrated. To buy myself some thinking time, I nibbled on my sandwich. The bread was stale. Then I had a sip of the ginger ale. It was flat. Philip took a bite of his roast beef, made a face, and pushed away the plate. He ignored the coffee. Which was probably wise.

"I don't believe Miriam ever told you she'd gotten a glimpse of a skirt that day at the school, either," I brought up at his juncture. "It was your way of diverting suspicion from yourself."

"You're wrong," Philip corrected pleasantly enough.

"In fact, who knows if she spoke to you at all about those attempts on her life during that lunch?"

"So how did I find out about them?"

"She could have mentioned the Coral Lake incident at any time in your relationship. And as to the ladder thing . . ." I left it to my smirk to convey what was only too apparent.

Philip gazed at me somberly. "I didn't heave any ladder at Miriam. And I didn't poison her. I never even heard of this . . . this tubocurarine chloride until the police told me about it. I wish I could convince you of that, Desiree." At this moment he looked so misunderstood, so appealing that it was necessary to give myself a mental pinch as a reminder that I was dealing with a murderer here. "And anyway," he added, "are you saying that when I couldn't get Miriam to see things my way, I gulped down my espresso, then rushed right out and picked up some poison?"

"Oh, no, you were prepared for that contingency. You had it with you—to administer later, in private, if it should turn out to be necessary."

"Well, I'm certainly efficient, aren't I?" Philip retorted, sarcasm entering his voice for the first time. He sat back in his chair. "Look, we don't seem to be getting anywhere, so unless you have any more accusations or you want to finish that"—he eyed my plate with distaste—"why don't we call it a day?"

"Yes, why don't we?" Disgusted, I stared down at the floor at my handbag, where the tape recorder continued to whir away—for all the good *that* was doing.

Hold it! It was going to be okay. Because just then that light in my head went on again. And I realized what I had to do.

I made a pretext of checking my watch. "Listen," I said to Philip, "can you wait a couple of minutes? I was supposed to make a telephone call about a half hour ago, and I'd better not postpone it any longer. And after that I'll need you to tell me how to find my way home—if you don't mind, that is."

"No, Desiree, I don't mind," Philip answered, even

managing a tolerant smile. *I ask you, is this man a treasure—or what?*

I retrieved my bag and headed for the phone booth a few feet behind Philip. Sure enough, there were a couple of directories inside the booth. And—surprise!—they were actually current. Riffling through the Yellow Pages, I found the heading I was looking for. I glanced around surreptitiously, gave one quick, well-executed rip, and jammed the entire section into my bag. And now, in case Philip should turn in my direction, I lifted the telephone receiver and pretended to hold a meaningful conversation.

As soon as I returned to the table, Philip provided me with instructions on getting back to Manhattan. Following which I allowed him to pay the tab. (Since he hadn't done me the favor of choking on his roast beef, this was the least he could do.) These things attended to, the ever-chivalrous Philip Chance helped me on with my coat. He even saw me to my car.

I was about to put my key in the lock when he placed his hand over mine to delay me. "I hope that after you've had an opportunity to think about this some more," he said earnestly, "you'll come to see that you're making too much of this mailbox business. I misspoke, sure. But it was an honest mistake, the result of a memory that was clouded by grief. Can't you understand that?" And when I didn't immediately respond: "I swear to you, Desiree, on my mother's grave"—I came close to gagging at this—"I didn't kill Miriam. In fact, there are times I still wake up in the middle of the night, close to tears at the realization that someone took the life of that wonderful lady."

Philip's eyes were moist now, and he'd concluded his piece with such wrenching emotion that I found I almost believed him.

Almost.

Chapter Thirty-five

"I swear to you on my mother's grave!"

He didn't really say that, did he? I mean, it was such a cliché! And even though I gave Philip Chance a subbasement rating on character, I never considered him totally lacking in smarts. So I'd have expected him to come up with something a shade more original than that.

Anyway, driving through the streets of New Haven en route to picking up I-95, I experienced a great sense of relief. It was one thing to identify the murderer; it was still another to be able to lay the homicide on his doorstep. But I had walked out of Shorty's confident I could do exactly that.

And while I was in this positive mode I even found a way to foist off some of the blame for my overlooking a clue that had been staring me in the face for so long. Let's not forget that I'd been lied to up the wazoo—and I mean by *everybody*. And most of these lies had to do with the personal qualities of the deceased, which as Hercule could have told you, is an absolutely crucial factor in solving a murder.

What I'm getting at is that if I hadn't been so preoccupied with sorting out the truth about Miriam, it's very possible—hey, let's say *probable*—that my mind might have been freer to concentrate on other aspects of the investigation. (At least, this is what I decided that evening. And to this day I'm trying to convince myself it's a fact.)

At any rate, just as I had on the trip up here, I was

soon occupied with some productive ruminating, this time satisfying myself as to the reasons I'd been misled.

I had understood almost at once—before she'd made any admissions at all—why my own client hadn't been exactly forthcoming with me. Norma Davis seemed to regard protecting a daughter's image as the number-one priority of motherhood. This became clearer still, of course, when I learned that this particular mother was wracked with guilt.

But mulling things over now, I also managed to fathom the underlying cause of Erna's whitewashed depiction of Miriam. Naturally, I couldn't swear to it on a stack of bibles, but I was pretty positive that the secretary had been deceiving me because she feared Deena had committed the murder. And apparently, by insisting that the victim was such a paragon, Erna had hoped to obliterate any motive Deena might have had for the crime. Bolstering that conclusion was the fact that when I'd handed her the opportunity to cast suspicion on someone other than the girl—specifically Philip—Erna was finally willing to concede that Miriam had been a flawed human being. A woman who urged her lover to reconsider their breakup—*or else*.

As to Deena, she—

Damn! It was still there. I had just made a right turn. And that light-colored car I'd casually noted in my rearview mirror about ten blocks back did the same. I felt a bit uneasy. Philip Chance drove a light-colored car.

Well, big deal, piped up this sensible little voice inside me. *So did millions of other people.*

True. But the car had been there, directly in back of me, for quite a while now.

Never mind. Philip had no reason to tail me. And certainly no reason to harm me. After all, what evidence did I have against him?

Then suddenly: CACHOONG! The clash of metal on metal exploded in my head.

My body lurched forward. The steering wheel cut

into my midsection, knocking the wind out of me. My hands shot up in the air. My foot slid off the gas pedal. *That bastard—whoever he or she was—had just rear-ended me!*

On its own now, the car careened to the left. I regained control barely in time to avoid colliding with an oncoming panel truck. After which, with the sound of the impact still reverberating in my ears, I tried to convince myself the ramming had been an accident. Being part ostrich, I might have managed it, too. *Only that's when he rear-ended me again!*

In spite of its being about eighty degrees inside my Chevy, all at once I was ice-cold. *What do I do now?* I demanded frantically as I prepared for another jolt.

But I hadn't a clue how to handle this; my brain had gone numb.

Then in the distance I heard the wail of a siren. And it was getting louder and louder. Abruptly, the attack car pulled out from behind me and sped past, taking the corner ahead on two wheels. It happened so quickly—and I was so shaken—that I didn't catch so much as a glimpse of the driver.

Was it a teenager fooling around? A would-be car-jacker? Or could it have been Philip Chance? I swallowed hard—twice. Following which I drove over to the curb and parked.

It didn't occur to me that this was a terrible neighborhood. (Predictably, I'd totally forgotten that I was in the company of my trusty thirty-two.) It didn't dawn on me, either, that the beige car might return. The only thought I had was that my nerves were too frazzled for me to even attempt the trip home just now.

Moments after this, that police car zoomed by, and I blessed it for saving me from I-didn't-know-what at the hands of I-didn't-know-who. Then I rested my forehead against the steering wheel, and for the next ten minutes I remained where I was, practically immobile. At last I pronounced myself, if not exactly calm, at least composed enough to make it into Manhattan.

*   *   *

Hours later, as I lay in bed coping with another one of my sleepless nights, I decided that it was very likely Philip in that car, engaging in some gentle persuasion to induce me to abandon my investigation of him. In other words, the man had been out to scare the hell out of me.

But, of course, I didn't really *know*. What's more it's extremely doubtful that I ever will.

Anyway, whether or not Philip was responsible for this evening's little adventure, of one thing I was certain: He was to blame for Miriam Weiden's death.

And I was about to prove it.

Chapter Thirty-six

Since I didn't drop off until the wee hours—it was three a.m. when I last peeked at the clock—dragging myself out of bed Tuesday morning was a job and a half. And I didn't exactly move at the speed of sound as I was getting ready for work, either. So it wasn't until after ten that I finally made it to the office.

Now, I hadn't phoned Jackie to let her know I'd be late. Which wasn't as courageous as you might think. I figured there was an excellent chance she wouldn't be in this morning. But she *was* in, looking all wrung out.

To give you an idea of her weakened condition, she didn't acknowledge my tardy arrival with a scowl. She didn't even check her watch. She simply said, "Hi, Dez," accompanying this with a wan little smile. I swear, if I hadn't known about the food poisoning, I'd have sworn an alien being had taken possession of poor Jackie's body.

"How do you feel?" I asked.

"Not too great."

"Maybe you should have stayed home another day or two."

"No, I'd feel just as lousy there. Oh, this is for you." She handed me a message slip. Then before I had a chance to so much as glance at it, Jackie proceeded to recite everything she'd jotted down practically verbatim. "Your client phoned. She said it was nothing important. You don't have to get back to her; she's going to be out most of the day anyway. She'll probably give you a ring when she comes home."

I suppressed a smile. "Thanks, Jackie," I threw out over my shoulder as I hurried down the hall to my cubbyhole.

I had two calls to make this morning. Two very important calls.

I started with my friend Felicia. Let me tell you a little about Felicia. She works in the circulation department of *Business Today,* and she is positively the most accomplished liar I know. Which is definitely intended as a compliment. I mean, the woman is an absolutely *brilliant* dissembler. Give her a little time, and she could make you believe the earth is flat.

She greeted me warmly. And then, since we hadn't spoken in a couple of months, we played catch-up for about five minutes. After which I laid out my request, providing her with a short bio of Philip Chance.

"Oh, sure," Felicia informed me happily. "I can find a way to get you this geek's picture. In fact, I'm looking forward to it." (Being overqualified for her job, Felicia is terribly bored at the magazine. So whenever I've asked for a favor like this she acts as if I'm the one doing something for *her.*)

Anyhow, once everything was set with Felicia, I dialed another old friend.

Harry Burgess is a semi-retired PI from Fort Lee, New Jersey, who has helped me out on a number of occasions. And he's always thrilled to do it. Not so much for the money, either, but because it's an escape from these keep-Harry-occupied projects his wife is constantly dreaming up for him. (Maybe she could conjure up a little task for Felicia one of these days.) He agreed to do some legwork for me almost before the proposition left my mouth.

"Obviously, Chance had to get the drug from somewhere," I said once I'd presented Harry with a brief summary of the case. "But how tough would it be for him to lay hands on one of his wife's prescription pads, write up an order for tubocurarine chloride, and forge her signature?"

Harry answered the rhetorical question with a wry, "Not very." And a second later: "What did you say was the name of that stuff again?"

"Tubocurarine chloride."

"Never heard of it."

"He probably came across it in one of his wife's medical books," I responded tersely. "But listen, the problem is, I haven't a clue where he would have had the prescription filled."

"Not right down the block, I bet," Harry offered.

"That's how I figure it, too. At any rate, I was able to get ahold of a New Haven Yellow Pages" (I didn't mention that I'd defaced Shorty's property in the process), "which also includes a bunch of suburbs—like North Haven, East Haven, West Haven, Branford, and I don't even remember what else. I did a quick count, and there seems to be close to seventy-five pharmacies listed. If I tried to canvass all of them on my own, I'd be ready for Social Security by the time I finished. On top of that, I can't even be certain Chance took the prescription to a store in that area— although I'm praying real hard that he did. If not, though, we'll eventually have to expand our efforts to other parts of Connecticut. Maybe even to Manhattan."

"And Vermont and Massachusetts," Harry chimed in to my dismay.

"I refuse to even consider anything like that at this stage. But I'll tell you one thing: I intend to get that bastard, Harry. Whatever it takes."

My old friend chuckled. "Knowing you, Dez, I'm not surprised to hear that."

I informed Harry that I'd fax him a copy of the Yellow Pages as soon as we were through making our plans. Also, that he'd be receiving a photo of the perp within the next few days.

And then we proceeded to divvy up the territory in

a manner that made sense geographically. As it turned out—and for no particular reason—I wound up with the towns west of New Haven, with Harry to check out those east of the city. The towns to the north we parceled out between us according to the number of pharmacies in each. As for New Haven itself, I'd opted to leave it for last—that is, if we didn't have any luck anywhere else. My reasoning—and you're going to think I'm nuts—had to do with Shorty's. You see, I figured that if Philip considered that neighborhood as sufficiently out-of-the-way for our little rendezvous, the same might be true when it came to his selecting a drugstore. What I'm trying to say is that I was holding the area in reserve. You know, as kind of my ace in the hole.

I was about to end the conversation when Harry put in, "Geez, it's been good talking to you again, Dez. And thanks for thinking of me for this thing. You saved my life."

"You wouldn't be exaggerating, would you, Harry?"

"Listen, wanna guess what Midge has in mind for me now?" He spared me the effort. "A mural."

"A *what*?"

"She wants me to paint a friggin' mural on the friggin' dining room wall."

"You're kidding."

"I am, huh? I took an art course a couple months ago—mostly so I wouldn't get stuck with another of those cockamamie chores of hers. So what happens? She decides I'm a friggin' Michelangelo!"

I couldn't offer much in the way of sympathy. I was too busy laughing.

It was an unusually nice day, and I intended to spend a good part of my lunch break window-shopping—with, I vowed to myself, the emphasis on "window." I had just gotten into my coat when the phone rang.

It was an obviously smug Felicia, reporting in. "Hi, I did you proud, if I say so myself."

"What happened?"

"You've heard me mention my sister Angelica, right?"

"I don't think so."

"It doesn't matter. Anyway, Angelica's husband has a cousin who's married to a guy who owns an executive search firm—Executive Decisions, it's called. So I telephoned this Philip Chance and said that I was with Executive Decisions and that someone had recommended I get in contact with him. He—"

"Didn't he ask who the someone was?"

"Sure, but I told him I didn't have the information right in front of me and that I'd get back to him later if he liked. I made it sound like he was being pretty anal, though," Felicia tittered, "so he said not to bother. At any rate, I claimed there were a couple of top corporations that I thought might be interested in a person with his qualifications—but, naturally, I wasn't free to give out any company names at this point. I said that before I could even make the proper inquiries I'd need some copies of his résumé—along with a few photos, of course. I informed him I required eight by tens. Oh, and I convinced him that it would be best to get these things off to me *instantly*."

Well, what did I tell you? The woman has an absolute gift! "You're wonderful, Felicia," I gushed.

She took the well-deserved compliment in stride. "The only problem I had was with Duane, my brother-in-law's cousin's husband. He gave me a hard time when I said that I'd be receiving a package at his place—the guy's a real prig—but eventually I managed to satisfy him that I wasn't involved in trying to overthrow the government or anything. At any rate, Chance will be FedExing the stuff to Duane's office today, and the receptionist over there promised to messenger the package to you immediately on receipt. You should have those pictures sometime tomorrow."

I thanked Felicia effusively. Then I let her know I owed her a dinner. A special dinner. "As soon as this is over, we have a date at the Four Seasons."

Felicia quickly amended the offer. "Make it Le Cirque."

I went to see my client that evening.

She cried—real tears again—on hearing that I'd finally unmasked Miriam's killer. Then a few minutes later she sat silently listening to my explanation, her lips pressed tightly together, her back ramrod straight, and her hands clenched into tight little fists.

When I was through she asked anxiously, "But you don't think you have enough evidence against him?"

"Not yet."

"I'm sure I don't have to tell you this, but I don't care how long it takes. Just find the proof you need." For an instant her voice was bitter. "He has to pay for what he did to Miriam."

"He will, Mrs. Davis."

"Thank you. Thank you for everything. I realize I didn't always make your job easy for you, and I'm sorry for that, but . . ." The moist eyes and the small, rueful smile both pleaded for understanding.

"It's all right. I can appreciate how you felt."

I was about to get to my feet when Mrs. Davis murmured, "First my husband, then my Ruth, then Miriam—all the people I loved have been taken from me. All but Deena. I thank God every night, Desiree, that I have that wonderful child in my life."

Miriam's miserable little secret flashed through my mind now. And I was more convinced than ever that the knowledge that Deena was in reality her own flesh and blood would, to some degree, ease Norma Davis's grief. Not only that, but the girl herself had a right to the truth, didn't she?

At that moment I promised myself that if Erna didn't reveal the circumstances of Deena's birth, I would.

Chapter Thirty-seven

Now, I had no idea how long it would take to track down the pharmacy at which Philip Chance had acquired his murder weapon. But I certainly didn't have any illusions about succeeding one-two-three. (The thought that I might strike out completely had been barred from my head.) Anyhow—wouldn't you know it?—on Wednesday I was offered a couple of new cases, the first by an insurance company and the second by Elliot Gilbert again. I mean, how's that for timing? Here I am, involved in this intense and, most likely, protracted canvassing thing, and I get not one, but two offers—and on the same day, too. I wanted to cut out my liver at having to turn them both down. But the last thing I needed was the added pressure of other commitments staring me in the face.

At any rate, that afternoon a messenger delivered an envelope containing a small supply of résumés and three eight-by-ten head shots of Philip Chance. I immediately FedExed one of the photos to Harry.

Then early Thursday morning I set off for Connecticut.

I'd elected to start with West Haven—which borders directly on New Haven. From there I would keep working my way farther west.

On arriving in the town, I stopped to ask directions to the first pharmacy on my list. A teenager with a spiked purple hairdo steered me back toward the highway. Then later an old woman had me riding around in a circle.

But my irritation dissipated when I eventually pulled up in front of the store and took stock of the neighborhood. It wasn't that different from the Shorty's location. In other words, it was definitely on the seedy side. A fine choice for an upper-crust killer who wanted to avoid meeting up with any of his acquaintances.

There were two pharmacists behind the counter—a middle-aged male and a somewhat younger female.

Well, while I was confident that Philip Chance's movie starish appearance would make an impression even on men—the majority of them, at least—I couldn't see *any* lady with a heterosexual bent failing to recall that face. (My nutso secretary Jackie possibly excepted.)

Which is why, although the man was unoccupied at this moment, I stood lurking—that's really the only way to describe it—a few yards away from the counter, biding my time until his feminine counterpart was free. Then, grabbing Chance's photograph out of my attaché case, I wasted no time in approaching her.

"I wonder if you could spare me a minute."

"I suppose so," the woman responded cautiously. "How can I help you?"

I held out the picture. "Would you happen to recognize him? He was probably in here a little over a month ago. But it might have been even earlier."

She barely glanced at my offering. "Over a month ago? Listen, we get a lot of customers in this store. I can't be expected to—"

"Please look again. It's important." I brought the photo within six inches of her face, so it was difficult for her *not* to oblige me. But after lingering over the likeness longer than I thought necessary, she shook her head.

"He's not familiar to you, I gather."

"No, he isn't."

I persisted. "You're sure?"

"A hundred percent positive."

"Are you and that gentleman over there the only pharmacists who work here?" I inquired.

"There's also Wanda, but she's out with the flu. And Renaldo—he gets in at three. But this morning it's just Milt and me."

Okay, I would have to come by again, that's all. And, in the meantime, there was still Milt. In spite of his not being the preferred gender, I showed him the head shot.

"Uh-uh," he said firmly. "What's this about, anyway?"

"We believe this man might have been involved in a serious criminal matter about a month ago."

"We?"

"I'm a detective," I informed him, knowing what he'd think and feeling no shame at all for allowing him to think it.

"I'm sorry I can't be of help to you, Detective. But I'm fairly certain I've never seen that fellow before."

I wasn't ready to quit yet. "He would have had a prescription for tubocurarine chloride," I said hopefully.

"Nope. And I'd remember if I got an order for that." And now he either got a twitch in his eye or he winked at me. "It's not exactly a best-seller here."

I had a heartening thought then: Philip Chance just might have outsmarted himself. What I'm saying is that while the exotic nature of the drug made it less apt to be detected in an autopsy, it was also more likely to stick in the mind of the dispensing pharmacist.

"But, of course," Milt continued, "one of the other pharmacists could have filled the prescription. I'll check it out on the computer for you if you can hang in for a little while. I have to give Ginger a hand now." Milt gestured toward the seven or eight people presently awaiting service, who seemed to have suddenly materialized en masse.

I told him I'd be glad to stick around, and it wasn't long before he rejoined me.

"Okay, what's the name?" he asked.

"Philip Chance. But he must have used an alias."

"I'd need either the name or the prescription number to look this up, Detective."

"Unfortunately, I don't have the prescription number, either."

"Well, let me find out if we do have a Philip Chance in the computer." He verified the spelling with me, then smiled encouragingly. "You never know; you might get lucky."

He stepped out of my line of vision now. When he returned a short time afterward, Milt's face told me what he had to say before he spoke. "No Philip Chance, I'm afraid."

"I didn't think so. Listen, would it be possible for you to go through the prescriptions themselves and see if you have any for tubocurarine chloride?"

"Well, yes, it's *possible*," the pharmacist responded without a hint of enthusiasm. "Can you tell me when he would have been in here?"

"By January twenty-first at the latest. But it could have been as early as December fifteenth." (This was my reasoning: Philip and Miriam had split up sometime toward the end of December, and she'd threatened him only days later. So it was conceivable he'd begun to gear up for the murder even at that point. By requesting that Milt examine those prescriptions from the fifteenth on, I would be playing it extra, *extra* safe.)

Milt sighed. "Tell you what. Our other pharmacists should both be in tomorrow afternoon. And if they can't help you, I'll go through everything we've got on file between December fifteenth and January twenty-first. But we make up about two hundred prescriptions a day, so it'll take some time. Depending on how busy we are, I might not have an answer for you until next—" He stopped abruptly, obviously embarrassed. "I'm sorry. I just realized that you haven't shown me any ID. It's not that I doubt you're who you say you are, but we have regulations. I shouldn't even have checked the computer for you until I saw some identification."

Uh-oh. Of course, I'd been aware that something like this could occur. Still, my hand trembled as I dug in my handbag. Fishing out a small leather case, I flipped it open to reveal my PI license—which was the best I could produce—then flashed it so quickly in front of Milt that it was, hopefully, a blur.

Before I could return the case to my bag, however, he held out his palm, and I placed the license in it per this silent command. He glared at the document. Following which he glared at me.

"Private. You're a private investigator." He punctuated the muttered words with a couple of *tsk-tsks* to further demonstrate his displeasure. "You ought to be ashamed," he lectured, "passing yourself off as a cop."

Skulking out of the store, I attempted to console myself by insisting that while being busted like that was slightly mortifying, it hadn't been the disaster I'd initially regarded it. After all, I didn't need to be a member of the police force to ask somebody to take a look at a picture, for heaven's sake. In a day or so I'd just go back and talk to Wilma and Roberto—or whatever their names were. I mean, if Philip Chance had filled his prescription here, one of them *had* to remember either the man or the tubocurarine chloride—right?

It was about a five-minute drive to my next stop, which, I noted with satisfaction, was situated in a part of the town that was even crappier than the one I'd just left.

Three customers were presently at the drug counter, each being attended to by one of the three pharmacists—two of whom were female.

I waited impatiently a short distance away, and after a few minutes both women became available almost simultaneously.

I walked over to the younger one, a tall, heavy-set

brunette with a ponytail and a liberal sprinkling of pimples. I figured her to be in her early twenties.

Indicating the photograph, I asked the appropriate question.

The brunette took the picture from my hand. But instead of responding directly, she smiled—appreciatively, it seemed to me—and then called over to the other female pharmacist, a lady probably twenty years her senior. "C'mere, Lena." And when Lena joined her: "Who does he look like?" She jabbed the photo with her forefinger.

Lena, who was considerably shorter, had to stand on her toes to examine it. "Cary Grant," she announced promptly.

"You mean *Hugh* Grant," her young coworker contradicted.

"No, Julie. *Cary* Grant."

"Never heard of him," Julie responded irritably. And now she turned to me for support. "He looks *exactly* like Hugh Grant, don't you think? I even told him that when he was in here."

It was a while before I could coax the words from my throat. "You're saying you recognize this man?"

"Sure I do. That's Mr. Green."

Chapter Thirty-eight

I was stunned.

I was elated.

But above all, I was lucky. *Incredibly* lucky.

I mean, what were the odds of connecting like this on only my second try? Okay, maybe not up there with my chances of winning the lottery, but still . . .

And now I finally permitted myself to think that darkest of thoughts: I could have canvassed every pharmacy on the east coast and come away with nothing. The fact is, in spite of my refusal to acknowledge any such possibility—and I still considered it very unlikely—Philip Chance just might have handed that prescription to a pharmacist who *wasn't* that bowled over by his looks.

But he didn't.

He handed it to Julie.

I wanted to vault the counter and throw my arms around that girl's neck. But it wouldn't have been appropriate. And besides, me—vault?

"Gregory Green," Julie was saying, her tone soft, caressing. "It's a nice name, isn't it? And it suits him, too, don't you agree?"

"I suppose it does," I answered.

She smiled then, recollecting. "He was in here a month or so ago, and Dominick—he's one of the other pharmacists, but today's his day off—was going to wait on him. I asked if I could take care of him instead, though. To tell you the truth, that man just knocked me out. Even the hat and dark glasses couldn't hide

how gorgeous he is. He has such incredible cheek-
bones, you know? And a fantastic smile. And this darling little dimple in his chin. He—"

"Cleft. It's called a cleft," Lena threw in before
walking off to help a customer.

Julie took a moment to snap, "Whatever," at her
departing coworker's back before turning to me again.
"He wasn't wearing a wedding ring, either, so—" Suddenly she looked apprehensive. "But what makes you
ask about Mr. Green, anyway?"

"I'm a detective, and we think he might have committed a crime. A very serious crime."

"Oh, no! Gee, that's just . . . it's just *terrible*." Julie
was obviously stricken. But after about five seconds'
worth of contemplation, she murmured, "Actually, I
did wonder about those dark glasses, since it was absolutely pouring outside that first time. I figured—"

"First time?" I interrupted. "He was here more
than once?"

"He had to come back the next day. He had a prescription for tubocurarine chloride—I even remember
the drug—and we didn't have any on hand."

Hallelujah! Here it was! The evidence I needed!

"Good-bye, Philip," I silently exulted, "you're about
to go away for a long, *long* time."

I think about the despicable Mr. Chance fairly often
these days, now that the trial date has finally been set.
And whenever he worms his way into my head, I take
great satisfaction from the delicious irony involved in
bringing him down.

Here was a man whose appearance had served as
an open sesame for him. After all, his attractiveness
had to have been at least partially responsible for net-
ting him his stunning physician wife and God knows
how many lovers. It had no doubt played its part,
too, in helping him launch what was, until recently,
a successful career. (Listen, it was hardly his sterling
character that had made those things possible.)

These same physical attributes, however, are what ultimately worked against him.

While another man might have gone virtually unnoticed in an out-of-town, out-of-the-way pharmacy, it was difficult *not* to notice Philip Chance.

So in the end, he'd simply proved too good-looking for his own good.

EGGPLANT PARMIGIANA

1 large eggplant (about 1¾ lbs.)
4 eggs, beaten
1½ cups packaged bread crumbs
1 cup (or more) olive oil
½ cup grated parmesan cheese
8 oz. mozarella cheese, cubed
Sauce recipe below or about 3 cups of your favorite store-bought marinara sauce

For eggplant
Cut eggplant crosswise into ¼-inch-thick slices. Dip first in egg, then in bread crumbs. Sauté slices in hot oil until golden brown; dry with paper towels. Lightly cover bottom of baking dish with sauce. Spread layer of eggplant, sprinkle with parmesan, top with mozarella, and cover with sauce. Repeat until all eggplant is used, topping last layer of sauce with mozarella. Bake ½ hour in 350° oven or until sauce is bubbly and cheese is melted.

For sauce
5–6 tbs. olive oil
2 cloves garlic, chopped
3 cups canned crushed
   tomatoes
2 cups water
2 six-oz. cans tomato
   paste

2 tbs. sugar
2 rounded tbs. salt
pinch of onion salt
pinch of cayenne
freshly ground pepper,
   dried oregano, and
   dried basil to taste

Sauté garlic in hot oil until golden. Add remaining ingredients. Simmer one hour, stirring occasionally.

Recipe serves 4 to 6, and I like this dish even better when it is completely baked, then rebaked the following day or baked, frozen, and rebaked whenever.

**Here is a preview of the next
exciting Desiree Shapiro mystery,
coming in early 2002 . . .**

"Your wife told me when she phoned this morning that you may be in danger."

I'd been focusing on John Lander when I said this, but it was Trudie Lander who responded. "Yes, I certainly did."

Oh, it's going to be like that, is it? Okay then, I'd just skip the middleman. "What makes you think so?" I put to the woman.

"Before I go into it, it would probably be best if we gave you a little background. Don't you agree, John?"

John, who obviously recognized this for the rhetorical question it was—owing, no doubt, to years of experience—didn't so much as nod before Trudie plowed ahead.

"Last month John's extremely wealthy uncle was told he had inoperable cancer. You may have heard of him, Ms. Shapiro—Victor Lander? No? He's really quite well-known—a pioneer in the plastics industry. Poor Victor. His illness is *so-o* tragic. He'd always been such a strong, vital man, hadn't he, John? And he's well into his eighties, too. But, sadly, in the fall, he began to deteriorate, and now the doctors are saying that he has only a few months to live, possibly less. At any rate, two weeks ago this past Tuesday— nine days after Uncle Victor revealed his diagnosis to the family—John's cousin Edward, Victor's principal heir, was *murdered*." As she uttered the word, Trudie shuddered, after which she swallowed a couple of times. When she spoke again there was an urgency in her tone. "What we're here about, though, is that this

Monday there was an attempt on John's life, too. He had been working late that night, and when he got home at around eleven-thirty, someone took a shot at him right in front of our building. John could actually hear the bullet whiz past his ear, couldn't you, dear?"

John knew better than to even attempt an answer. But at that moment Trudie took a couple of seconds out to pick some imaginary lint off her skirt, and I used the opportunity to slip in a few words. "Have you spoken to the police about this?"

She looked up, eyes blazing. "The police!" she spat. "The morning after it happened, I went to see one of the detectives investigating Edward's death. He wrote down the information and promised they'd follow up, but I'm sure they've merely been going through the motions. I don't believe that detective gave any credence at all to what I had to say."

"Why do you think that?"

"It was apparent to me he regarded the whole thing as a ploy to divert attention from the fact that John had a very good motive for wanting Edward dead. And unfortunately, there were no witnesses."

"What motive are we talking about?"

"Oh, didn't I tell you? John is next in line."

"For what?"

Trudie eyed me rather pityingly. I got the impression she'd concluded that I was more than a little slow-witted.

"Why," she informed me, "to inherit Uncle Victor's millions, of course."